A NEW WORLD ROMANCE

A NEW WORLD ROMANCE

Susham Bedi
Translated by Astri Ghosh

zubaan

ZUBAAN
128 B Shahpur Jat, 1st floor
NEW DELHI 110 049
Email: contact@zubaanbooks.com
Website: www.zubaanbooks.com

First published by Zubaan Publishers Pvt. Ltd 2024

10 9 8 7 6 5 4 3 2 1

ISBN 978 93 90514 73 1 (paperback)
ISBN 978 93 90514 75 5 (ebook)

Zubaan is an independent feminist publishing house based in New Delhi with a strong academic and general list. It was set up as an imprint of India's first feminist publishing house, Kali for Women, and carries forward Kali's tradition of publishing world quality books to high editorial and production standards. *Zubaan* means tongue, voice, language, speech in Hindustani. Zubaan publishes in the areas of the humanities, social sciences, as well as in fiction, general non-fiction, and books for children and young adults under its Young Zubaan imprint.

Typeset in Sabon 11/16.
Printed and bound at Chaman Offset.

For Rahul

The Story of Two People

This is the story of two people who live in Navabhum, or the New World. Navabhum is often called Gaurbhum or the Land of the Fair-complexioned.

They live in Navabhum but were not born there. They were born in Purabhum, the Old World.

Which makes it difficult to say where they are from.

Well, maybe it doesn't matter where one comes from. Especially if you are talking about emotions like the flavour of love, which encapsulates all feelings, all you need for that is two hearts that beat. It can happen anywhere—on earth, in the heavens or even the space between heaven and earth.

It's true that hearts exist in certain bodies, and bodies grow in a particular soil, breathe in a particular air, connect with a particular kind of sunlight and water, and are formed and take shape in a particular manner.

This is why anyone who settles in Navabhum still bears the fragrance of the soil they were created in. The real smell lingers no matter how much you wash, scrub, or spray yourself with perfume.

Every soil bears a colour of its own, sometimes white, sometimes yellow, sometimes brown and sometimes red. Once a colour has set in, it won't go away, no matter how much powder and rouge you rub on or how much kajal you smear. As Radhika said after being tinted by the colour of her love for Krishna, "*Kāli kamri pe sakhī chaṛho na dūjo rang*," meaning that you can dye something that has other colours black, but if a cloth is black, it will not take other colours well in the dyeing process. Not that this is valid anymore. Nothing is impossible, thanks to the science of chemistry. You can remove the black by bleaching.

Scientific methods today can change a dark colour to a lighter one. I've heard that a famous singer in the New World changed the colour of the skin he was born with. But he still gets counted among those who have his original colour. I am trying to say that the colour of one's soil does not wash off. Or that people don't let you wash it off.

Even if your colour changes, does everything inside also change? Some colours might be able to cover attitudes, but it's just a very thin veneer. If you look closely, you can see the variations and layers inside.

And the quality of colours tends to vary as well. Some colours stick, others don't. If a colour is not fast, it will fade when washed a couple of times. Then it is easy to dye it another colour. Even black, if the dye is not fast, can be covered by other colours easily. It must be seen which and how many colours are mixed in our hero and heroine, which ones are fast and which wash off.

The fact is that people have been coming and going from Purabhum for ages. No one kept track of which place they left, where they settled, and where they went again; people in Purabhum are remarkably incapable of keeping track of things. They only know how to scuttle around all day long. Not to keep accounts of things. So, we are still determining who will meet and who should be matched with whom. In Navabhum, people do not believe just about anything. This is why they are incredibly proud that they have invented a machine capable of keeping track of everything, a computer, and that you can turn it on at any time and read what is on the screen. The people in Gaurbhum write down details of every activity of theirs. Everything holds a historical significance for them. What George Washington ate, on which side of the bed he slept, and everything he did from the minute he got up until he went to bed must be documented. The matter has reached a stage where every being in Navabhum considers himself as important as his ancestors and fills the computer with descriptions of all he does. Who knows when it might be of historical interest?

The only thing we know of the hero and heroine of this story is that one is from the East and one is from the West. When they left the old country and settled in the new world, one settled on the East Coast and one on the West Coast. In a way, both come from opposing directions, and their colours and castes are mixed. Both consider themselves the offspring of the Aryans. Their mother tongues are derived from Sanskrit, and they are both coloured by the language of Gaurbhum.

Another thing to note about colours is that if a colour is diluted, you can tell because it will always be different from the original colours it came from. Yes, it can be more beautiful than the original colours and a bit strange. But it is distinctive.

This is how we can say that, had this story occurred in Purabhum, it would have taken another form. Particularly because the story's main characters have their roots and upbringing in the old country—they reached adulthood there, which means the plants grew there. They were full-grown trees, in a way, and were uprooted in their entirety and replanted in Gaurbhum. They were luxuriant and laden with tiny, light green leaves when they arrived. Because they were promising plants, they kept their inner desire to live and their passion contained for a long time. They didn't wither. But how long can a tree last without its roots? While some trees might be able to set down new roots in new soil, it depends on whether they thrive in the new atmosphere. And a tree can be saved from withering away. But what is the point of saving it if it just does not grow new leaves? If not now, then tomorrow, it will give up and die anyway. How long can the leaves remain lush and green? It's like a Christmas tree. Uproot it and bring it home and decorate it. Then, when the holidays are over, throw it out again.

Our hero and heroine are Christmas trees that have been strung with colourful decorations but whose roots are firmly planted in the soil from which they were uprooted. The hero claims he was brought here, roots and all, and replanted.

To return to our original question about whether the story would have been different had it happened in Purabhum. After all, the old world is vast. Spread over thousands of miles from north to south, east to west. Who knows which part of the country it would occur in, which village or city, or even era? Had it been the age of Kalidas, our heroine would have been born in an ashram or a royal palace. The hero would surely be a prince or a king who had lost his way or gone out on a hunt. They would have friends who would help them meet or reveal their inner feelings. They would probably have a Gandharva wedding in the quiet. The heroine would get pregnant, and her father would go in search of the guilty person.

If the storyteller aimed to write a pleasant story, then the hero would have turned out to be a mighty king so that the heroine would have been married according to social customs and would then have become the queen consort of the king's many queens.

In the normal course, the story would have ended here. If it were taken forward, it would only be by hindering the union of the hero and heroine. The main obstacle is usually that the heroine gets pregnant. The hero would get the heroine pregnant and run away like most sages do with apsaras. In the case of sages, it would be the apsaras who would disappear because heroes such as these would usually be called licentious heroes, and no storyteller has dared to call a sage licentious, so in this matter, it is the woman who gets saddled with the blame. But the trouble is that in the new world, such excellent means of contraception are available that our heroine would be a fool to get pregnant. And then the question of whether or not to have an abortion would give the story a political slant. Conservatives would say that abortion is a sin, and liberals would say that it is the right of a woman to choose what to do. One new conservative politician even said that women who abort foetuses should get the death penalty. In this way, instead of focusing on the heroine, the question would be about the woman's right to choose an abortion or whether abortion is legal or illegal. Love would get lost in all of this, in the hustle and bustle of media coverage, and no flavour of love would be left in it. This is why, in a proper romance, these elements, usually essential to the stories of people from Purabhum, cannot feature.

And here, should one want to add a tragic element, the hero or heroine would have to suffer from some curse, so they would be separated. A long poem would be written about the pangs of separation, which would be sent to the lover by a cloud messenger. But the long distances of Navabhum can be covered in a day by plane, so there is no scope for a long separation. The hero and heroine can meet each other whenever they feel like it.

Even if you live in a faraway city, you can still meet on weekends. And if you can't meet, you can speak on the phone for ages. And if you don't get a chance to talk on the phone, you can leave messages on each other's answering machines. And one can say whatever the heart desires in a message. The right person can get the message at the right time, so there are no groans of separation or despair; those appear only when you depend on clouds or birds as messengers.

You can't rely on clouds anyway; they can turn and change direction at any point and take the message somewhere other than the beloved's hometown. I am sure you know that people who forecast the weather might be right but, clouds have minds of their own. They seem to be drifting towards Pallampur but end up pouring down on Gallampur. So if a lover doesn't know where he himself is heading, how will he predict what the clouds will do? He only has the wealth of trust and can spend as much of it as he feels. The rest is up to God.

They say that God is scared of lovers. He even sends back sealed dead bodies from Yamalok. That is how Savitri brought back Satyavan. Not only did she get her husband back from the King of the Dead but she also threatened and scared him into sending back a hundred sons like her husband.

Many lovers have started calling God their 'beloved' so that God, confused about whether they are referring to him or some mysterious earthling, fulfils their wishes by considering himself the object of their love. Yes, this has happened in many places. Not only in Purabhum but also in the world of crows, Shyambhum, and many other places. While you won't find many examples of this in Navabhum, similar things must have happened here.

Even without the element of pregnancy, many interesting stories are unique to the old world. If you consider more recent times, the tales of Laila-Majnu and Sohni-Mahiwal or Heer-Ranjha are from Purabhum, but in them both the hero and heroine usually die. In this love story, the hero and heroine neither die nor live. They are like those straws that neither drown nor swim; all they do is float along with the water and the wind.

In modern times, in the old country, new short stories are written about love all the time. There are so many films about love, some that make it, some that flop. So many lovers who face calamities die or are killed for love, so many love marriages. But all that happens on the silver screen. In real life, people are married off before they have the chance to fall in love or love is strangled at the outset. People only do what is expected of them or what society and their families want them to do, and this is how their lives are spent, being dragged into the daily grind. They are saved from the fate or doom of love; they get happiness and sorrow from this kind of security.

Many so-called real stories also come to light. One always mentions culture in such cases. There are the problems of poverty-stricken families. There is tension between the hero and the heroine due to class and caste differences or a love triangle. Nowadays, there might even be talk of divorce sometimes.

At the same time, the tales of the new world are very different from those of our hero and heroine. As I have said earlier, they were not born in the new world but have just been decorated like Christmas trees in Gaurbhum. Water and fertilizer get added to the soil to make the plants last longer. But the soil and water that actually nourishes them comes from the old country.

One interesting aspect of every story in Gaurbhum is that the hero and the heroine get separated after meeting once because the father or some father-like personality disapproves of one of them or there is a villain. Ultimately, the heroes and heroines either reunite or die in the name of love, like Romeo and Juliet. Whatever else happens, there is always a triangle in these tales.

There is neither a triangle nor any obstacle in our love story that can be removed so that the hero and heroine can meet again and the story might have a happy ending. Our story has neither a happy ending like marriage nor a tragic one like death.

In this Gaurbhum, there are only happy endings; here, people are always running around to get something, and it has become their nature to sacrifice everything to get it.

This means that in this hybrid story of ours, there will definitely be some elements of Gaurbhum and some of Purabhum, but it also means that the story will be somewhat different from its parts. It is said that when colours are mixed, the mixed colour is of a new kind, different from all the original colours—it can be more beautiful than the original or vulgar or ugly, sometimes even disgusting.

This story could be anything—a precious combination of colours and shapes like a multicoloured Iranian carpet or an ugly sackcloth bordered with tattered strips.

It would be best if you decided what it is. On my part, I have woven a precious fabric and presented it to you.

***

Now, let us hear the love story of the original inhabitants of Purabhum, who are based in Gaurbhum.

Well, first of all, the writer of this story is not claiming in any way that she is the first woman to write a love story. Such stories have been written since time immemorial. They have been written and are being written in every land. Stories of new kinds and new styles every day. Hybrid or mongrel, all sorts of stories. However, the work of writing love stories has mostly been done by men. Should women write, they become mystics. Even if love and affection are born out of air, they get absorbed in smoke, clouds, etc. One notable property of my romance is its unique blend, rarely found in this world. Due to this, the taste of this story will be of its own kind, just like a classical dancer presenting a dance according to the rules but adding his ideas to it—in other words, improvising. Or when the head chef of a restaurant prepares a well-known dish using his recipe and adds new flavours to it.

Have you started suspecting that I am distracting you with talk of all kinds of things and taking you away from the real story? Or that I don't have a story, like Satyanarayan, so I am talking about this and that rather than the story? Have you ever heard the story of Satyanarayan? Even after listening to the whole story, the listener is waiting to know the real story.

No, this long introduction is so that we can listen to and enjoy the real story in all its dimensions.

So listen—in our story, these two lovers living in Purabhum are divorced. It's strange, isn't it? In the love stories of Purabhum, the hero and heroine are often teenagers, especially the heroine, a very pure girl. And if the heroine marries someone else, the poet will remain silent about it. Even if one finds out later, no one will be ready to say what the truth is. Some will say yes, perhaps there was a marriage, and some will say no, brother, they have been in love since childhood. There is so much speculation about Radha that it is impossible to know what the actual circumstances of her life were. There are some contradictions; the heroine may also be married, but generally, the matter is dealt with as described above. There is often talk of betrothal and fiancés to preserve that girlish innocence and the story's interest.

But in this love story, not only has the heroine lost her virginity, but it has also been publicly trumpeted because marriage itself means the loss of virginity or a social declaration of virginity being lost. So, the fact that the hero loves her despite knowing everything or can do so is a new thing, especially in the context of the old world. There is no prohibition on this love in Purabhum, especially in modern times. But most lovers remain silent about it because the issue of age is also a serious one there. If you are going to live for forty years, the period meant for love is only ten years, that is, between the ages of twenty and thirty. Before that you have childhood, and after that comes old age. Before you turn twenty, you will be tightly bound in chains, and after thirty, you will be ridiculed. If the heroine's age is factored into the categories of heroines given by the sages, then she can be a love interest only between the ages of thirteen and twenty-four.

Meanwhile, the hero is eternally young (no matter what his age may be). In Gaurbhum, as life expectancy increases, the maximum age for love also increases from forty or fifty to eighty or ninety. Similarly, its other limit has also gone down from sixteen years to between ten to twelve years. New research here has gone so far as to state that attachment starts from when you are five to six years old, which means that it is only now that the stories of Purabhum have started influencing them.

Well, now you will say that the character of the hero and heroine will be hybrid—a combination of both countries. Just as a change of soil changes air quality, it affects human nature, too. In the nature of Purabhumis, there was a lot of salt as well as sweets and hot spices. Similarly, in the nature of Navabhum, everything sweet, sour, or salty tastes bland. They also have a habit of cooling everything from meat to tea with ice. Things whose job is to keep the body warm are used to provide coolness. In the last few years, people in Navabhum have started importing many spices and spicy foods. Hence, the nature of the people here has also become mixed. Sometimes very excitable and sometimes downright cold.

How much air or water and sunlight the hero and heroine got from where, and what spices have nourished their flesh and blood should become evident from their behaviour during the story. Therefore, I will leave you to decide about their nature and character. Let me explain: our hero's nature is like the sun, and our heroine's is like the wind. The hero is not only warm like the sun and interested in spreading his light everywhere but is also constantly in search of light. That was why he came to Navabhum in the first place.

The innate nature of the heroine is that of the wind. The wind, meaning that which flows and reaches anywhere. It is not the earth that remains firm in its place. She flies and carries many things with her. Have you heard the story of the race between the sun and the wind? When the wind challenged the sun to see who could get a jacket off a traveller faster, do you know who won? Well, let's let that be. Our hero and heroine are not in a competition. But their inclinations are certainly different according to their elements.

If people were named according to their nature, no names like 'Air' or 'Heat' would exist. The name should suit the love story—Madhumalati, Radhika, Roopmanjari, Lavanyavati, Padmavati, Kanaklata, Laila, Heer or any such melodious name. But these names are very commonplace now. Purabhumis who settle in Gaurbhum either adopt new names or shorten their existing names, like Harry for Harikrishna, Sam for Sampat Ram, Neel for Neelkanth, while Jai Kishan becomes Jay, etc. Our hero and heroine must have names that don't need to be changed or shortened. My friend's name is Ketaki. Let me keep that. Yes, the sun can have many names—Ravi Dinkar, Diwakar, Arun, etc. Ketaki's friend is Aditya. How about Aditya? It is another name for the sun. Aditya reeks of Adipurusha, the original man. But if there is a smell, why avoid it? Doesn't every man smell of the Adipurusha?

Let us hear the story of Aditya and Ketaki.

You may ask who this story's 'I' or narrator is. So, let me also tell you that it is none other than Susham Bedi, a storyteller from both Purabhum and Navabhum. You don't need to accept the fact without questioning it. The author could be someone else in Susham Bedi's clothes. Or Susham Bedi herself could have created another Susham Bedi utterly different from the real her. And if you like the story's flavour, this name will become famous, like Valmiki, Tulsidas, or Kalidas.

Sorry, I have to go now. A friend of mine has just come to me and is very upset. Something has gone wrong in her life, too. Some love-related incident or accident has happened. I will come back soon and tell you my love story. Just wait a little.

[illegible] of the land that [illegible] the [illegible] can have many names [illegible] Dupleix [illegible] etc. Kerala's [illegible] How About [illegible] on this [illegible] of Ashvatthama, the [illegible] man? But is there is a smell [illegible] Does every man smell of the Adipur [illegible]?

Let us hear the song of [illegible] in Kerala.

You may ask who this [illegible]. The narrator is Son[illegible] let me tell you that it is none other than Sushama [illegible] a [illegible] and [illegible]. You don't need to accept the fact without any question. [illegible] the author could be someone else. [illegible] Sushama [illegible]. Or [illegible] could have created another Sushama [illegible] different from the real her. And if you like the story [illegible] name will become famous, like [illegible] Taslima [illegible].

Sorry, I [illegible] to go now. [illegible] to me and [illegible] I will come back soon and tell you [illegible].

Purvarag
The Dawning of Love

Exposition

The first stage in every love story is the purvarag or exposition, that is to say, an account of the moments when the seeds of love were first sown in the hero and the heroine. This seed can be of many kinds, like a relationship in a previous life, a revelation in a dream, or heaps of praises from friends for the future lover, which might have kindled an interest in the mind in advance.

A relationship in a previous life is the most well-known option. It is even said that Rama and Krishna were incarnations of Vishnu, so Vishnu's consort, Lakshmi, was born as Radha and Sita to be with him in each of his incarnations. Padmavati saw Ratnasen in a dream. Even in Banabhatta's *Kadambari*, things happen because of a vision in a dream.

The question is, how did our hero and heroine meet for the first time? Did they know about each other before, or did they have a connection in a previous life?

Sure, they did have a connection because they came from Purabhum, the old country, but even though they were from the same land, it was not like they had a village-and-town relationship. Let us see how far back this relationship went.

Lovers in the new world do not believe in dreams and things like that. For them, a dream expresses suppressed wishes and desires; it is not a prophecy. There is no need to meet in dreams over here because there are so many opportunities for people to meet. Especially if they are gainfully employed, when they can meet at conferences, gatherings, meetings, at the office, while travelling by plane—there are thousands of opportunities to meet. One can meet while walking in a park, on the street, or at a friend's house. Since people from Purabhum who come to Navabhum have usually left their country in search of work, our hero and heroine are most likely professors, doctors, or engineers.

I know that you are losing patience by now. And I do not want to lose a sensitive reader like you. So, let me get right to the story and save the other stuff for later. Our heroine, whose name you are acquainted with already—and if you aren't let me remind you of it: Miss Ketaki—had to get to a conference that day in a town four or five hundred miles from where she lived. She was going to present a paper there. But she was in two minds. Should she go or not? A lot of work was pending. The university was in session. But then she bought a ticket the week before the conference and took a plane there. The conference was at a five-star hotel. Ketaki had phoned ahead to book a room.

A crowd had gathered in the lobby of the hotel. Some of it consisted of the people who had come for the conference. But it looked like there was a festival on in that town that weekend as well. There was a long queue at the reception. Ketaki went over and stood in line. Aditya came and stood right behind her in the same queue. Ketaki was overwhelmed by the crowd and kept glancing at the hotel staff checking in the guests at the reception. Sometimes, she would turn around and take a quick look behind her. Once, when she turned to sneak a look, she noticed the person standing right behind her who was looking at her with interest.

Ketaki turned back quickly and started to count the people in front of her. Her Old World upbringing had taught her not to look at a man and smile but to turn her gaze away. She had also guessed that he was a man from Purabhum. He must think she was a very restless woman. So Ketaki steadied herself and stood in one place. But after a few moments, she suddenly turned back again. This time, the man smiled, and Ketaki suppressed a smile as she turned her gaze to look ahead again. Suddenly, it occurred to her that it was considered impolite to avoid looking someone in the eye in Navabhum, so she turned around and gave him the full impact of her smile. This time, the vivacious smile took the man by surprise. When he realised what was happening, his lips responded, and he nodded; the woman had turned around again.

Ketaki was so self-conscious by now that she kept telling herself she must not turn around and look. Still, as if out of habit, she would start to turn around to look; she would stop herself halfway and begin to look at whatever came into her range of vision as if it were something she had stood in line to look at. In this way, she saw a lot—the floral design of the sofas in the lobby, the colour and shape of the suitcases of the other guests waiting in line, lots of people entering or coming out of the golden elevators, hotel employees pulling trolleys with luggage, on the right-hand side a bit further away the glass windows of fashionable shops that displayed clothes, ties, and watches, and in a part of the sun-soaked section of the lobby cordoned off by a railing on the left, happy unknown faces sitting and chatting at an open restaurant that was full of plants and flower decorations. It was a bit like a mela. Only Ketaki was watching it like a stranger from another world. Suddenly, she became aware of the person standing behind her. Was he, like her, feeling distant from all of this as well?

When it was Ketaki's turn to talk to the receptionist, she was told there was no reservation in the name of Miss Ketaki Tarleja. Ketaki started to frown. How was it possible that there was no room? She had made a reservation. But the computer or the clerk had messed up things. They could not find Ketaki's name. And Ketaki did not have any proof that she had made a booking. She had not written down the confirmation number. Even if she had written it somewhere, she had not bothered to bring it with her to hand it over. She had never arrived at a hotel with a booking before and found that things had gone wrong like this. She kept saying, "How is this possible? How can you do this? How can you lose my reservation?" When it became clear that there was no way around it, she got worried. What would she do now? She did not know a soul in this city. Where would she stay? For a moment, the image of homeless people sleeping on the pavements downtown flashed before her eyes. No. These people would have to do something. She had to spend the night in a proper place. Her paper presentation was scheduled for the following day. Was there no other option? The receptionist was in a hurry. Since there was a crowd, she wanted to deal with each person quickly. "Miss Ketaki Tarleja, I am sorry. There is nothing available at the moment. Every room has been booked."

Ketaki kept standing there. "Please, do what you can. Anything. I have to stay somewhere. I have to present a paper tomorrow morning. I need to have a place to stay. Please do something."

Aditya was all ears when the receptionist said 'Miss Ketaki Tarleja'. He was acquainted with the name. He had read Ketaki's book a few months earlier and liked it. He was still thinking about some of the things she had written. When the receptionist did not respond to

Ketaki's request, Aditya suddenly came up from behind and said, "Please give my room to this lady; here is the confirmation of my reservation."

Even though Ketaki felt relieved, she wondered where this person would go if she were to take him up on his offer.

"What about you?" was all she was able to say.

"Don't worry about me. A lot of my friends are here at the conference. I will stay with one of them."

"Really?"

"Please don't worry about me at all. How many days do you need a room for?"

"Just one day. I have to go back tomorrow."

"Just one day. That makes it very easy. Finding a place for a night is relatively easy. And if you want to stay on for a bit longer, that can be figured out as well."

The receptionist said she could not transfer the room to another person's name for a day. Ketaki said it did not matter to her whose name the room was booked in. She told Aditya, "Put your luggage in the room for the time being if you like. When you find a friend to stay with, you can come and fetch it."

It was only fitting. Aditya couldn't just leave his stuff anywhere; this was the only way to do things. It was just a matter of dropping off the luggage. The conference had already started.

"Is there an interesting panel at noon?" asked Ketaki. She hadn't been able to read the programme properly yet.

"There is something, I think. Let's register first. We will get a up-to-date copy of the programme as well. Then we can decide."

It felt a bit bizarre to Ketaki that she was unexpectedly entering a hotel room like this with a strange man. Had he been from the New World, it might not have seemed so weird, as she could have kept up a front of ordinary politeness. But he was from the Old World. There is a lot of baggage one carries from one's own country. It was a bit filmy as well. Still, she was happy that this person had saved her today, and she felt grateful to him. A feeling of contentment, too, that it was someone like her, from her part of the world. It would be good to have someone to talk to. After all, meeting new people was one of the attractions of going to conferences. He must be around 45 or 46. She had heard his name before—Aditya Ghosh. She had been going through the *Journal of Asian Studies* on her way there and had seen his name. Was it a review of his book? She could not recall the title of the book. She had perhaps read something of his earlier as well. Her thoughts were running wild; she wanted to know more.

"Should we have tea or coffee before heading to the panel discussion? Have you had lunch?" asked Aditya.

"I had lunch on the plane. But I would love to have a cup of coffee. It will wake me up. I had to get up very early this morning."

"So did I. Let's go. The café at this hotel is good. We can go there."

"Looks like you have been here before."

"Three years ago, the conference was held here."

"I couldn't come that year."

They sat in the café and talked for hours. About the research they were doing. About common acquaintances. Eager to know more about each other. An unwearied curiosity. An unwearied conversation.

The more they learnt, the more there was to learn.

"The last panel must have started by now."

"Shall we go?"

"Isn't it too late now? There wasn't anything particular we had to listen to."

"So should we just sit here?"

"The reception is in an hour. We'll go then."

"Okay, let's just sit here. Would you like a drink?"

"Already?"

"Is there a special time for drinking?"

"No, it's not that... I could have a gin and lime or maybe even a campari."

"What would you prefer?"

"The sun is still shining... an afternoon drink would be nice."

"It looks like you are thinking of colonised, warm countries."

"Shouldn't I, when I look at you?"

"A lot of the people here will remind you of them. On that note, let's have something tropical then."

"Right! Exactly!"

"So what will you have?"

"What about that Hawaiian drink... mai tai? Or maybe a Mexican one, a margarita?"

"Sounds good. I will have one, too."

And the conversation wove on.

"How is it possible that we have never met before?"

"I don't go to many conferences. People say, don't they, that real work only takes place within the four walls of a home."

"That is how you manage to do so much. I read an article of yours in the last issue of the *Journal of Asian Studies* as well."

"Well, are you less productive? I was turning the journal pages on my flight and saw that one of your books has just come out from Princeton University Press. I have read a book of yours, *Civil War and Domestic Policies*." Suddenly, Ketaki remembered everything.

Aditya was uncomfortable when the conversation veered towards him.

"What are you working on now?"

"Communalism and nationalism."

"What are you focusing on?"

"On the problems in Kashmir."

"Tomorrow's paper?"

"It's on the same subject. I am analysing the effects of Indira Gandhi's policies."

"When is your panel?"

"Will you come?"

"Since we now know each other, of course I will. Unless I have to attend a very important meeting."

"Eleven in the morning?"

"I will be sure to come. My meeting is at seven in the morning. I should be free by nine or half past nine."

"Oh my God! You are actually going to come. I need to prepare properly, then."

Teasingly, Aditya said, "There's no time for that now. It looks like we are late for the reception as well. I have to go to the dinner. Are you planning on going?"

"To the All-Conference Dinner?"

"Yes. That's where I will meet my friends with whom I might be able to stay tonight. Or else I will have to sleep on the street."

"No, no, how can that be permitted? You have first rights on the room, anyway. Go to the room if you'd like to freshen up a bit. I will be sitting here."

"Why don't you go and get ready? I will come up after that."

"Fine. I will go up first."

"I will call you in half an hour. Let me know if you are ready, and I will come up."

"Sure. I'm not going to need more than that."

Both of them were very conscious that they had to be tread cautiously. They had to look out for each other's needs and stick to formality.

When Ketaki had first entered the room with Aditya, she had felt weird. They had just put their luggage in the room and rushed downstairs for a coffee. Coming to the room alone, she looked at Aditya's suitcase, and it did not seem weird that it was there. At the same time, she felt as if her presence was a bit like that of a thief.

The room was quite large. The city's lush greenery stretched out below its large glass windows. The occasional lofty high-rise could be seen in the distance. On the room's left wall were two vibrant frames with paintings of waterfalls that sprang out and gurgled down from mountains. There were two double beds. They were covered with flowery bedspreads that reflected the colours of the paintings. Ketaki found the colours of the bedspreads soothing to her eyes. The colours were pleasant and delicate. In one corner, a round table was surrounded by easy chairs covered with fabric that matched the bedcovers. Along the right-hand wall was a long table. One of side of it was a patterned iron frame with a mirror. On the other side stood a table lamp. There was a large wardrobe near the door to the room. The television was in a cabinet.

She was surrounded by images of herself when she switched on the bathroom light. There were full-length mirrors on three of the walls. Ketaki became aware of herself. She examined herself from the front, side, and back. Then she thought, *I'm looking fine.* She just needed to freshen up. She took out some liquid face wash from her vanity kit and smeared it onto her face. As she splashed cold water on her face, she felt it revive her skin. She put on some lipstick carefully and changed her sari quickly. She had brought a deep green Kanjeevaram sari for dinner that night. It had a broad blue border embroidered in gold with long lines and geometrical shapes. She had bought a few saris to use at conferences that looked stylish with their deep colours but were not too bright or flashy. She was glad she had brought this sari. It would make her feel elegant in front of Aditya. There were times when she was careless about what she wore. Luckily, it was ironed and ready to wear. She had had a haircut a week earlier. Her hair had been styled to let it flow from the sides of her face towards the nape of her neck. This way, her hair stayed out of her eyes and her face looked neat and tidy. She was happy. Enthusiastic too. She felt a bit anxious about the paper the next day, but still, more enthusiasm than anxiety. It would be powerful. She remembered a couple of points that she wanted to highlight. If she had the chance this evening, she would also discuss them with Aditya. She might even get some new ideas. The way he thought was quite impressive. How much she had learnt in the past few hours! When the phone rang, she was putting on emerald-studded golden earrings that matched her sari.

Picking up the phone, she said, "What timing! Come up. I am ready."

As soon as she said it, she thought, *what if someone else is calling*? But hearing Aditya's voice, she felt reassured. "I am calling from the lobby. Will be there in two minutes."

When Aditya knocked on the door, Ketaki was on her way out. She thought she had better go down and see if she saw any familiar faces. She burst out quickly, "I will wait in the lobby. Should we go to the dinner together? I don't know that many people. If you are with someone you are not scared, or you will end up being all by yourself. Because that is what I dread most about these conferences—being all alone in a crowd."

Aditya wondered what he had done to deserve such benisons. "Need you ask? Thanks for waiting. I won't take more than ten minutes."

***

With all the food and drink, meeting people, and the chief guest's speech, the dinner went on till midnight. Aditya kept getting up from the table and going out to make phone calls. He spoke to some people to learn that they were already sharing a room with someone or had brought their wives with them. Then he asked the hotel operator about a few other friends and found that his friends had either not checked into the hotel or were not in their rooms.

By the time it was midnight, Aditya started getting worried. Where could he go at this time of the night? Where would he wander? He did not want to say anything to Ketaki in case she took it the wrong way. He kept racking his brains for a solution. In the end, he decided to go to the room, call a few hotels, and move wherever he could find the first available place. What would he do if he could not find a room at that late hour? He had meetings that started early in the morning. He had to give a speech as well. Would he have to spend the night awake in the lobby? He panicked. Turning to Ketaki, he said, "I am going to the room. I will call other hotels to see if a room is available. When you want to come up—"

"No, I will come up with you. It is late anyway. I have a paper tomorrow. I want a full night's sleep."

Aditya got on the phone the minute they reached the room. He even asked the receptionist if they could help. But they replied that all the hotels in the town were full and there was nothing they could do at that time of the night. There were a couple of hotels that were far away. It might be possible that they had rooms available. Aditya was trying to find a room in one of them.

Ketaki sat in an armchair in the corner, observing Aditya's efforts. What should she do? What was it her duty to do? The man was decent, which is why he had given her his room. Should she then let him wander about like this? You wouldn't call that being humane, would you? Just because she was a woman, would allowing a man to sleep in the same room as her be improper? She was not a little girl. She was over forty. He was a civilised, decent man. She had just spent the entire evening with this man. If his behaviour had not been inappropriate for a second, what would he do now that could have been improper?

Even if he did manage to find a room at a hotel far away, should she let him go there? She had heard that the area of town they were in was unsafe at night. All kinds of thieves, drunkards, and drug addicts would be roaming the streets right now. Should anything happen to Aditya, would she be able to forgive herself? The poor fellow had just wanted to do good, and she was willing to thrust him into the mouth of death just for the sake of some foolish social norm. Aditya was a decent man, so should his decency and decorum be rewarded with putting his life in danger? Her thoughts agitated Ketaki.

"Please, Aditya! It is very late. It is dangerous to go out now. This city is not safe at night. Why don't you go to sleep here?"

Aditya was aware of the fact that it was not safe outside. He had a meeting at seven in the morning. But still, he thought he should leave because it was the appropriate thing to do. His old-world mind knew how inappropriate it was to spend the night in a room with a woman. Ketaki was a well-educated woman of good character. He wanted to show his respect for her by leaving the room. She deserved the respect that any woman who was of good repute did. Formality forced Ketaki to say what she was saying, but if he were to stay, things would be bizarre for both of them.

"No, Ketaki. I will take a taxi. It is relatively safe. I will get a taxi outside the hotel. Don't worry."

"Well, there are two huge beds over here. What difference does it make if you stay here?"

Aditya thought that if he stayed, he would probably be unable to sleep a wink. How could he sleep in the same room as a strange woman? It would feel highly unnatural. He upped his efforts to find another room, no matter what happened. He called every place where there was the slightest possibility that he might find a room. He felt he had to find a room under any circumstances, as if he were trying to prove to Ketaki that his intentions were honourable.

While Aditya was getting distressed looking for hotels, Ketaki saw there were no rooms available and she was convinced of the necessity for him to stay.

"I don't understand, Aditya, why are you so upset? There's no big deal in you spending the night here. Why are you being so old-fashioned? What sin will we commit by sharing a hotel room?"

Aditya wondered if he was blowing things out of proportion.

Then the receptionist, who was searching for vacant rooms on her computer, called, "Sir, I am sorry! I could not find a room."

Aditya hung up with a sigh and said with a weary voice, "I couldn't get a room."

"Well, then. Please relax."

Ketaki got up from her chair, came and stood in front of Aditya, and said, as if they were close friends, "It is late now, and you should sleep. It's only a question of six hours. Then it will be morning. You have to go to your meeting at seven o'clock."

Aditya looked at her as if he were weighing something in his mind. To make the atmosphere less tense, Ketaki said, "We have spent more time than that already together. It did not seem strange then. Why now?"

Aditya couldn't think of anything to say. Ketaki said, "I will go to the bathroom first. Change and all that. Think about it in the meantime. I need to sleep, or my paper tomorrow will be ruined."

While Ketaki was in the bathroom, Aditya remembered he had not brought any nightclothes. He usually slept without anything. He didn't carry kurtas or pyjamas to hotels. Of course, it was different if he were to stay in someone's house. He had thought of bringing nightclothes when he was packing. Then he thought it would make the suitcase heavier, so he dropped the idea. What would he do now? He felt a bit uncomfortable. Never mind, he would manage, somehow.

When Ketaki returned, he was still searching through his suitcase. Ketaki said, "I am going to sleep," and got into bed. Ketaki felt that if she shut her eyes and went to sleep, Aditya would feel more comfortable moving around in the room.

When Aditya returned from the bathroom after brushing his teeth, he was still wearing his pants and shirt. Hearing him enter the room, Ketaki opened her eyes and was surprised to see him lying down fully dressed, but she didn't say anything. It felt as if her extreme drowsiness had vanished suddenly. Her mind was buzzing. Having a man in the room was no ordinary thing. It was not as if she had never had another person in her room, but how this had happened amazed her. Because these things only happen in Hindi films. Was this going to end up like a film? Would they both suddenly lose self-control and indulge in frenzied love-making, and would the hero and heroine fall in love? In cinema, the heroine gets pregnant after an incident like this. But before that, it rains, of course, so they have to seek shelter from the storm in some lonely place. What a load of rubbish they had in films! *Just look at us; we are in the same room.* How ridiculous it was to think that suddenly something like that would happen. Ketaki could feel a warmth rising inside her while her mind filled with thoughts. A sweet, tender feeling engulfed her.

As soon as he switched off the lights, Aditya felt a jungle awaken within him. How wrong everything had turned out. He would probably end up staying awake all night. He felt he was going to head towards Ketaki's bed any moment. He had never before had a beautiful woman sleeping in his room while he was tossing and turning on another bed. He remembered how, during his research, he had become friendly with a student from Gaurbhumi, the land of the fair-complexioned. She lived near his home. He would often give her a lift in his car. She would come to his apartment and wait in his living room if she got ready early. One day, when he came out of his bathroom after a shower, he found Judy lying in his bed. She had got there earlier that day and gone into his bedroom to wait for him.

Seeing Judy spread out on his bed was nothing less than an invitation for the unmarried Aditya. He was only wearing a towel tied at his waist. When Judy greeted him with a longing look, Aditya leant over her, clasping his towel at his waist with one hand. Judy tugged at the towel mischievously, and he dropped it and climbed onto the bed quickly. Judy opened her arms and hugged him tight as if she had been waiting for this. And then she started coming over early every morning. This arrangement continued for a few months until he left town. After that, he had not been in touch with Judy. It was like a physical toying of sorts. That finished on the same bed where it had started.

But now, an extremely improbable thing was happening. He wondered whether, if he were to reach out and touch Ketaki, she would push him away or accept him. He kept thinking he should at least try and find out. But no. There was no invitation from Ketaki.

He would never do anything like that. Ketaki had let him stay there because she thought he was decent. He was not going to surprise himself or her. After all, he was surprising both of them by not doing anything. Was Ketaki, by any chance, expecting them to do something? He thought of the Spanish film he had seen a few weeks ago. In the movie, the main character does not have intercourse with the girl out of respect for her, but the girl is disappointed and gets involved with someone else who satisfies her physical needs. Sad and broken-hearted, the hero languishes in the illusion of idealism for the rest of his life. No, Aditya is not a hero like that, nor will he ever be. But to do something right now would be to take advantage of the situation. He does not want to be that kind of person, not in his own eyes nor Ketaki's. If he felt attracted to Ketaki, he should leave it at that. There was no need to spoil it by giving it another shape.

But it was not possible to fall asleep. His mind was too restless. Even if they just chatted, at least they would have got through the night. But Ketaki must be fast asleep. *And she is very nervous about tomorrow's paper anyway.* If he were to wake her up, it would be very wrong. One can't sleep anyway while wearing pants. His legs were itching. He unclasped his belt. Unbuttoned the first button. As he continued to fidget, Aditya thought that Ketaki was probably in the throes of deep sleep by now, and he pulled off his trousers slowly under the blanket and tried to fall asleep. As soon as he loosened his clothes, his mind began to relax. He had a great urge to clasp Ketaki in his arms and hug her tightly, feeling her close to his body.

Now Ketaki had started to imagine some wild things herself. If Aditya were to come to her bed, what would she do—scream, shout, scold, or quietly take him into her arms and rest her head on his chest? In the dark, Ketaki could hear him removing his trousers under the blanket, and she wondered what he was up to. Then, for quite a while, she kept speculating—Aditya has left his bed and is standing next to mine; he is a bit hesitant; she opens her eyes and looks at him; she smiles, signing with her eye for him to sit down at the foot of her bed. Aditya sits down and clasps her hand, which has come out from under the sheet, in his hands. Then, stroking her hand, unable to stop, he kisses it. Ketaki heaves a deep sigh; Aditya leans forward, then comes closer and touches her lips with his.

Despite thinking all this, Ketaki was sure that nothing would happen because a decent person like Aditya would never stoop to that level. And should he do so, Ketaki would give him a piece of her mind. Perhaps she was enjoying this flight of fantasy because there was no danger of it materialising, nor was she being unfaithful to the man with whom she currently was in a relationship. She had no intention of doing so either.

Aditya's divorce proceedings with his wife had ended just three months earlier. He was free in his mind to start a new relationship, but he did not wish to be tied down without thinking it through properly, nor did he want to do anything that would cause him to be ashamed of himself in the morning. Living in the land of the fair-complexioned, he had never found it difficult to get hold of a body. There was magic in physical relationships, but he also wanted a relationship of the mind. And she was a lady from Purabhum. It would probably be easier to open one's mind to her. This would be a problem for Aditya, too. Why ask for trouble unnecessarily? It looked like Ketaki had all the qualities needed for an emotional relationship, and it was, therefore, necessary to protect her from lust so that, when they had established an emotional relationship, they could start thinking of physical needs. He must not do anything to spoil an emotional relationship or ruin the chances of having one in the future. If bodies meet without minds meeting, it's something else. Aditya had experienced that, and it was an experience he did not want to repeat. Because he had kept waiting for a long time for the emotional connection. Whatever was happening now was a momentary weakness, and it was possible to control it. While being divorced meant his heart was free, he was pretty weak. He had certain needs. Lost in these thoughts, he dozed off.

When Ketaki woke up, the room was awash with light. She could hear the sound of the shower from the bathroom. She hadn't noticed that Aditya had gotten up and started getting ready. She looked at her watch; it was six thirty. She thought back to the night. She felt at peace. So, nothing had happened. She had slept well. But she felt a pleasing sensation, as if the night had held a secret for both of them.

Whatever she thought or felt about last night was her own. But she would have liked for him to be a part of it. Would Aditya be able to guess what had passed through her mind, what she had fantasised about? Had he also thought similar thoughts? It is natural to think. But maybe he was attached to someone, so he could not think of Ketaki that way or even feel attracted to her at all. Aditya's face had not expressed any such feeling. But she must have seemed attractive to him; otherwise, surely they would not have enjoyed spending the whole afternoon and evening together? Many people had come across to say hello to Aditya, but he had not spoken to them much and had turned his attention back to Ketaki. Was he like that? A couple of women had been rather enthusiastic, but he had fobbed them off. That was because he wanted to stay focused on Ketaki. So why wouldn't he have had fantasies last night? But he was a very decent man. He didn't reveal anything of the sort. Just went to sleep quietly, the poor thing.

Aditya came out of the bathroom fully dressed, perhaps to save Ketaki and himself from embarrassment. Seeing Ketaki awake, he smiled.

"Did you get to sleep properly?"

Ketaki remembered the secret the two of them shared. She smiled back at him.

"Oh, I slept very well. I will get ready and start looking at my paper as soon as you leave. My brain is buzzing."

"Let's have breakfast together."

"Sure."

"We could meet downstairs after my meeting. Would nine o'clock be okay?"

"Yes. I will meet you outside the restaurant."

Ketaki got out of bed after Aditya left and went to the bathroom. Seeing Aditya's shaving kit and other toiletries sent a thrill through her body.

The words of an old song came to her:

> Blowing away in the wind, my red scarf of muslin
> My red scarf of muslin, ji, oh yeah
> Here and there it flutters, my red scarf of muslin
> Oh, my red scarf of muslin, oh yeah.

She hummed as she got ready. She spent a lot of time getting ready.

During breakfast, Ketaki, with a naughty look in her eyes, said, "I forgot to ask you how you slept. After all, you were my guest."

She wasn't sure what she saw in his eyes.

"Are you asking me this for the sake of asking, or do you really want to know?"

There was mischief in the way Aditya asked her this. Ketaki felt embarrassed suddenly. She tried hard to cover her embarrassment.

"It's a damnable nuisance to lie quietly when a beautiful woman is in the room with you. You must have wondered what kind of an impotent man you were with."

A fountain of laughter spilt from Ketaki's mouth that she could not control.

"How right you are. That is precisely what I thought. You could have tried, at least. I would have had the opportunity to pretend to flirt, at least. Now I don't know whether to blame my age or—"

"No, no, come on, your age doesn't show. You are still very capable of bowling someone over."

"So you weren't scared I would get you locked up for date rape or something?"

"You can't trust girls these days. Who knows when they might think of something? There are cases of sexual harassment and rape every other day."

Both of them were laughing uncontrollably and not making any sense.

It was natural to be like that after what had happened the night before.

"Goodness, it's half past ten. I need to get going."

"Did you rehearse?"

"Absolutely. You are coming, aren't you?"

"I was planning on it. Why, if you don't want me to, I won't come."

"That's not what I meant at all.Your comments will make me wiser."

"I can't promise that. I will come, of course. But I have to meet someone right now for fifteen minutes or so. I will probably be a bit late."

"My paper is at the end. Come late, it's no problem."

Aditya did get delayed but managed to listen to the whole of Ketaki's presentation. He was impressed by her mental abilities anyway, but after he got to hear her, he was even more impressed. There was originality in what she said, and depth. She raised some very pertinent points in her paper. Even though the panel was over, the question and answer session continued informally. Aditya got involved in talking to some people he knew. When he finished and went towards the dais to congratulate Ketaki, he found her eyes on him. He congratulated her and said, "Your thoughts are heading in the right direction. Are you going to work more on this?"

"Yes, this is a chapter from my next book."

"How far have you got?"

"It's a long way to Delhi." Ketaki seemed to be in a hurry. Perhaps some people were waiting for her. Aditya felt like talking to her. He said, "What is your plan now? Lunch somewhere?"

"There's a lunch with the others in the panel. Why don't you join us?"

"No, I have another commitment. Let's meet afterwards. When is your flight?"

"At six in the evening. I will have to leave right after lunch."

"You will be done by three or half past three. Let's talk then. I will take the key to the room from you then."

"Good. We can meet in the room between three and three-thirty."

Ketaki was with the other panelists, and yet she wasn't. While talking, she would suddenly remember the night before and smile at her secret.

She reached the room at five minutes to three to find Aditya there.

"How did you get in? I had the key."

"The housekeeping staff were cleaning the room."

"Did you come a while ago?"

She had suddenly used the familiar form of you in Hindi, "tum", and did not correct herself, as if it were natural to say "tum" and not the more formal ap.

"Around two thirty. Are you packed?" He was using *tum* as well now.

"There's hardly anything. I will do it right away. I brought a book with me. If I give it to you, will you read it?" She was back to using "ap" again.

"Of course! Thank you."

"This is my second book. Reflections on Hindu-Sikh relations from a historical viewpoint. Tell me what you think about it when you have read it."

"I have not brought any of my books."

"Famous writers do not wander around carrying their books."

"You are taunting me now."

"Well, ask yourself why. Am I not right?"

"The speed at which you are moving will leave us all behind."

"You too!" She smiled. "Far from leaving anyone behind, if I manage to keep pace, that will be wonderful."

"Aren't we moving at the same pace?"

"Of course not! Your fourth or fifth book is out; I am still on my third."

"Humility is a good thing. Keep at it. That's how one gets ahead."

"Thank you. I should leave now."

"Is it already time to leave? Can't you stay a bit longer?"

"Well, it's time to go."

"Must you go today?"

"I don't have to go today."

"So why don't you stay on then?"

Ketaki gave it some thought. Would it be correct to stay? What work did she have to get done by the next day? Not anything, really. So she could stay on.

"Let me think." She thought of the night before. Of repeating the embarrassment. Now, when there was no compulsion, Aditya will believe I've been wanting all of that and be encouraged, in a way. Did she want to get stuck in this quagmire? Aditya had been her protector until now; she had been in his care, but now there was no need for such a responsibility. The bindings on both of them would loosen quickly.

While Aditya was thinking that if Ketaki stayed on, she would be giving him a go-ahead. He wouldn't stop this time. He would let himself be carried away.

As she stood in the door on her way out, Aditya touched Ketaki's shoulder lightly and asked her for the last time, "Think about it. Stay, please." His voice pleaded softly.

"Aditya, no."

"Alright. Let me drop you to the airport."

"There's no need for that."

"We'll get a little more time together."

Ketaki liked the idea.

After checking in the luggage, they sat down to have a coffee.

By now, they had guessed they were starting to mean something to each other. This meeting was no ordinary meeting. But the dilemmas, doubts, and suspicions were still there, so neither was willing to admit how special this was. Aditya said, "It would have been nice if you'd stayed on for the evening. There are a couple of great panels tonight."

"I was keen. If you had insisted, I might have stayed on."

"Then let me do it now. Stay."

"Now, when I am here at the airport?"

"So what? I have to go back anyway. We can go together."

"No, baba. Now that I am here, I am here. Had I stayed, I would have stayed on. What will be will be."

"You are pretty fatalistic, aren't you!"

"Of course. If it is fated, we will meet again."

"Well, then, I will have to control our destiny."

"Try. Who knows... we might meet again."

"Sure. I will remember your words."

Both of them were bubbling over with laughter.

When the flight was announced over the loudspeaker, Aditya asked, "Can one hope we will meet again?"

"Like I said, if you keep trying, we will surely meet again."

"You mean I did not try hard enough this time to stop you from going."

"Maybe not enough."

A poet in the Old World once compared the relationship between men and women to the earth's play by saying that the earth stays in its place, but the male bounces like a ball, and thanks to gravity, even though a ball may bounce many times, it keeps returning to the earth. Our hero and heroine were playing a ball game like that.

But the game lasted only a short while because Ketaki had to go. Aditya reached out to say goodbye, and Ketaki smiled and shook his hand. Both pairs of hands were moist and warm. They held on to each other's hands for a few moments. When they let go, a lot that had been unclear seemed to have been added. As Ketaki went towards the plane, Aditya stood still, looking at her till he could see her no more.

Ketaki could still see his eyes. She could see them all over. Even when she sat down in her seat, those eyes were still open inside her eyes. Those eyes had somehow captured the whole sky. Deep, quiet and filled with curious mystery. There was moisture in them, a softness, and a shine that mirrored his intellectual intensity. Throughout the flight, Ketaki felt surrounded by those eyes, and with her eyes shut, she kept looking at and reliving scenes from the last 24 hours. Sometimes, she would alter the scenes according to her desires—her answers would change, and so would Aditya's. And the answers and questions, questions and answers, the sweet innuendo, kept running through her head. The whole trip had been quite piquant. For the first time in her life, Ketaki felt that memories could be pleasing. Especially if fantasy were mixed into the memories; it increased the pleasure. Man would be deprived of so much were it not for memories. If anyone were watching Ketaki right now, they would think she was crazy because she was smiling with her eyes closed, or maybe they would think she was dreaming.

Aditya took a taxi right back to the hotel. He kept thinking of how the pallu of Ketaki's sari had slipped and his eyes had settled on the valley between two hills. While Ketaki looked out the window, he stared at her, transfixed. And then, as soon as Ketaki turned her face, he composed himself. Ketaki had sensed the direction of

Aditya's gaze and tucked one edge of her pallu under the side of her blouse that covered her left shoulder while she kept her eyes on the scenery outside the window. She had drawn a curtain over the scintillating scene that was fascinating Aditya.

In her absence, his mind kept replaying the scene. He felt a bit lost, perplexed.

As soon as he entered the room, he felt a strange emptiness inside. He went to the conference but felt uneasy there as well. He didn't feel like talking to anyone or want to listen to anything. He had lost interest in the whole thing. He phoned the airlines. There were no flights that evening. He took the first flight he could get the following day and left the town. He forgot that he had to head a panel at the conference the next morning.

The Seeds of Love

So this was the purvaraga or exposition, where the seeds of love were planted before the lovers met. In fact, the story of our hero and heroine does not have any of the elements of a purvaraga. They met because they actually saw each other, so this section should not apply to them. They had read each other's books, so it could be said that, like in the case of the act of hearing (one of the traditionally recognised avenues for cultivating devotion), reading had caused the seed to be sown. But I find that a bit difficult to believe. As both of them are intellectuals, they read many books and even praise them. To count reading as a seed of the feeling of love would mean that hundreds of lovers would start sprouting, and that is just not possible. Reading books is their profession. Sure, it did make meeting like this easier. They knew of each other, but you can't call that purvanurag, love that arises before lovers have met. Their story is not one of traditional love songs but more like the sixteenth-century epic poem *Dhola Maru Ru Duha* from Rajasthan, which is a story about love after marriage, so it can't be counted as one of the romantic tales of heroes and heroines ready to be put to death for their love. Instead of seeing one's future lover in a vision before they meet, in this case, everything happens face to face on this earth. Although the Rupmanjari of Nand Das is married, the seed of her love gets planted when she sees Krishna in a dream. She leaves all the hindrances and obligations of home and flows away like a river swelling in the monsoons. But here, the hero and heroine, who have seen each other in real life, are afraid of feeling love for each other or, to put it another way, are not taking it seriously. On the contrary, they start suppressing the feeling of love as soon as it arises, considering it a false emotion, and in this way, they deny love and themselves as well. If anyone looks at them from the outside, they will clearly see that the symptoms are the same as in the love stories.

When Ketaki got home, she felt Aditya's face was keeping her in the circuit of his attraction like a magnet. Instead of being happy, she got alarmed and tried to move out of this circuit. She thought that maybe it was the fact that she was not as busy with work as usual that made her spend her time thinking about Aditya.

She started thinking about a new research project. She was, of course, working on a subject already. She had committed herself to teaching a new course at the university. She started getting involved with so many activities that there should not have been a moment to think of anything else. But what began to happen was that Aditya would sneak in and sit down on a chair when she was taking a class. He would start whispering in her ear if she was at a meeting. If she were eating, he would sit across from her so that she would look at him and forget to eat. When she went to bed, he would speak to her until sleep fully took her in its grip. And she more or less stopped talking to and meeting her old friends.

Aditya decided every day that he would call Ketaki, but he would get scared. What would she think? She might even think he was stalking her and tell him off. He kept preparing himself to do it, and he kept losing courage. Just the thought of making a phone call sent the blood rushing through his arteries, and he would get anxious and postpone the call. And because this thought would make his blood speed out of control, quite a lot of time passed in procrastination. And putting things off was something that caused him a lot of anxiety. Baffled and bewildered, he would try to think of some way to gain control over his troubled mental state and take the matter one step further.

As you might know, in any love story, the hero sets off in pursuit of the heroine the minute the seed of love starts sprouting. And he makes all kinds of efforts to get her. This is why, when listing the characteristics of a story, the Sanskrit critic Acharya Bhamaha says that the theme of a story is Kanyā Haran, i.e. the acquisition of the heroine or beloved, war and separation. What I mean is that acquiring the girl does not happen by itself. To get her, every hero has to struggle and fight. It is in this struggle that the story emerges. If there is no battle, there is no story.

Let's see how much truth there is in what the critic says.

It is not that I doubt the excellent Acharya's words. But our hero does not look like a brave warrior. What if I were to fail the Sanskrit critic's test and be deprived of the privilege of storytelling? He will have to fight some battle, or else I will have to find another way.

Let us now consider the hero's situation. As far as the seed of love goes, he had no feelings about that. He wished to get to know Ketaki better; he wanted to meet her frequently, and this was all he understood. Nothing more than that. So when he felt the blood in his veins rushing several times faster than usual, he did not think about fighting. He only thought his nervous system was malfunctioning and that he needed to speak to a specialist.

And the question of a battle does not arise because the heroine is not anybody's possession or charge. She is like a waterfall that cascades freely without any hindrances. Nor is she in hiding, requiring one to go in search of her. It is only a matter of lifting the receiver and dialling her number.

Strangely, despite having access to such technical conveniences, our hero was pining for her and yet sitting around doing nothing.

Either the hero of today needs more self-knowledge, or he runs away from what his heart tells him or cannot grasp what his heart whispers in his ear. It has to be something like that. Even though there were phones at his desk and in his bedroom, toilet, kitchen, dining room, and everywhere else, why didn't he make the call? He certainly called others all day long. Every so often, his voice could even be heard in his motherland. Then why couldn't he call the woman he loved?

Well, it has yet to be determined that the heroine is the beloved. If the hero does not feel the pangs of love, it is morally wrong to call the heroine his beloved. The heroine might not approve, either. For all we know, she may be modern and have declared love dead or know nothing about love. Only those who read literature know about such meaningless stuff. Some others know, and some don't.

But I am unwilling to believe that the hero of my story is a coward. One would usually regard avoiding conflict or struggle as cowardice. But even though he is Bengali, unlike the hero of any Bengali film or novel, he is not submissive, faint-hearted or lily-livered. He seems to have a logic of his own. Maybe he does not, like a conventional hero, believe that you get the girl if you go out searching for her, meaning a heroine might have a mind of her own. Maybe the heroine does not want him, and then the whole search would be useless. Or, perhaps the heroine has some other lover or a husband. A husband one can fight and defeat, but a lover would be someone the heroine had chosen. Confronting him might make the heroine recede further. So that needs to be known first. In these days of women's liberation, if one does not know what the woman wants, what can one do?

What I am trying to say is that many questions were bothering our hero. He didn't want to believe in following his emotions. There was the chance of disappointment, and he had been there. But that is an old story, and I don't want to spoil things by talking about it now.

He had many leading ladies in his life, not just one. Some just came along, not because of anything he had done. Meaning the responsibility did not necessarily lie with our hero. So, he did not give much weight to risking his life to get the heroine or undertakings of that sort. Sometimes, the heroine would even show up in his bed by herself. The manners and customs of the new world are different. Sometimes, the heroines start out in search of the hero. It's nothing special. These things happen in tales of love. While searching for the main heroine, our hero is often the redemption of many beautiful women along the way and moves them to the inner chambers of his palace. Similarly, many heroines wander around crazed in search of their hero, such as beauties like Hidimba, who followed Bhima, and innumerable gopis who went after Krishna. It proves that this story's hero is a bit special and he is particularly accomplished when it comes to attracting beautiful women.

But the hero was not interested in such heroines at the moment. Nor was he convinced that Ketaki would come to him all by herself. There was possibly a little bit of pride involved, as heroines made it a habit of coming to him on their own, which may have been why he was hesitant about getting in touch with the heroine of this story. But as far as I know, Aditya is a serious sort of hero, not full of self-praise or false pride. He did contact her—in a very civilised and serene manner, so that she would not suspect that he was contacting her for no reason.

You might recall that Ketaki gave Aditya her book before leaving the hotel and expressed the wish that he read it and give his opinion. Now, what better reason could there be to contact her than that? He dropped everything else and sat down to read the five hundred pages of the book. He didn't sleep all night. Just kept reading. The book was fascinating. So, staying up all night was no punishment. But the night is the night, after all. It is meant for sleeping. Why else would the sun, birds, plants and trees all go to sleep?

Having stayed up all night, Aditya made a bleary-eyed phone call when the day broke. Thank heavens it was before the time of video calls, because if Ketaki had seen what his eyes looked like she would have had to change her relationship with those eyes.

The benefit of living in Navabhum was that a person could use the local language, in which there was no distinction between the honorific 'āp' and the more familiar 'tum' when one wanted to say 'you'. This meant that one did not have to decide immediately when talking to somebody how much of a distance one wanted to keep. What happens sometimes is that you feel close to somebody, and if that person doesn't feel the same, they get offended when you use 'tum'. The same is true if you use 'āp'. Someone might get offended at the use of this instrument of pushing people away because they might be expecting intimacy from you. While Aditya had already gone from 'āp' to 'tum', getting in touch after such a long time made him hesitate. Using the language of Navabhum saved him from his predicament for the time being.

Ketaki felt a thrill the moment she heard Aditya say his name.

"I read your book," Aditya started by saying.

Ketaki felt her hair stand on end, as if she were guilty of murder, standing in front of a judge and waiting for the verdict.

As soon as Aditya said he liked the book, Ketaki felt the sword tip had move away from her head to bequeath her a life.

She wrote each thing he said with an invisible pen on the pages of her mind. She would think about all of it later. Aditya was generous with his commentary. Each comment showed his ability to analyse and was expressed with clarity of thought, weighed and measured, clean and tidy. She wasn't just listening; she was preserving each thing he said within her.

When they stopped talking about the book, Ketaki wished they hadn't. It wasn't easy to decide whether it was aural pleasure, mental pleasure or just the joy of a vocal exchange. She only knew that she wanted to hear Aditya speak or to speak to him herself, and she wanted this conversation to last forever. Everything he said was significant. There was not one superfluous word.

"Tell me about yourself. What ideas are you working on nowadays?"

"I am trying to find questions to work on in the context of the current world situation."

"Like what?"

"The breakup of the Soviet Union has brought about a lot of changes at the national level, so many new nations have been born... The victory of democracy has been declared in the whole world, but what will the real effect be on different countries? I am considering writing about that."

"Do you believe that the whole world is becoming a market for Western countries, especially America, in the name of democracy?"

"Well, on the surface, that is what it looks like. Democracy is not a simple formula you can apply anywhere. Every country has its own traditions, history, and economy, and democracy grows from within that. Any form of government is generated from the situation in that country and the conduct of its people; why else was there no revolution in India despite all the fuss that was made about Marxism? Why did it only happen in Russia and China? No matter what we say about the democratisation of Russia, whatever political structure takes shape over there will be different from our concept of democracy, and that difference is what I want to examine. That is what I am thinking about at the moment. I might just have to go there next summer."

"What do you think is the fundamental difference between American and Indian democracy?"

"Look here, there are mainly two types of democracies—those that are based on the sentiment of the majority and those that are based on the concept of equal rights. America has had the majoritarian type of democracy until now. In India, when you talk of the majority, it becomes the Bharatiya Janata Party's Hindu nation. If you emphasise equal rights, it's the Mandal Commission, which a multitude of other people have started opposing. One needs a balance between the two. Here in the States, the two-party system is quite simple. In India, elections are extremely complex; different regions have their own political parties. So, one has to bring about a consensus among different opposing elements. In addition, the mental world of the voters of the two countries are also different; there is a great need to educate society about democracy. But it is a complicated issue. It is difficult to answer without a long analysis."

"I look forward to your book on the subject."

Just then, her phone notified her of another waiting call, so Ketaki said she would answer it and get back to him. It was a cosmetic company calling to conduct a survey. Ketaki broke off the call quickly, but when she called Aditya back, the spark of the conversation had fizzled out. Aditya said he had to go somewhere and that he would call later. Ketaki felt bad. Had she not answered the other call, she and Aditya would have gone on speaking for a while. Now, she had no clue how long she would have to wait for him to call.

But then she realised that she could call him herself. True, but she would have to think of an excuse. Just call to chat? Did they have that sort of friendship? Ketaki felt that she needed to learn how much one should use the phone, ideally. A friend's husband had once said, "Why does Ketaki leave such long messages on the phone? Does she have nothing else to do?"

That made Ketaki think she spent a lot of time talking on the phone. Perhaps that wasn't such a good thing. She had better control herself.

I told Ketaki a couple of times myself, "Look, I am a bit busy. I can't talk right now." She was quite upset. Perhaps that was when she became conscious of how much time she spent on the phone. Poor Aditya. He kept waiting for her call. How was he to know she was waiting for him to call?

Ketaki had no clue what was going on inside her. As far as she knew, love descended upon you like a gale or a storm and blew away everything. No such whirlwind had hit her life. How was she to know that even though the ground seemed calm and tranquil, there were forces underneath that were active and shook the earth during an earthquake and destroyed everything at once? Ketaki was unaware of the changes underway within her. All she knew was that she had never felt this way before, longing to hear Aditya's voice, to meet and see him.

Then, suddenly, one day a parcel arrived. Ketaki was curious. Who had sent it? She turned the parcel upside down. She spotted the name of Aditya's university. What had Aditya sent her?

The packaging was so thorough that it was impossible to tear it open. She had to locate a pair of scissors. They weren't where they were supposed to be. She did not have the patience to look for them. She took a knife from the kitchen and cut one side of the package open to find a book inside. There was a handwritten note from Aditya as well.

> Dear Ketaki,
> After I read your book, I thought you might like this one. The point of view expressed in it is quite like yours. Since it is from another discipline, you might enjoy looking at things from a different angle. Please read it and let me know what your reaction is.
> With love,
> Aditya

It struck Ketaki that Aditya must be thinking of her as well. That was why he had thought of sending the book. And maybe, by sending it, he was giving her an excuse, no, an opportunity, to call him. Which would mean he was keen to talk to her, too.

A book is a very rare and precious thing for modern-day lovers. In a way, it is like a mantra; the minute you chant it, you get a chance to contact your lover. Contact over a book then makes it possible to converse or take your relationship a bit further, whereas, in our medieval tales of love, the hero and heroine do not have anything to say beyond exchanging feelings of love. And suppose they are too embarrassed to express their love. I—in that case, they must make do with silence, or the storyteller takes refuge in describing nature.

Ketaki started reading the book the very same night. By the next morning, she had left a message on Aditya's answering machine: "Thanks for sending the book. I just started reading it. Let me know when you are free so we can have a long chat about it."

Ketaki was not home when his message came in on her answering machine: "I am free on Sunday morning. Let me know if that suits you. I could call you at 10. If you can't talk then, suggest another time."

Ketaki left him another message: "I usually go to the gym on Sunday mornings. But I won't now. I can go later. I'll wait for your call."

And so the phone dates started. Then Aditya said once, "Why do we speak to each other for hours on the phone? Wouldn't it be better if we met sometime? We could meet and talk."

Ketaki beamed. "Sure. But when? And where?"

"Let me think."

The next time they spoke on the phone, Aditya said, "I have to come to your town next month."

"Really! When? For how long?"

"Two days."

"For work?"

"Yes, I have a meeting. Would you like to meet up?"

"Absolutely!"

When Vidyapati's heroine wanted to meet her lover, she had to search everywhere for a secret message-bearer who could carry messages for her. Prithviraj had to attack Sanyogita's father's kingdom to meet her. To meet

Mahiwal, Sohni had to cross the river on a large earthen jar. Here, one just has to make a phone call, and a date is fixed. Well, one does need to take a flight. And one cannot deny the dangers of flying.

But it is yet to be decided whether Aditya and Ketaki are, in fact, lovers. Do they show all the signs of lovers?

What are the signs of lovers? Do we really know?

Shouldn't we decide first whether these two are helplessly in love, failing which the entire undertaking of writing a story will be pointless? The time that I have spent writing and you have spent reading will have been needlessly wasted. And you must know that although time might be the cheapest and most useless commodity in Purabhum, in Navabhum, people are ready to give up their lives to save the slightest bit of time. Ever since he came to the new world, our hero had used time very measuredly. Ketaki didn't believe in sitting and twiddling her thumbs, languishing over her lover.

On the contrary, she was so involved in her work and a bunch of tasks that she had not noticed the bullet of love digging into her. She was wandering around, absorbed in her work, making new plans. She is the kind of lover who doesn't even think the serpent of love can sting her. She believes that falling in love is the domain of those princesses who have been raised in comfort and leisure and have nothing to think about or do. According to Ketaki, a woman in love looks beautiful, has a weak mind, is innocent at heart, is eager to please her lover, and is someone who sighs and bursts into tears at the drop of a hat. Ketaki has none of these characteristics, so she cannot be counted as a woman in love or one of the heroines of medieval romances.

She still could not stop thinking about Aditya, waiting for his calls or remembering conversations they had and things he had said.

But she did not consider these things the characteristics of a woman in love.

Could you call them the characteristics of a modern lover?

Let us not forget the hero. The characteristics of a lover have been described since the time of the first sage, Bharata. However, according to the writers of the Shastras, a hero is not just a lover. He has many tasks to do, and while he is busy dealing with them, he meets the heroine, who attracts his attention. This is similar to the story of Shakuntala, in which the hero, Dushyant, goes out to hunt and comes upon Shakuntala. And then, for a while, the whole story centres around them. Until the hero brings the heroine to the queen's chambers, the main focus is on their love. The minute the queen reaches the palace, the story of that love ends. The heroine becomes one of many queens, and the hero feels he has done what is expected of him for love. In the love story of Padmavati, the hero hears of Padmavati from a parrot and goes out in search of her for no other reason. And when he does marry her, he brings her home to be the rival of his wife, Nagmati. After the wedding night, Padmavati spends the rest of her life dealing with her co-wife. And if one wants to write a tragedy, then there is only one kind of ending to a love story: the hero dies and the heroine commits sati. When Padmavati's husband Ratnasen gets killed in a battle with Allauddin Khilji, Padmavati and her co-wife Nagmati throw themselves on the funeral pyre of their husband.

Our hero will surely fit in some category mentioned in the Shastras. Due to his enlightened mind, one might call him dhīrapraśānta—a self-controlled and calm hero. A bit like the heroes of Tagore. Like Ratnasen, he can't be just a lover. In a way, it would be an injustice to him if we were to look in him for characteristics of an old-world hero. He has made Gaurbhum his home for the last twenty-five years, understood their ways, and made them his own, so what does he have to do with a Purabhum hero, especially one from the Shastras? He is very different from the modern heroes of Purabhum. His views and opinions have changed a lot. While looks and appearances still stay the same, as does the colour of the skin, inside him there has certainly been a transformation.

Could one call him a postcolonial hero?

Bhojaraja has given a lot of thought to the virtues of a hero. At the same time, most other authors of the Shastras have got entangled in elaborating on the virtues of a heroine and never been able to leave. But whether one defers to Bhojaraja or Bharata, one can only classify our hero as a supreme male character.

Well, the point is that Ketaki came to see me yesterday, looked at my unfinished novel and said, "Why have you called this chapter 'The First Sighting'? That is over and done with." And she was right. And she wasn't. Since love did not appear the first time they saw each other, I believe the first sighting has not occurred yet. Only if they feel filled with love the moment they look at each other can you regard it as the actual first sighting. In a country like Gaurbhum, intellectuals say that love that does not spring at first sight can hardly be counted as love.

It is possible that I, the narrator, do not know how to define whatever happened between Ketaki and Aditya. I can only take what Ketaki tells me and put what I understand into words. Much of it may be beyond my comprehension, so I cannot get it across to you. But I trust that you will understand it all by yourself if you are sharp enough.

There are, after all, many categories of love, and there is the kind of love that develops slowly. It doesn't burst into flame at first glance. Sages in the old world linked love directly with beauty. Love that smoulders on slowly doesn't fit into the highest category. But they consider love to be the raw sugar that a mute person can savour but cannot express with words. The same goes for thinkers of the new world. No one has ever been able to define love properly, so one starts to doubt whether it exists. Especially when love is considered God, this doubt becomes real because anyone and everyone questions God's existence.

So we were talking about the first meeting, which is a tale in itself. Both of them wanted to meet and wanted to avoid meeting as well. They were scared that it would be hard to avoid further involvement if they met.

Aditya's meeting was being held quite far away from Ketaki's university. Ketaki was busy as well. Finding a time when they would both be free was hard. Earlier, a hero would be involved in work while the heroine sat at home and waited for him to come. But now, our heroine was just as involved in all kinds of work as our hero. The fact is that after the divorce, she had no other way of getting by. You had to dig your own well to drink the water. It was impossible to manage without a job. There was no one to take care of her. This is the price the heroine had to pay for freedom.

So, meeting each other was quite a complex matter. Getting to the heroine was not hard for him; no guards were watching over her. Even her parents were dead and gone. Nor did she have a guardian uncle. But being busy is a hindrance in itself. Anyhow, they met for lunch, as that was the only time in the day they could make the time to meet.

Just think about it—in a beautiful restaurant in Gaurbhum—dressed up in the latest apparel of Gaurbhum, but the produce of Purabhum—a heroine and a hero.

At the centre of the restaurant was a huge decorative display of fresh flowers. Gathering in her voluminous black skirt as she sat in her chair, Ketaki looked at the flowers and remarked, "These tropical flowers are so beautiful. Highly unusual. That anthurium's bright red looks almost like a dash of sindoor. The fragrance of that flower arrangement pervades the whole restaurant."

"Do you like flowers?"

"I have always loved flowers. But since I was always surrounded by them, I didn't give them much thought. Now that I am deprived of them in my apartment, I try and enjoy beautiful flowers whenever I see them."

Just then, the waiter turned up. And the talk turned to the food.

The waiter started listing the special dishes they were serving that afternoon.

Ketaki chose a salad of radicchio and arugula as an appetiser and three kinds of baked fish as her main course. She asked, "What would you like to eat?" Aditya said he would have the same. He immediately felt that whatever Ketaki had chosen would be suitable for him as well. Maybe he wanted to give little thought to food. He liked the fact that Ketaki was ordering tasty food. There was something about it that gave him a feeling of deja vu. Could it be that she reminded him of his mother always ordering food for him at restaurants? Only his mother knew precisely what Aditya liked to eat! He loved fish in any form. Perhaps Ketaki had associated his being a Bengali with fish and that was why she had ordered some for herself. His taste matched that of his mother's, or rather, he had grown to prefer the things his mother liked. Often, it would be hard for Aditya to tell whether his mother had ordered what she liked or only his favourites. Aditya felt he had come home. He sat Ketaki at the dining table at home and asked, "How come you like fish?"

"What do you mean? Was fish invented exclusively for you Bengalis? But then, you guys only eat river fish."

"People in your part of the woods usually prefer to eat meat and chicken."

"My birth sign is Pisces. When I was little, my mother often fed me a whole fish. Until I saw the whole fish, eyes included, I would create a fuss and say, 'What kind of fish is this?'"

"Wow, you are a step ahead of me."

"Hmm, have you ever eaten the head of a fish?"

"No. I am not up for that."

"But that is the delicacy." Ketaki started to laugh loudly as if she had won.

The point was that despite being where they were, they were in another place together. You could feel it in what they were saying—every conversation they had, carried a sense of the present and the nostalgia of the past, in the new love and the memory of old companions. Both of them were drowning in the other as well as in their living history.

They spent quite a long time talking about this and that. What his meeting was about, studying, teaching, politics, history, and economics—things related to their daily lives. What was not being said or done was what was foremost in their thoughts.

When it was time to leave, Aditya felt he had been unable to say anything significant, so he said candidly, "Why are we speaking of everything under the sun? I came here to meet you. I want to hear more about what you are up to."

Ketaki couldn't say anything. "What news could there be about me? Life goes on, that's all."

Suddenly, Aditya said, "I have been thinking a lot about you."

Ketaki said, "So have I." She caught her tongue in her teeth and stared down at her plate.

"There hasn't been a day that I haven't thought about you since the day we met. You might consider this distasteful or cheap emotionalism, but the fact is that you have awakened something inside me, shaken me up inside. I am not fully aware of the changes within me, but whatever is happening, I might let it happen. Would you like to say anything?"

"I don't know what to say at the moment."

"I am not asking you to commit yourself in any way."

"I understand."

"Would you like to meet me again?"

"Sure."

"Are you going to the Asian Pacific conference next month? I have to go there."

"I hadn't decided yet. But maybe I will come."

Aditya understood that Ketaki was experiencing the same emotions as him. She was also eager to meet Aditya, which made him keener to meet her. He didn't particularly want to go to the conference. But now he was determined to go, so he tried convincing Ketaki to go with him.

When Aditya helped Ketaki put her coat on as they were leaving the restaurant, his fingers accidentally touched her shoulder. He felt a buzz as if he had been struck by lightning. Ketaki extended her hand after getting her coat on to say goodbye. Aditya felt as if he had dipped frozen fingers in warm water to stop his fingers from shaking. He felt like holding onto her hand. As if asking a question, he said, "So then, see you."

With a smile in her eyes, Ketaki answered the question in Aditya's eyes and reassured him.

Ayog
Semi-union

Venus and The New Moon

When you see Venus next to the new moon, it always feels like they must be old lovers. Together like this for centuries. Always at the same distance. They are gazing at each other, chatting. And yet you feel that maybe they will never be able to meet, that a distance will always remain between them. The lovers' destinies are often close but not close, far but not far.

Perhaps this is just my way of looking at things.

People might think that this is the way unions are. Not too close, not too far. That's how they last. Because if the distance persists, a lover turns and finds a new path, and if one gets too close, the sweetness is so intense that ants get at it. And you know that once ants attack something sweet, it isn't edible any longer, or they devour it themselves. Which is why Buddha suggested one should choose the middle path.

Now, the middle path cannot be the path of love. How can someone, blinded by impulse, who can't see the way clearly, stick to the middle of the clean road before him? Love is born when a person leaves the middle path, or rather, love, when it is born, forces you to leave the middle path. Love is nurtured by following a twisting path. And sometimes, lovers leave the path and start moving through the heavens. As a result, they land on the ground with a bump at times or remain suspended in midair. "The path of love is very straight," as the poet said, but he was talking about it being as straight as the slice of a sword. Those who do not want to kill or die but just want to follow an easy road cannot love. One can only love if one is willing to be crucified.

In any love story, the union of hero and heroine is challenging. For a long time, they remain in a state of semi-union or ayog, i.e. they experience desire and anxiety. Many obstacles come their way, and they must face many adversities. Farhad had to dig up a mountain to get water, but he still did not get his beloved. Matters of pride and honour often appear as obstacles. The poor heroine suffers greatly because those fights are mainly related to men's ego issues. Even the men who are closest to her. On one side is her brother or father, and on the other is her lover. A thousand years ago, the Rajput king Prithviraj kidnapped his brother's daughter Sanyogita from her swayamvar because Sanyogita's father did not want to marry her off to Prithviraj. While Prithviraj was the most powerful king of his time and Sanyogita loved only him, it was precisely because of this conflict that a fierce battle occurred.

There are two types of union. One is for a short while; the hero and heroine can sit together in a restaurant for an hour, have coffee, walk in a garden, or stand in the corner of the college classroom and chat. The second one binds the two together for life; the hero takes the heroine as his bride and brings her to his home forever. As far as the traditional love story is concerned, the latter lasts throughout life and for many births. This relationship is often said to have begun in a previous life. It gets fulfilled in the era in which the story is set, like in the story of the parrot and the mynah; their relationship has been going on since time immemorial. But once the bride comes home, either the love story ends there, or if the story continues further, then it deals with the domestic disputes of the mother-in-law and sister-in-law or the issues of the co-wife. When that happens, the romantic fun disappears. Yes, one gets a taste of domesticity, but the spice of the fights between mother-in-law and sister-in-law is sometimes so pungent that one's tongue gets burnt.

In theory, there is a great difference between meeting briefly and staying together for a lifetime. Perhaps that is why Acharya Dhananjay, the author of *Dasarupaka*, conceived of 'ayog shringar'. Ayog is basically purvarag or the moments before the lovers meet. The seer also described its ten stages—desire, anxiety, memory, statement of virtues, excitement, delirium, frenzy, fever, and inertia; he even included death. In contrast, the stages chosen by Acharya Mammat under 'sanyog' or union are sighting, hugging, kissing, water sports, etc. Desire, delirium, etc., only last during ayog, i.e. until the hero meets the heroine; after that, the only things that remain are kissing and sexual intercourse.

For this reason, perhaps Ketaki and Aditya are afraid of a full union despite wanting to get closer to each other. Perhaps they do not want to lose the pleasure of desire, excitement, or memory and are forced to remain in a state of purvarag or ayog. I want to call this disjunction "ardha yoga", or semi-union, because even though the hero and heroine connect on many levels, they are not entirely connected. Some distances remain.

This may not be a simple thing to explain. They are not doing it intentionally, but because of circumstances. So, what are these circumstances? They are probably trying to protect themselves. It's a matter of self-respect. Not only Freud but even our old teacher Bhojraj noted that the fundamental relationship of love is with one's own ego. This means that you love others so that you can be loved, that is, to satisfy your ego. A profound concept. I will consider it later. It will lead to too much digression now, making the story difficult to handle.

There is one more thing: Adi Acharya Bharat has also described three types of union according to the hero's point of view. 'Dharma shringar'—where the hero establishes a love relationship with his wife according to 'garhasthya dharma'. 'Artha shringar'—where the hero enters into a relationship with another woman based on money. 'Kam shringar'—here, the hero and heroine meet purely for work's sake. Actually, Bhojraj Ji also emphasised one more difference, which he called 'moksha shringar', but no one accepted that difference because, in a way, it got absorbed in religion.

The problem is that our hero and heroine do not fit neatly into any category. The sages have not defined any category on the basis of the way these two develop intellectual attraction for each other. There is a feeling of lust in both of them. Still, desire and intelligence have become so fused that it seems wrong to look at them separately. One thing is clear: while they are capable of conquering sexual attraction, they do not want to avoid an intellectual connection; hence, whenever they meet, intellectual connection remains in the forefront. Their intellectual connection made it difficult for them to consider the sexual attraction significant. Even if there is a desire for it, it remains unspoken or suppressed.

The strangeness of their situation is that they remain parallel in the states of union, separation, and semi-union. They live on two opposite ends of the land, a thousand miles between them. Therefore, the meeting of bodies is impossible. But the meeting of minds happens now and then on the telephone. They meet each other every few months in connection with some academic activity. In this way, they keep getting the mental satisfaction through which union occurs. Yet, they do not get complete satisfaction, and the desires of ayog—adornment, excitement, praise, etc.—also keep coming and going. Many separations or 'vipralambh shringar' also take place. Migration is the main problem, both the cause and the result of their separation. (We will discuss separation at the appropriate place.)

In today's era, it is necessary to interpret the statements of the sages by modern standards; otherwise, how will our readers know if what I am saying is correct? They will say that it is better to study the Acharyas than to study you. Why would anyone read writers like me, especially when ancient sources are available?

With all the developments in modern psychology, it seems fitting to say that these situations keep arising in the minds of the hero and heroine; that is, separation can be experienced alongside union, and union can be experienced alongside separation. How did all this happen? Hopefully, we can demonstrate that through the story.

So, as I was saying, the first union between our hero and heroine flourishes only on the level of intellectual growth. Today's scholars will even ask you to explain what you mean by intelligence. Is it the intercourse of the intellects with each other, or is it the reaching of the intellect through the body, or something else? It would be best if you decided on this matter yourself. I am concerned with the pace of the story and the departure. The storyteller should not enter the world of analysis. That destroys the story and the analysis because it has no solid basis. Why would anyone read the storyteller for an analysis? Let us talk only about the story.

So Aditya returned to his West Coast city after lunch that day. But his mind was still sitting on the eastern coast of Navabhum. He thought he would write a letter to Ketaki. But there was no time to write letters. Sometimes, people do not even give you their address. The interaction is completed by simply exchanging phone numbers. But he had kept Ketaki's visiting card carefully, and her address was on it.

One day, another parcel arrived at Ketaki's house. Her guess when she saw the envelope was accurate. Upon opening the packet, she found two of Aditya's books. So he had remembered to send her a parcel. Ketaki had considered buying the books, but he seemed to have sent them as soon as she had returned.

Ketaki put everything else aside and devoured both books for 4–5 days.

Then she wrote to Aditya for the first time. Her letter discussed the two books. In the end, she wrote that she would be thrilled to meet him and discuss the issues mentioned in the book because she would not be able to write everything in a letter. What she couldn't write about had to do nothing with books. There were some personal matters as well. Readers must understand that women hesitate to say everything clearly.

This time, Aditya called her. "There is no need to wait until the conference, why don't you come here on the next long weekend?"

"So far!"

"There is a conference at our university. You could come for that. There might be some funds available as well. Here, too, there is considerable discussion about communalism."

"But you are so far away."

"Once you board the plane, it doesn't make much difference whether it's 3 or 5 hours."

"That's true."

"I'll meet you at the airport. Would you like to stay at my place, or shall I arrange a hotel?"

She thought about that for a few moments.

"A hotel would be fine."

"I will call you after finalising everything. You book your plane tickets."

"I will check out tickets today."

When Ketaki put the phone down, it was as if there were rollerblades under her feet. She moved quickly from room to room as if she were about to board a plane. The airline operator asked her to stay on the line. Ketaki flipped through books with her cordless phone pressed to her ear, opened the fridge, filled a glass with something to drink, and made lists and notes of essential tasks.

During the flight, she was lost in thought. What would Aditya think? He had called, and she had come. That was why she had decided to stay at a hotel. But was there anything wrong with that belief? Wasn't she eager to meet Aditya? Why was she denying that truth? The happiness attainable from that truth? Wasn't it just a matter of ego? Hiding the needs of the heart from oneself. Denial. Because there will always be the danger of the ego getting hurt and of rejection.

She had always made mistakes like this. She would not do so this time. Even before her marriage, she had not listened to her heart. She had listened to her father and married the man of his choice. What a mistake that was! The man was educated, came to America to study on a scholarship, and started his practice here. But how Ketaki suffocated under his ego and success! When she asked about finding a job, the answer was, "I have so much work to do. You can take care of all the secretarial work. That way whatever we earn stays with us." Or "Why do you want to take on a job? There's so much money coming in. Why don't you handle that?"

Then, other changes started happening in her life. Ketaki had been busy with her PhD. Her husband had started becoming interested in one of the student interns at his hospital. That girl became a part of his practice and his personal life. All this happened when Ketaki was completing her doctoral thesis.

A crack began to appear in Ketaki's heart.

Thankfully, she had postponed her wifely duties until she finished her doctorate.

No. All that happened a long time ago. She refused to think about it.

Upon completing her doctorate, she even worked as an assistant professor at a college. After that, teaching, reading, writing and publishing were allowed to remain the centre of her life, and everything else was left out.

One or two sporadic relationships. Only to get rid of her intense loneliness. Protect her from depression. They allowed her husband to get rid of her by slandering her. Then, it seemed as if those relationships became a medicine—healing the wounds caused by the divorce. Somewhere, she was exacting revenge for the way her husband had insulted her.

But this time, that was not all. Aditya was truly growing in her life. Ketaki was bursting with the first redness of the morning.

As soon as she emerged from the flight at the airport, she saw Aditya sitting in the lounge, right in front, flipping through a magazine. His searching eyes had found her immediately too. When he got up, they reached for each other with both hands.

"You disembarked very quickly. I started flipping through the magazines to pass the time." He had the latest issue of *The Economist* in his hand.

"My seat was right in front," said Ketaki. She looked at him. He was wearing a dark blue shirt and beige cotton trousers. A lock of hair fell over his forehead.

"Did you check in your luggage, or is it just this bag?" asked Aditya as he took it from her.

"I believe in travelling light," Ketaki said, throwing her handbag on her left shoulder, putting her right hand in her pocket, and standing in a relaxed pose.

Aditya looked at her and said, "Let's go to your hotel... or do we want to go somewhere else first?"

"I'm in your hands. Wherever you want to go," she said, swinging the purse from her left shoulder to the right.

"Such trust in a stranger? No, no, that could be dangerous." Aditya was smiling.

"I don't even know the difference between who is mine and who is a stranger any longer." By the end of the sentence, there was a trace of embarrassment in Ketaki's voice.

"That is even more dangerous." Aditya ignored the embarrassment.

"Playing with danger is considered good in this country. It is the culture here. If I don't take risks now, when will I take them?"

"The philosophy is valid. Danger does make life more interesting."

"Not only interesting, dangers also make life worth living."

A trace of curiosity appeared on Aditya's face. Ketaki smiled. She said something and left something unsaid. "Had I not taken the risk, I would have returned to my country. Then how would I have met you?" Now Ketaki smiled and fixed her gaze on Aditya's face.

Aditya wanted to know more about this woman. She had reached here after so many journeys. Her history must be complex. He didn't know how many layers it was wrapped in. After unwrapping each layer, he would find something attractive and exciting. Maybe that was why he was drifting towards her. He wanted to keep opening her—in every way, from every direction, on every surface.

On coming to Navabhum, all the creatures of Purabhum first try to get to know each other through their personal histories. First, they revolve around personal history, then learn more about each other's families and social, urban, or class-specific circles.

The interests of the hero and heroine have yet to be completely satisfied in the realm of personal history.

"When, why and how did you come to Navabhum? Ambition? A habit of running away from home? Or circumstances?"

Ketaki told him. "I wanted to come here to visit. Not to settle down. But the strange thing is that whenever the subject of marriage was raised at home, only some foreign-based groom would come to my parents' mind. There may be a shortage of brides here. Everyone wants to get married to someone over there, and it seems like an excellent proposal for girls like me, whose parents are looking for a prosperous and secure life for their daughters. They need to realise that, while the solidity of prosperity may be necessary for marriage, it is more important for a relationship to be solid. One-sided prosperity collapses by itself or like a three-legged table—it does not have a well-balanced base. So this, sir, was the beginning of my expatriate life."

"So the groom brought you here in a palanquin?"

"Not a palanquin, but on a flying carpet."

"You must have enjoyed the flying carpet a lot."

"The story is more complex than you think. I had been here before. Papa was posted here for three years, so I returned home after finishing college. That's why I was not an innocent or a country bumpkin bride."

That means our heroine was already steeped in Navabhum.

"And so your parents were familiar with this world, and they didn't have the same fear of leaving you here that other parents in this situation do."

"Correct. Not only that, they also thought that I could put my education to good use by coming here."

"Which is what happened."

"But it could only be put to use properly after I managed to get out of the trap in which they had entangled me."

"Well, your studies turned out useful after all."

"Yes, in many ways, wherever I am now is because of my studies."

"Then what is the story of that three-legged table?"

"The table is still standing on three legs. My head is propping up the fourth corner."

"So now just one axe is needed." Aditya was laughing.

"Sure. And you can do the chopping."

"No. I only consider a table with four legs a table. Everything else is a compromise."

"Please tell me, what do you think those four legs are?"

"The sages of our country have given them precise names."

"So tell me what they are."

"Oh, you know—dharma, artha, kama, and moksha. According to me, I stand on two legs, but the other two..."

"Which are the two legs you don't have?"

"Does that need to be specified? I am not dissatisfied on the religious and monetary fronts... but the rest..."

Aditya gave her a mischievous look and started to laugh.

Ketaki kept looking into his eyes. She could see a whole world there. Then she looked outside the car window. The mountain ranges laden with pine trees were spread far and wide. She exclaimed, "What a beautiful place you live in!"

Aditya loved his city very much, but hearing this from Ketaki made it seem like she was complimenting him.

"You've never been to the West Coast before?"

"I have, but only visited the capital. I was so struck by the miles and miles of nature, such denseness of greenery, beautiful serrated hills, and such bright transparent sunlight."

"This state is lovely. If you are interested, I will take you on a long drive one day. There are redwood forests where trees that are thousands of years old await you. You have everything there: the high waterfalls, the expansive ocean, the dense mountains. If you like the desert, you don't have to go very far for that, either. You can find a whole world of variety in some hundred miles."

"Such beautiful wildflowers add colour to this landscape." She had been looking at the flowers outside the window for a long time.

Then, because she loved looking at the beauty of nature, Ketaki said, "I don't have anything to do in the hotel right now. Leave the luggage in the car. Let's go to your conference first."

"Are you sure?"

"Yes, yes, I came properly prepared. This is not like a train journey in our country, where one has to have a bath before doing anything else."

Aditya couldn´t help laughing at the way she had said that in Hindi, with a Haryanvi accent.

She met a lot of people at the conference that evening. She already knew some of them, but Aditya introduced her to everyone as his special guest. About two hours later, Ketaki began to feel the jet lag. When

Aditya saw her fight sleep off, he reacted immediately. "Let me drop you back. We have to make an early start in the morning."

Aditya picked up Ketaki from her hotel early the next day. She was dressed in jeans and a sweater and was in a holiday mood. She had tied her cut hair tightly into a ponytail. On a face like the open sky, light red lipstick marked her lips as if the sun was about to rise between them.

They drove towards the hills. The infinite expanse of beauty intoxicated Ketaki. Many parts of the forests on the mountains were on fire. The fires spread with the wind. It was not in anyone's power to stop the spread. It was being brought under control with great difficulty.

Incidentally, that evening, it was reported in the news that parks were now open to the public. Aditya decided to go to one of them the following day.

The entire route looked like a bed of beauty to Ketaki: dense forests, an endless expanse of greenery, and high, strong rocks. Spreading far and wide like memory, the rocky cliffs held ancient histories. Ketaki felt that the histories of the stones extended far beyond the history of humans. These stones had seen, heard, endured, and appreciated so much. How small a person becomes when she encounters such vastness and depth. But when it descends within her, whether it makes her great or not, it definitely makes her feel that she can be part of the greatness for years, by tasting, smelling, and drinking in the vastness. If only she could be a part of it! Would this experience remain with her? Would it survive and stay alive or get lost again and disappear in the hustle and bustle of the city and work? No, this time, she would try to keep it safe.

She felt as if Aditya were also a part of her experience, as if, alongside the vastness of history, she was simultaneously drinking in Aditya's presence. Aditya was like a thread woven into her entire experience, which, along with the atmosphere, was running in her veins.

"It has been a long time since I have been so close to beauty." Aditya smiled, for seeing the effect of the view on her made him feel good; while meditating on this pleasure, he said, "You live in beauty; I mean, you personify it ... yourself."

Ketaki started to blush. At that moment, she appeared extremely beautiful to Aditya, just like the rocks bathed in the redness of the rising sun, whose reflection also washed Ketaki's face in colour. He felt like kissing her. All the details of the night flashed across his mind like lightning. His hair stood on end. Aditya felt his mind spinning as if he had left the steering wheel and fallen into her arms.

Then, as if with a jerk, he pulled himself together.

Perhaps Ketaki would find his behaviour rude. He started paying full attention to the road as he drove.

But within a few moments, he realised that Ketaki was looking at him. Aditya kept his eyes fixed on the road. He felt rather than saw Ketaki turn towards him.

He looked at her for a moment. When Aditya turned his face towards Ketaki, she saw the morning's red sun reflected in his eyes. That light was pleasant. Not dazzling. The light that gives living things life does not scorch you. They exchanged smiles as they looked at each other.

"Where should we stop?"

"You decide."

"Why not sit somewhere and enjoy the sun before it rises too high?"

At the next stop, Aditya turned the car and brought it to a halt in front of a small café nestled among the rocks.

No one was there so early in the morning; the owner had just arrived. As soon as they opened the door, the smell of fresh coffee hit their nostrils.

Aditya asked the woman at the counter, "Can we get breakfast?" She nodded and said that they could sit wherever they wanted.

Shortly after they sat down, the lady came to take their order.

After ordering an omelette, toast, and coffee, as soon as the lady turned towards the kitchen, Ketaki said, "I feel like settling here among these rocks."

"Not a bad thought. It will be easy to write a book in such a rugged environment. You won't find any library nearby, though."

"One could pick up one's entire library and bring it here."

"It's worth thinking about once you become a pensioner. If the library were here now, you'd only be able to read during the holidays. You'll spend the rest of the year waiting to reach here."

"You don't like living in the wilderness."

"I do, but it is not practical. Business is in the city."

"To be honest, I have tried to live in the wilderness. My ex-husband bought a house in an area like this, but it was not as beautiful as this. Well, the big problem was that I started getting bored after a few months. I felt like I was cut off from the whole world. I am blessed to live in the middle of civilisation. Otherwise, the eternal silence and desolation would bore me."

"You are right. I want to live as close or far away from my university as I am now. It helps me maintain balance in my life."

"Is your house on a hill?"

"It is not very high but can be called a hill. You can see for yourself and decide. Will you come and see my house?

"Of course, will you show it to me?"

"If you wish."

"Do you even need to ask?"

Peals of laughter again. Like foam that rises from the water when you row a boat.

Breakfast arrived. Ketaki spread butter on Aditya's toast as well. When she was handing him the toast she had buttered, he looked confused. Then suddenly, as if she had become self-conscious, she said, "Once one has been a housewife, one doesn't forget this for the rest of one's life."

Aditya said, "As a matter of fact, I like it when someone else butters the bread. Especially if it is a beautiful person." His eyes were gleaming with mischief.

"A slave of habit!" She laughed.

"No, of the hand." The pinky of Aditya's left hand crept towards and nearly touched Ketaki's hand on the table.

Aditya's eyes were still mischievous.

"So we have descended from history and politics to the real thing," she said, hiding her shyness.

"Politics and history have their role. So do feelings. There is no contradiction there. Both swords can stay in one sheath."

"But are both swords?"

"Absolutely, and double-edged ones as well. They cut from both sides, and if you have been struck and are about to die, no one will ask if you want a drink of water."

"But still, you want to give space to feelings in your life."

"I haven't done that for a long time. Now, I feel compelled to do so. It also feels as if this is happening for the first and last time in my life. I have started loving you, Ketaki. Will you be able to take it?" He said everything in one breath.

Ketaki was stunned, dazzled by the brightness of a thousand flowers.

Aditya murmured, "Will you be able to bear my love?"

Sunlight slanted through the glass walls of the café and illuminated Ketaki's face. When Aditya talked about loving her, he felt as if Ketaki was the whole world; she was the light or that radiant beauty he had always been searching for, whom he had no hope of finding. Suddenly, Ketaki had awakened one of his semi-conscious dreams.

Ketaki seemed to be frozen as if she could not hear what she was hearing, as if it was a thought, a stray leaf flying in the wind, a fragrance passing by in a breath, or a single sunlit drop from the sky. Was it true? Had she genuinely heard what she had heard?

Aditya had said what he had to say; perhaps he was waiting for Ketaki's answer, but she was lost. She was still trying to hear the words he had said a moment ago again and felt that he was about to say something. There was an expectation on both sides that something would be said by the other. Ketaki wanted to be assured that what had been said had been said. Aditya felt that perhaps too much had been said, and he remained silent in great suspense, waiting to see Ketaki's reaction.

Hours of silence passed between them.

Aditya tried to speak. "Will you say something? Do you want to say anything? You can even scold me for my nonsense if you like."

Now Ketaki was sure that whatever she had heard had been said.

But what was the answer? What could she say?

There are very few moments in life when it seems as if you can put your whole life at stake just for that moment, as if everything has been a preparation, a waiting for that one moment.

Ketaki felt that she was saying this and Aditya was listening.

In fact, Aditya had heard it.

She started watching the play of light on the rocks outside. The sun had come out completely. Shimmering golden sunlight had begun to take hold everywhere.

Suddenly, Ketaki's hand trembled on the table. Aditya had touched her with his finger to get her attention. Ketaki felt as if a ray of the sun had turned into electricity. Then she controlled herself, turned to Aditya and said, "Are you really waiting for my answer?"

"If... if you can give it."

"Do you think one can answer your question with a yes or a no?"

"If I can be sure... I am not saying that... you do not need to answer immediately. I do not want to put such a burden on you; even if you do not answer, it doesn't matter."

Ketaki was deep in thought. Should she say something and commit herself with her words? Get trapped by them? Was she ready for this encirclement, this bondage? She kept wondering what to do for a long time.

Aditya told her, "You seem to have forgotten that someone else is also sitting here, right before you."

"It was not forgetting; on the contrary, it was remembering; I was connecting all the memories from the inside out."

"Do you live more in memories than in the present?"

"Don't we all live in memories? The present also becomes a memory in the next moment. Can any measure of time be called present? One day, one year, the past, or an approaching or passing moment. The present never happens; it is only history; we are born out of history, live in it and then become a part of it."

"You are not only a history scholar; you have also lived it."

"I have lived it. That is why history seems most true to me, the destiny of all of us."

"Destiny as well as karma."

"Rightly said. If there are fragments of deeds, they get organised and become destiny; that is, they become history. Our personal history."

"Do you know, we got so engrossed in these things that we spent one and a half hours at breakfast. Now we should finish it."

"Okay. You keep track of time."

"For you, that's already history."

"But my history contains not only events but also dates."

"We will keep track of them as well. But the date of what has happened is not as important as its impact."

"You keep track of economic impacts and consequences, so they will seem important to you. I am also concerned with the current form of political history. Still, dates are important to me because they become stopping points. Without them, there would be no pauses in history."

"Why the need for pause? Why not look at the flow of something uninterrupted and continuous?"

"Well, flow can be the subject matter of poetry, not of history. We have spent a lot of time on nonsense. It looks like we will never reach our destination."

"If we cannot get there, we will turn back midway—an excuse for you to return."

"How do you know that I am so interested in reaching my destination?"

"Let's both keep wandering."

"Just as history is continuous, so are the paths. Destination is a state of mind, only one date in history. But I don't want any pause in my life. The pause happens only once. Ultimately, that pause gets lost in the pace of history itself."

"Have you ever read historical philosophy or the history of philosophy?"

"You must be joking!"

"Your interest is obvious."

"I am interested in many things. If I could do everything, you wouldn't be able to recognise whether I was a dancer, a singer, or a painter."

"So, you have so much talent, but you are a creature of this earth, right?"

"No, I have come from Gandharvaloka."

"By mistake or on purpose?"

"After getting to know you, perhaps I should say intentionally."

The foam of laughter rose in the air again.

A Redwood Forest

A dense forest of tall redwood trees and trails covered in their shade. Ketaki and Aditya were walking.

It was getting dark, and Aditya was thinking about the fact that there was only one day left for Ketaki to leave, and he could not express his feelings to her. Whatever they had discussed remained incomplete. He did not know when they would meet again. He couldn't say all this over the phone. That's why it was imperative to talk right then.

He began, "I have an idea of your answer, but I still wanted to know. You..."

"I won't be able to say anything very clearly. You asked this question too soon. Right now, I am trying to figure out what is happening to me. I don't usually understand anything about myself."

"I am not asking you to commit anything. I only know about myself. I will only talk about myself. But my love... do you accept it? Will it make you feel burdened?"

Ketaki saw that many fireflies were illuminating the darkness. She even tried to catch one of them but could not. Maybe these were just childhood games.

"Why are you talking about burdens?"

"Unwanted love can be a burden."

"But how did you imagine it was unwanted?"

"I don't know anything about you. You might have had a lot of love in your life; and you may have no place or need for it. What else would it be then, other than a burden, another living being to take care of?"

"So you assume that love is a responsibility."

"You don't have to do anything but let me keep loving you, that's all I ask."

Ketaki's body trembled again. She felt that the cold in the forest had increased a lot.

Aditya started speaking again, "If you don't want me to I won't even come near you. Whenever you want, you can push me out. But if you can accept me, then let me know."

Ketaki's body was trembling badly. She could not clearly hear what Aditya was saying, as if these words were pervading her entire being like the powerful sound of a symphony. Ketaki felt that the music was making her flow. She could not walk properly. When she stumbled on a few pebbles, she lost her balance. She said softly, "Aditya, should we sit down?"

And Aditya took the crumpling Ketaki in his arms. Ketaki clung to him like a swaying creeper. Then, a moment later, she drew away. Aditya caught her with his left arm and said, "You look tired. Let's go back." And he took her back to the wooden cottage.

Ketaki still hadn't answered his question. He took her to her bed. Ketaki remained sitting on the edge of the bed. She was exhausted. They had been walking for miles on end; she had been trying to absorb as much as possible—the beauty of nature and Aditya's words—and trying to understand him.

Aditya kept hovering around her for some time so he could provide whatever she needed. Then he gently placed his hand on her shoulder and said, "You sleep for an hour; after that, we will go for dinner." And he went to his room and lay down.

Ketaki slept and did not wake up. When she woke up at 5:00 in the morning, she saw that Aditya was awake. She started to worry about catching the afternoon flight. She had to teach the next day.

"Let's leave quickly. Else, I might miss the flight."

Aditya had not been able to sleep the whole night. He kept thinking about himself and Ketaki. His heart was yearning for Ketaki's company the whole time. Ketaki was like a full cup, with no place for more water. Aditya felt that Ketaki was not aware of his loving heart. Nor did she see any need or place for Aditya's love in her life. But still, Ketaki was as eager to meet him as he was to meet her. So, did Ketaki love him too? Ketaki was becoming a puzzle; whatever Aditya would have liked to hear, Ketaki had not said any of it. She weighed each word before she spoke.

Did she not want to reveal her thoughts, or was there nothing special on her mind? What could she say? Would it be right for Aditya to continue to reveal himself? His feelings for Ketaki, should he let the feelings flourish and keep growing? But if they kept growing like this, he would certainly have to face disappointment one day. If Ketaki suddenly told him one day that enough was enough and she no longer wanted to meet him, what would he do? He had no rights over Ketaki. Are there rights in love? Does loving in itself give one any rights? Only the recipient of the love can offer those rights; the lover cannot claim them.

But is the right given or taken?

Did he have any rights without Ketaki's consent?

Did he have the right to love?

Or were all rights Ketaki's?

But Ketaki was confused herself. She didn't say anything. She didn't want to say anything. Something in her life was stopping her from opening up to Aditya. What was it? Was it another man? Or was it her nature not to open up? Would Ketaki have come to visit Aditya like this if there was another man?

Maybe she needed to figure out Aditya. That's why she was afraid to open herself up.

Ketaki was becoming a strange puzzle for Aditya. The more he thought about their relationship, the more confused he got and the less he knew his next step.

If Ketaki had no feelings for him, he did not want to touch her. He had no desire for a mere physical relationship with her. Aditya felt that just being around Ketaki filled him with freshness. A kind of energy, an enthusiasm, bathed every pore of his body. He wanted to maintain that feeling. It would be okay if Ketaki wanted him from a distance. But the feeling that Ketaki reciprocated his love lifted him higher. His enthusiasm increased many times. The blood in his arteries started to pump like that of a 20-year-old man. All this happened the moment she came into his life. Before that, his life had been like a river flowing on the plains. No movement, no storm, no collision with any stones. Just a monotonous, slow pace. Lots of writing, publications, speeches, honours, travels, the occasional casual relationship, that was all the excitement he had in his life. If you looked at it, there was no excitement of any kind. There was no sense of the commotion going on now, at every moment, in that life.

Aditya wanted to feel that commotion more deeply. Wanted to make it a permanent part of his life.

But why was Ketaki so anxious to go home?

Sunny Paths

As she moved towards the boarding gate, Ketaki said, "A goodbye kiss," and extended her cheek towards Aditya; Aditya kissed her lightly.

Then Ketaki moved forward and left a lipstick mark on his cheek. Laughing, she said, "Wipe your cheek; otherwise, people will wonder what you have been up to."

Aditya couldn't laugh. He suddenly felt miserable, perhaps because Ketaki was leaving. He did not want to think about how lonely he would feel.

"No one is going to think anything," he said, feeling wretched.

Ketaki didn't seem to have heard him, or perhaps she just did not want to listen. She quickly said, "Bye," and walked into the aerobridge. Aditya stood there for some time, watching her walk away. She turned once.

Seeing Aditya standing there, she waved at him and continued moving.

She had a lot on her mind: worries about work at the university, teaching and writing. She had a lot of preparation to do as soon as she got back. There was a deadline coming up for a paper she wanted to submit to a journal. It was truly like being on death row. One felt that if one could not do it on time, one would have to face death. Every month, there was some such death to face. There was another deadline for a conference paper the next month. But there was still a lot of research left to be done for the book she was working on. She needed to spend some hours at the library.

But as soon as she boarded the plane, Aditya came and sat inside her. His face, smile, sadness, everything kept revolving around her. Who was this person who was growing on her like this, without any warning? Should she stop him here and not let him go forward? What should she do? She had just said goodbye to Aditya and was sitting in the plane and thinking about the next opportunity she would get to meet him. Was Aditya so prominent in her life? Was she falling in love with Aditya? Was it love at all or momentary attraction, curiosity, or infatuation? How could one know right away that it was love? If he stayed on, then love would happen. But suppose everything returned to normal after a few days, and the turmoil in her mind stopped? In that case, it would only have been a momentary curiosity or infatuation. How would she know? When would she know? She didn't want to tie herself down without knowing. She wanted to be free anyway. Not get tied to anyone, not be associated with anyone. Separate even after being together, free even after connecting. That was what ideal love was. No burden. But she had yet to make up her mind. What should she do? What decision should she take? Aditya had probably decided already. He was waiting for Ketaki to make a decision. What would she say to him? That she was his, she loved him. Or that he should never have asked such a question. Whatever it was, she wanted to let things go on.

But Aditya was not in favour of letting it go on like that. He needed very clear, very definite answers. Ketaki never had definite answers. She was not sure even about herself. Wherever life took her, she went. After divorcing her husband, she never bothered to take her relationships seriously. Wherever there was a turn, she turned. Wherever it flowed, she let it flow. She felt that nothing was in her control. Relationships were formed and then came to an end. As if they started in order to end! She had no right over anyone else's mind. Nor did her mind state everything clearly. Then why worry about keeping it in her control?

But Aditya was sure. And he wanted her to think clearly, too. For him, this was crucial, not a laughing matter. Ketaki didn't want to be as serious as Aditya was. At that moment, she did not regard it as the most important question of her life. She was just watching which way the stream was turning. She smiled, remembered a saying, and said, "See on which side the camel sits."

If this coming and going was attraction, she did not want to create a world of disappointment for herself and him by getting closer to Aditya. But she also knew that she did not want to lose Aditya.

Ketaki wanted to test herself to know whether the feelings in her heart for Aditya were everlasting and permanent. If other men still interested her. She wanted to avoid single-mindedly immersing herself in Aditya. But if she kept thinking about Aditya even after getting close to another man, it had to be love. She could commit to Aditya only once she had taken the test.

Why is love so ethereal that we cannot grasp it? When she was studying in college, how often had she thought she was going through the experience of love? Back then, she had not doubted that it was love. Manik had been a senior in college. There had been only two or three students from Purabhum in the entire college. Therefore, it had been normal for them to become friends. They had never formally expressed their love for each other in words, but Ketaki knew in her heart that she liked Manik and that he liked her, too. Upon completing his studies, he returned to Purabhum. He'd got a good job in a foreign firm. After he had been working for a couple of years, a proposal asking for Ketaki's hand in marriage came from his home. Ketaki was very happy. So, her teenage dream of love was about to come true. Then her father asked her, "Do you want to get married, or do you want to study further? I thought that you wanted to have a career first. You won't be able to do anything after just a BA. You should study for a few years more."

She nodded, agreeing with her father mindlessly, and said immediately, "Yes, Papa, I will study now and not get married."

Then I heard that Manik got married to someone else. But Ketaki had deleted Manik from her mind the moment she had decided to focus on her career. Never again did she remember him in remorse or regret or pain. Life went on at its own pace. And she only had good feelings when she thought about Manik. You couldn't call it love. It was just a pleasant and optimistic feeling. Like you generally feel towards your friends. Love is special, something beyond friendship.

That's why Ketaki often started doubting whether such a thing as love existed in this world or if it was an illusion of the mind—a game of make-believe. Perhaps when a person starts having fewer interests and pursuits, he develops the disease of love to make life enjoyable. For example, many people develop hobbies like playing cards, horse riding, collecting artefacts, or other similar things, which become passions. Love, too, is nurtured like a hobby and becomes a passion. And perhaps it becomes a passion because the pleasure increases a lot more when it is a passion. People start discussing it, and being at the centre of attention or becoming a topic of discussion because of your love brings additional joy. This is why once a person falls in love, they cannot get out of it or do not want to, despite all its negative aspects.

Ketaki knew this aspect of love. Why whould she take the trouble again?

The only thing Ketaki did not understand was whether the love she had at eighteen would be the same when she was forty.

If someone could have told her there was no difference between love at forty and love at eighteen, then perhaps she would have automatically retreated. She would have jumped into it fearlessly if someone had told her there was a big difference. But here, no one knew anything. She had read many books and watched many dramas and movies about young and middle-aged love. Still, she could not find the truth anywhere.

She felt that everyone was confused. Then, the second important doubt was that, if one didn't know whether love existed or not, how could any questions about middle-aged love or young love arise?

Ketaki had read many definitions of love—love as romance, social contract, romantic worship, souls merging, etc. She felt that scholars had yet to explain it correctly despite thousands of years of studying ideas.

While there was truth in whatever every scholar said about love, the commentary was as abstract as love itself. The question remains the same. Is love God or is love an expression of the soul or is love the best emotion of human life? How far can all these definitions explain love? They only tell us that it is truly something that is neti-neti or neither this nor that, like the Supreme Spirit. Then what was Ketaki to do?

When the plane started cruising above the clouds, Ketaki looked out of the window at the billowing mass spread like a fluffy white carpet and said to herself that she would not do anything. She would not think anything. Like the clouds, she would start flying, sometimes she would settle down, sometimes she would collide, and sometimes she would rain. Clouds do not make their own destiny. The surrounding elements determine their fate. Was there any harm if she also allowed this to happen? This may be the only way to know the truth, to reach the unfathomable, the unknown. To touch the deepest depths and highest peaks of love.

She started thinking about those sun-washed paths on which she had walked the day before with Aditya.

Poetry had started flowing from Aditya's words. She had been surprised.

Once or twice, he had even quoted a couple of poets.

She had said, "Are you also interested in poetry! I thought that social scientists only use and understand the language of the mind."

"I feel weird too. This could only be the effect of your presence. I must admit I tried my hand at poetry while I was in college. But earning a living does not leave me much time for poetry."

"You used to write poetry?"

"Sometimes."

"Do you still have your poems?"

"They may be lying around somewhere."

"Will you let me read them?"

"I think you are more interested in my poems than me."

"I have never seen that version of you. I would like to see him. Look for them, please. Wherever they are, look for them and send them to me."

"Did you also write poems?"

"Every social scientist probably first starts with poetry. When they fail to become poets, they quietly immerse themselves in literary criticism, social science or history. I used to write occasionally, but I don't have even one left. In moving from one country to another, only the poetry gets lost; the rest of the stuff always gets here."

"It's true what you said; the poetry itself gets lost. But can't you write those poems again? Other poems?"

"You might be able to write again. But it will not be the same poetry. And if it is going to be something else, then it does not matter whether it is poetry or sociology!"

"Why do you say this, Ketaki? Poetry is poetry, it will remain poetry no matter when it was created. No sociology can match it. It is above all else. But our poetry has indeed been lost... We who have adopted societies and cultures, endured their conflicts, we have lost our poetry."

"We have become cut off from society and culture. That is why we have lost our poetry. It is also born when we add feelings to society and culture."

"Come on, let us both search for poetry."

"Forget it; I have come too far. I can't look for poetry now. And what need is there to do so?

"Is there really no need?"

"Do you need to?"

"What if I say yes?"

"Then I will also have to think. I might follow you but will not make any promises yet."

In Search of Poetry

On the flight, she relived the memories of their meeting and suddenly wanted to write a poem.

"Aditya, look, I have really written a poem, I am sending it to you."

Feelings 1

Should I put this out to air?
Lay it in the sun to dry?
Leave it to get covered by dust?
It will spread colours in the light
It will fill the air with fragrance
and sway in the breeze
soak in the rain
And take me in its embrace

But what if an eagle swoops down?
Or a storm takes it away?
Or it gets scorched in the sun?

Melts in the pouring rain?
Tell me
Wherein lies the danger? In the light?
Or in darkness and desolation?
What risk will you take?
To burn or to melt?

Like the five elements
Feelings only change form
They don't die
They melt
They burn

But they do not die
Breaking out of a lifeless shell
They flow out
And scatter
Again in some new
Human home
And shimmer
And glow
Burst
Spill out

Till they take over
The sky again
And set out on a new journey
Of sentiments

"Look what has happened to me, Aditya: I had not written a poem for so many years, and now I can't stop. The lines spill out on their own. Perhaps by completely cutting myself off from my daily routine when I spent time with you in the lap of such immense beauty... living on a different plane and being with you... thinking about you... that has to be the reason why the poems erupted. You also said that you began searching for poetry in my presence. Look at this... this second poem was written in the flow of the first one."

Feelings 2

It blocks my way
Doesn't let me move forward
Doesn't let me climb higher
Soft and
Ludicrous
Why don't I let it go
Why not bury it
In a dark cave
Why not let it float away
Into the deep sea?

So I can't see it
Nor hear it
Nor let it near me
Will it still pierce me
Make my hair stand on end
Twist my insides
Or if it has to go and return
Despite being unseen, unheard and untouched
There is a rustling somewhere inside
Why should I bother?
Why not let it stay by my side?
Free it from the trouble
Of coming and going
And myself, too

On the same day, Aditya sent her a letter addressing her with all kinds of terms of endearment like "sweetheart", "beloved", "my sweetness". He wrote, "You are the freshness of my mornings. Drops of dew floating on the petals of the morning. I have never loved anyone so passionately, so deeply. Today, I am grateful to you for the flame that you have awakened within me and for everything you have provided to keep that flame alive. Yes, I will say this, Ketaki. I am really grateful for what you have given me. Otherwise, who knows where this flame lit by you would have taken me and scorched me?

"Right now, I can't say what magic you have in you or what charm it is that has cast its spell on me—your gaze, your laughter, or your words. The life-giving power of your eyes, like nectar or wine, intoxicates me. You kill and give life at the same time. Do you know that you have such power?"

As she read his letter, Ketaki recognized the same feelings in herself but realized she lacked the words to express them like this. Aditya wrote in response to her poems, "I can see you in these poems of yours. Whatever you were saying, your conflicts, dilemmas, problems, compulsions... like the essence inside you, it's all there in these poems. Keep writing, Ketaki. A lot of things that you want to say... or don't want to say... you tell me through these poems. That night when you fell asleep...I wanted to hear you tell me a lot more... never mind, some other time."

Later, one day, Aditya commented again, "You have indeed written a lot of poems! But one question keeps troubling me after reading them. You are afraid of drowning. Why? Have you ever thought about this?"

"That is what I am. This is the kind of clay I am made of."

"But why? I have seen a lot of love within you. Full to the brim. You try to tie yourself in knots."

"I am not used to the speed with which you move forward, without any resistance. I have to move slowly, stop and think."

"That's fine, but I see that you take your steps a little more cautiously, as if some deep obstacle within you is stopping you from moving forward."

"I want to think carefully before I let myself drown completely."

"I am not asking for a commitment from you. Then why do you shy away from saying anything about yourself?

"I don't seem to know anything about myself or what I want. Not wanting to be tied down is probably the basic thing; every relationship eventually becomes a bond. That is why I shy away from making decisions."

"So I was right."

"What?"

"About being a burden."

"I enjoy the feeling of your presence, your being around me. I don't want to lose that feeling. That's the poetry of my life, the melody, or whatever you call it!"

"But why do you think it's a hindrance? I would definitely like your love. But I will never tie you down against your will. You are free. You will remain free. I would, however, like to know more about my place in your world. Is there a place there for me or not? Do I have the right to ask you that?"

Ketaki did not reply. But a few days later, she wrote, "To tell you the truth, I don't think about anything else except you. Not about anyone. The people that I used to know are almost all gone. Still, I want to keep myself free from you. I also know that your company is my biggest source of happiness. Even the possibility of being with you fills me with energy. Still, I feel nervous that you might drain me. I don't understand why. But I know I cannot dedicate myself to one person."

When Aditya called, he said, "No one is demanding surrender. But as I said, what kind of relationship do you want? That both of us remain open? Or that we completely belong to each other?"

"Do you need answers to these questions now?"

"If you don't want to say anything now, I will wait for whenever you can."

"Why are you in such a hurry? Why are you demanding answers from me so quickly? We have only just met! We don't even know each other properly."

"I don't feel the need to know much more. Yeah, you're probably not sure about me yet."

"I am sure, and I am not. The only problem that bothers me is that I never have the direct answers you ask for."

"Okay, I won't ask you any questions."

"No one is asking you not to ask questions. But don't feel bad if the answer doesn't satisfy you."

"Your second problem was that you don't know enough about me. Tell me, what do you want to know? My life is like an open book. You can ask me anything."

"It is impossible to know someone completely in just a few months, and that too in just a few meetings."

"So, how much more do you want to know?"

"How can I tell you? But I want to know more than I know."

"So ask me stuff... see how I open up to you."

"Questions? Should I ask a horrible question? You won't be upset? I'm asking to start the questions. This question's answer can be very long or short. It depends on how much you can open up about yourself, and how much you can trust me."

"Ask me. Why are you thinking so much? You keep laying the ground for something."

"So tell me, how many women have you told that you love them?"

"I get it. You don't trust me right now."

"I trust you, and maybe I don't. What can I do? My mother taught me not to trust any man right from when I was little."

"It was the correct thing to do at the time, to protect you. So, I will not blame your mother. But now there is no need for that."

"It is a habit with me."

"You think I'm luring you with lies."

"It doesn't seem so. But you could be."

"What will I achieve by luring you with lies?"

"Well..."

"Your body, at the most."

"Sure."

"But I have no interest in having your body without getting you. Do you understand?"

"There's a difference between understanding and trusting."

"So what is the process of trusting someone or getting them to trust you?"

"You can't rush it. It'll happen on its own. It needs time."

"Ketaki, I will not force you if you do not want to meet me. I will end the matter here."

"Why are you saying this? I do want to meet you. I want to know you better. You didn't answer my question."

"Do you really want to know?"

"Every single detail."

"I will give you details, but for now, I want you to know I only ever told one woman that I loved her, and that was in college. After that, I never fell in love or said those words."

"You mean no one came into your life after that? Have you been completely celibate?"

"No, no! Who said so? I had a few small affairs but was never in love."

"What about your wife?"

"Just something that happened, as things do. I did whatever seemed right for the marriage. Family expectations. There are many types of adjustments. The one who gets married is just a pawn, and the players who play the game are the others."

"Then suddenly, one day, the pawn's horns grow, his legs grow, and he breaks the rope and runs away."

"Interesting! Your story is almost the same as that of most men who come from Purabhum."

"The stories may or may not be the same. They also have some characteristics of their own."

"For example?"

"For example, the twist you wrought in my story does not happen to everyone. I never expected that I would be able to discover something new at this stage of my life. That I would be able to feel the way I do now. I thought that my age of love and discovery was over."

"What definition would you give to this feeling?"

"It is hard to find words for it. It's like asking what poetry is. That could be poetry itself. Poetry may be a combination of some words or a pattern, but only a lover knows the effect it creates. Similarly, music can be seen only as some fingers hitting an instrument, but what comes out of that makes us forget even the presence of those fingers. That is what love is, Ketaki. You stimulate me. But you don't realize where I have reached and the sublime experience it has given me. No one can take this feeling away, even if you are not with me. You gave me what you had to offer. Now, you will never be able to take it back, not even if you want to. That is your gift, but now it is my possession. Just mine."

All Ketaki understood was that there was some inner compulsion that was constantly pulling her towards Aditya. She couldn't pass up a single opportunity to spend time with him. On the contrary, she kept waiting for those moments with unending enthusiasm.

Aditya felt good to her. Someone whom she could easily trust. Someone with whom she would be safe from the dangers of the world. But why? What about Aditya made her feel this way?

Was it that his love was spontaneous and free, given without any expectation of reciprocation?

And this was her reaction to Aditya's love. Ketaki's response came from her subconscious. The brightness of Aditya's spirit was reflected within Ketaki.

She wrote another poem that day:

My being

When I am by myself
When I am on my own
That is when I am most with you
When I cannot find myself
Then you too are gone
Or perhaps you wait
Patient and quiet
In sleep or in dreams
In a rush of work, a crowd of people
Or when the body rests, is at peace
You too are somewhere, relaxed, alert
As I awake into consciousness
You are there, quiet, unnoticed

Awake, you rise
Stirring my nerves
Filling my veins
With a rush of blood
That makes me feel faint
I think
You are the companion of awakening
Why are you throwing me back
Into a state of stupor
Where you and I may lose ourselves again

Golden Trails

Another brief meeting.

The river flowed right through town. Colourful flowers, dense shady trees, and small bridges on the promenade for pedestrians on both sides of the river. Vehicles, people, and crowds passed through there. If you climbed the stairs from the promenade and came up, you saw many cafés, restaurants, and boutiques on either side of the street. Ketaki was watching the flow of the river with Aditya. Occasionally, boats full of passengers would pass by. Travellers dressed in the bright hues of summer waved and smiled at the pedestrians walking along the shore.

The character of the promenade also changed as you walked. Sometimes there would be a café along the promenade, sometimes the river bank was deserted, with not a soul in sight. As the river meandered, the promenade also wound along with it. Ketaki was enjoying the uniqueness of every new turn. Of the power it had to awaken astonishment. They came upon a very densely shaded spot at one turn. Lots of magnolias covered the steps of the pier.

"Should we sit here for a while?" she asked Aditya, and without waiting for him to reply, she plonked herself down on the corner stairs. Aditya sat down as well.

"Are you tired?"

"A bit."

"If we had gone to a café, you could have had something to drink and felt refreshed."

"I don't have the energy to go to a café. Let's wait for ten minutes, then we can go on."

Suddenly, Ketaki tilted her head towards Aditya, almost resting it on Aditya's shoulder, and said, "Let me close my eyes for two minutes."

Aditya felt like kissing Ketaki. Maybe Ketaki wanted that too. Perhaps that was why she said she wanted to lay down her head.

He took Ketaki's face in both hands and lightly kissed her lips. Ketaki smiled with closed eyes and nuzzled her face against his shoulder. Suddenly, something inside her had opened up.

She said, "When I was very young, there was a river near our house. I loved watching it flow. But I was not allowed to go there alone. I used to wait all day for my father to come home in the evening. Once he was back, I would ask him to take me there. But Papa did not have the time to sit with me on the river bank for hours. He would take me there and bring me back quite quickly. I would have to go somewhere with Mummy, or else Mummy would be waiting for us to come home for dinner. I still feel bad that I could never gaze at that river to my heart's content. I used to go there every season. I even saw it when it was in spate and was fascinated by its meandering flow. I was scared, too. Once it was completely dry. I was astounded that its bed, which had always been so mysterious, was now exposed like this. At first, I found it difficult to believe this was the same river. But then, when Papa reassured me that it was, I touched its sandy bottom, threw stones, and got a feeling of joy mixed with victory, thinking that I could even walk on the river. That day, I felt that, after discovering the river's secret, my fascination with it had ended. I want to be a river, Aditya. Today, I feel like asking you to sit with me on the banks of this river for hours."

Aditya again had Ketaki's face in his hands. This time, he kissed her deeply. Then he pressed her hand and said, "I would have wanted to do that too. It's great that you said it."

"Aditya, it has been so many months since we first met. Then we..."

"I also want to ask you. But I did not want to sound too eager. I have already told you that a physical relationship with you is not everything for me. The level I can reach with you depends on the rest of the relationship. We can only get there with all the dimensions of a relationship, not just the body alone. Still, the connection of bodies also creates a kind of intimacy. It washes away the awkwardness which is always present in a man–woman relationship. How do you feel about it?"

"I understand what you mean about removing the awkwardness. But the awkwardness can increase with physical intimacy instead of being washed away."

"This could also happen, but more dimensions are added, and perhaps completeness comes into the relationship."

"Adi, may I ask you something?"

"Hmmm."

"Have you ever tried to define love? By yourself. I don't want to hear other people's definitions."

"You think that along with writing about the principles of economics, one also acquires specialist qualifications in love?"

"No, it's not that. But after all, we keep creating definitions for ourselves from our life experiences. Don't say that you have never thought about love or have no opinion about it."

"I would never say that, especially not to you. Especially when it has become clear to you. You want to know my definition, right?"

"Yes, what you feel in your heart."

"For me, love means complete dissolution—completely merging with each other, getting lost; in the language of spirituality, you could call it two souls becoming one. You already know that I am not religious or a believer or anything. Still, I am using the example of souls to get the expression right. Because many things that are not visible are abstract; they are only felt, we have to resort to abstract ways of speaking about them, and we all have some conception of the soul."

"How can two people merge into each other? What do you mean?"

"I mean removing all masks and exposing oneself. Becoming completely naked in front of each other. Like one mirror in front of another mirror. Where whatever is reflected in one mirror is also reflected in the other mirror. When it is visible, the shadows become multi-dimensional. Nothing remains suppressed or hidden."

As he was saying this, Aditya's face had become completely transparent. His eyes became brighter as they grew moist. He went on to say, "You don't need anyone else to make you feel special about yourself. In the eyes of love, you and your self become illuminated. Accepting it makes your existence authentic."

Ketaki did not like what he had said about merging. "But in becoming one with the other, an individual's personal existence ends. This is a love that devours the other. For me, love is liberating. The desire to be together while liberating each other."

"There is freedom even in a complete merger. If the mind is stable, then it remains free—that is freedom. Wanderings end. It is as if one finds one's pivot. There is freedom from impermanence, strangeness, and loneliness, not from the lover. Perhaps we both have different definitions of liberation."

"I have no problem with your definition. I am also happy with merging. But I don't know how long it will last. Ultimately, people like me cannot be happy by losing themselves. Deep inside, they will demand something more. But I like your definition."

Aditya started to laugh. "What does it matter if you like it? That is a matter of consent. It is more about assent than consent, which does not come about by saying or convincing anyone but by attitude and faith. If you do not agree, then nothing has any meaning, but let's leave it there. At least you are not protesting; there's some hope for the future."

Before Ketaki could say anything, Aditya suggested, "How about it, would you like to go to a café?"

"I don't feel like getting up from here. Let's just sit at the café on the river bank, then we won't have to go far from the river."

"So get up; let's go to the café we left behind."

But Ketaki's mind had already started off on a different path, far behind—the trail of the past. While getting up, she said, "Have you ever made a paper boat?"

"I used to make paper aeroplanes. They would fly for a while, and then they would fall down."

"My boat used to float for a long time. I would keep looking at it. Then, when it started getting bent, I would scream loudly, as if I was drowning."

"Are you afraid of drowning?"

"I used to be. Not anymore. But when I was little, I remember that when a train passed over a bridge, I was scared of drowning in the river. Whereas when the river was near the house, everything seemed under control. Like now, I can't say that I fear water. Maybe I was very fascinated by water and equally scared of it. By learning to swim, I found a cure for fear and fascination. How wonderful it is to find solutions to such fundamental fears. Are you scared?"

"Of water?"

"Of water or air or height or darkness. There are so many types of fears. You know, I used to be afraid of the dark earlier. Now I like the dark very much. Very romantic. Like right now, I feel like sitting here even in the twilight. Then, you won't have to go anywhere when night falls."

"And if you are alone in the dark, won't you feel afraid?"

"No! Now, not even when I am alone. I start meditating. I will bring you to me in my thoughts. Why, do I still look timid to you?"

"No, not at all. You look very strong, maybe stronger than me."

"I may be better than you in some things. In fact, although they say that women are emotionally and physically weaker than men, my experience has been the opposite. A man may be physically strong, but as far as emotion or determination is concerned, I do not find any deficiency in myself; rather, I find myself stronger than men. Now I laugh when I think that I used to be afraid of men once upon a time."

"Really? But why?"

"When I was little, I felt I would be eaten up. A lot of men stare in our country, you know. When I was studying in the eighth grade, a man followed me on my way back from school. I was terrified. Then I told my father, and he started picking me up from school. I never saw that man again. But the occasional incident would occur. One day, maybe in the tenth or eleventh, I was the only girl on the school bus. It was just before Holi. In fact, maybe the next day was Holi. Most of the girls would have decided not to come to school a day before because usually, you ran the risk of people throwing colour at you all over town. But I refused to sit at home in fear. The boys kept making a lot of noise the whole way. They could even have put colour on each other. But I sat quietly in the front seat, and no boy harassed me. I was very studious, read the whole way on the bus, and did not talk much. Maybe that's why they didn't have the courage. Some might have been frightened by my serious attitude or might have felt pity for me. Why bother a girl on her own."

Aditya, engrossed in Ketaki's words, said, "Why does it happen that when I am with you, my past comes alive, and I start reliving it with you?"

"We both reach home. I was thinking that I was there the year you got married too. I was giving lectures on new theoretical discoveries. We could have met then."

"True, our lives would have been so different then."

"You would have been with me wherever I went. I would have introduced you to Papa. He would have most definitely liked you; I could have made him happy. He passed away feeling bad for me." Talking about it made Ketaki sad.

Aditya teased her to change her mood. "It is also possible that you wouldn't have paid any attention to me then."

"Why?"

"What do we know about these things? What if you were involved with someone else?"

"If I was, I would have left him. Really. I wish I had met you. Why did we meet so late? More than half our life is over, Adi."

"Is that all you plan on living? Who knows, you might still have another fifty years left to live."

"I don't think I will make it past sixty."

"Is that written in your fate?"

"Yes, my astrologer said so."

Aditya found the opportunity to joke, "I also have an astrologer, but he says that you will live for a hundred years."

"Maybe whatever happens, its time is fixed; if we had met earlier, the relationship would have ended in a fight by now."

Now it was Aditya's turn to get serious. "Do you think we can't stay together for long?"

"No, not at all. On the contrary, you understand my needs so well. You are such a sensitive person. No matter how much time I spend with you, living together for years and wishing to live together are different. You may meet many people that you think you can live with, but when you start living together, will life become hell?"

"Do you know this from experience, or are you just saying it?"

"Many of my friends have been through such experiences. I am always afraid of them. No matter how attractive you are, it is the destiny of a human being to get bored. No matter how much love or desire one has, one will eventually get bored."

"According to you, no relationship can be full of love till the end."

"This quality, which was there initially, is no longer there."

"Then one shouldn't get married at all."

"I say that marriage is the declaration of the death of love."

"So our relationship is doomed to die as well."

"I am trying to save it; that is why I keep talking about space and freedom. When you give each other freedom, love doesn't go away. Because there is no burden or imposition, you draw together with someone of your own will and can separate whenever you want."

"Well, you can end it when you want as well."

"Suppose it is necessary to end the relationship. In that case, end it, but if you wish to remain bound together, why would you do that?"

"But you said that if people are constantly together, it leads to boredom, didn't you?"

"I never felt that about you, that I could get bored with you. You always keep creating something or the other, some idea or the other. You keep me entangled in thoughts, I just feel like being with you and being bound to you. You have really made me forget everything and concentrate on you. I can't think of anything else."

"But your words scare me."

"Why?"

"Tomorrow, you might tell me you are bored with me. Let us end this story."

"Never. There is so much in you that I will not be able to finish talking to you for the rest of my life. This lifetime is not long enough to live with you."

"It was good that I met you late in life. You will not be afraid of spending the rest of your life with me."

"No, I will ask for a long life so that I can spend time with you."

Aditya felt confused when Ketaki spoke like this. Did she really love him, or was she just interested in having a casual relationship that she could end quickly? She didn't seem to take her relationships with men seriously. She had also said she had had other relationships. Were they relationships or just friendships? It wasn't clear.

Meanwhile, something had happened that had troubled Aditya. Still, he tried to convince himself that Ketaki was entirely within her rights, whatever she was saying or doing. It would not be right of him to interfere with her personal matters.

When they talked about attending the last Alabama conference, she told Aditya she would not go. Then, when the conference was near, and Aditya had decided he would participate in another meeting, Ketaki told him she would go to Alabama.

Aditya felt terrible that they had missed an opportunity to meet. But Ketaki had not been in touch with him that whole week. For some reason, Aditya thought that perhaps Ketaki had another friend she wanted to meet in Alabama. Which was why she did not want Aditya to be there. When he mentioned this to Ketaki, she said, "Aditya, I hope you don't believe I have no other friends except you. Please, don't behave like ordinary people. Why do you guys start getting jealous over such small things? I am not anyone's property. I am my own master. I can meet whoever I feel like. These things really irritate me. If I did not need you, why would I keep telling you I wanted to meet you over and over again? No one is taking your place, nor will anyone be able to. There is no reason for jealousy or to get hurt."

Aditya found Ketaki's words to be partially true. If she had not admitted anything, she had not denied it either. He was a little upset. Ketaki did not leave anything for him to say. In her opinion, he was reacting like a jealous man. He could not find the energy within himself to change her attitude. Maybe she was right. Then he thought he would raise the issue some other day. She could get annoyed if he raised such questions. He would keep quiet about this for the time being. But the relationship he pictured in his mind and the joy of the complete dissolution of souls he wanted to have with Ketaki... would remain only his imagination. Would Ketaki ever be able to pay attention to his inner needs?

The Path of Dreams

On the phone:

"I wonder what it would be like to be together if we ever got together?"

"Maybe it won't be like it has been so far."

"How can you say such a thing? Ultimately, a person remains true to their nature."

"Surely that depends on the person you are with."

"This may also be true and must be so. But one can't change human destiny. Living together cannot achieve the love that flourishes at a distance."

"People become closer when they live close to each other," Aditya said firmly.

"At the same time, there is an inner distancing too. A boredom, monotony, a feeling of helplessness, feeling like you can't get away, or a fear of getting stuck in one place."

"You always talk about the pain of being tied down. I think you and I can live together without invading each other's spaces because we have almost the same needs. We can spend time together, understanding each other's needs and respecting them."

"Maybe you are right. I just fear that the truth is never what it seems. The expectations of the household are different."

"I find it pleasant to imagine sharing a household with you. I often imagine you in the living room, in the kitchen, the veranda, everywhere, and enjoying your company."

"I also find the fantasy pleasant. But when I think about the reality of household life, all the romance of love gets overshadowed by buying groceries, cooking, cleaning, paying bills, and a variety of miscellaneous tasks. Running a household over here is even more difficult than at home. Modern thinkers are not wrong when they say that love dies as soon as you get married, or if you want to bring about the death of love, then get married."

"I think that the success or failure of a marriage depends on the kind of partner you have. But you view the whole institution of marriage negatively."

"Marriage is like that. No matter how desirable or loved one is, the simple burdens of daily life tend to suppress one's sensuality and softness. The fundamental issues of marriage become how to be on good terms with your relatives, what to give to whom, and what kind of house to build. All these issues become so important that the two people who were most important to each other, whose wishes were paramount, now become the biggest problem. Your greatest urge is to cut that person out of your life whose company is most important, for whose company's sake you took on the yoke of marriage."

"I see all this very differently. For example, I don't see you alone in the kitchen. We are together. We are doing something together. I cook for you. On Sundays, we do gardening together or go grocery shopping together. I find the pleasure of romance in all of that—the joy of a domestic romance."

"There is no such thing as the romance of domesticity. All I know is that the woman spends all her time in the kitchen. The man chats or watches TV in the living room. Where is the romance in this? There is only the daily grind." Ketaki was twisting the telephone cords in her hands while trying to untangle them, making them even more intertwined.

"But at the stage of life we both are in, our household will be very different. We are both working professionals. No one will have the exact expectations from you that they would have had in your first marriage. And the beauty of the kind of household I imagine with you is that you get the space you want."

"You may be right. One should try and see what it is like." This time, when she started rotating the wire in the opposite direction, it seemed to be unravelling.

"So, are you coming to stay here then?"

"Sure! Let me know when I should arrive."

"Tomorrow!"

"Why not today?"

"Well, then, come right now."

"When everything is more fun in one's imagination than in real life, why not live in the world of imagination?"

"As far as I know, reality is more beautiful than imagination."

"Are you sure?" This wire still needed to be completely untangled. Maybe if she unravelled the whole wire and moved it around after putting the phone down, it would be fine.

"Of course. And I will urge you to listen to me. I want to see you happy and cheerful and be content seeing you live happily."

"Let's do one thing then. Let's return to Purabhum and find a cottage on a hill somewhere. Have a cook and someone to look after the rest of it. We could both go for walks together on sunlit paths and do our work. That would be a wonderful life." Ketaki was sitting on a revolving chair, swinging back and forth; her fingers were still playing with the telephone wire.

"There is nothing wrong with that. This dream can be fulfilled whenever you want. Are you ready to return?"

"Are you ready?"

"I need seven to eight years, then I will retire and will not feel the need to go there. After all, that was where I worked earlier."

"So did I. I like working here. I may not want to work after returning. Just research and writing, which you can do anywhere if you get the books and journals you need."

"So, should we start planning for it?"

"Sure. Should we return together, or will you go and set up base first?"

"Whatever you wish."

"Okay, you go and get hold of a house first, then I will join you.

"What if I reach there with bag and baggage and you just stay on here?"

"If I promise to come, I will definitely do so. You aren't asking me to make a promise right now, are you? Right now, we are just enjoying a fantasy, right?"

"You don't want to commit to anything right now, do you?"

"No, and anyway, what you are talking about is far off right now. Who knows what will happen? I don't know whether I will still be alive then."

"You mean you can't see yourself alive even in the next three years?"

"You can't be sure of it."

"Then you should see a doctor. Such fear of death! Such pessimism!"

"You don't know about this aspect of my personality yet."

"I would certainly like to know about this part of you also. But Ketaki, this is not your true you. There is some veil which I will try to remove. You are basically optimistic and positive, you have faith. The success you have achieved in life cannot be the work of a pessimist. You may be flirting with these ideas, but fundamentally, you are very religious and positive."

"Are you trying your hand at some kind of psychoanalysis? All that can be dangerous."

"Intuition is also a thing. Not everything requires a diploma."

"So you are a born psychologist. There must be some truth in what you say. There are many types of fears inside me, and I get rid of them by talking about them. They say that if you talk about something, it will not affect you. So, if you express the worries in your mind, you become free from them."

"That is a very positive theory."

"So your psychoanalysis worked."

"But tell me something, why do you shy away from answering personal questions?"

"I am not in the habit of answering personal questions." Ketaki stood up and started pacing in a circle whose radius was the length of the telephone wire.

"Has your relationship with me not yet reached such a level that I can ask you personal questions?"

"That's not what I meant."

"That means you believe I have the right to ask you personal questions?"

The wire had been stretched too much. The base of the phone was about to fall, but Ketaki came forward and caught it.

"Sure! And you also have the right to get answers to every question. You can whittle away if you don't get an answer. I also keep asking you questions, and you give me satisfactory answers, but I don't know what happens to me. I don't have fixed opinions about myself, I am on the move. My answers may change, they may be different tomorrow. This is why I feel nervous about giving answers. I change."

"There is nothing to worry about. Everyone's views keep changing. If the environment and context of questions change, the answers also change. But the basic viewpoint of people generally remains the same. That is why you may not be aware of it, but basically, you also do not change or cannot change."

"Perhaps you are right. If it is my nature to change, my essential nature does not change. But it is not easy for me to answer."

"Perhaps you don't want to take responsibility for your answers."

"What do you mean?" Ketaki started turning the pages of the magazine on the telephone table. It was as if Aditya's words showed her a mirror she wanted to but was scared to look into.

"I was wondering why you were nervous. The liberation you keep talking about seems linked to your nervousness about responding. You don't want to take responsibility for the effect your words have on others or their reaction. Whatever the other person feels is their choice, and you are not responsible for it."

"You are right; I will never hold myself responsible for the experiences of others. Everyone has their own turn of mind. I do not have any influence, nor can I interfere with it. So how can that be my responsibility?"

"No one is asking you to be responsible for it. But if you do not express your feelings openly, our relationship can never progress or reach another level. In this connection, I was saying that the fear of saying it will disappear if you start taking responsibility for what you say."

Ketaki did not know why, but she felt hurt when Aditya said this. What did Aditya think about her? Did he not consider her a responsible person? Did he think she was playing with him??

But it was also true that she did not curb herself. She did not commit herself in any way. Nor did she free herself entirely from her past relationships. It was as if somewhere in her subconscious mind, she believed that Aditya, too, would go his own way and that this relationship would probably end. Then, would she build a new palace on the ruins of all those old relationships? What a crazy thought. Did that ever happen? Did she want to revive those relationships again? Could something new be built from debris? The foul smell, the mire, the stench, could she bear all that?

So what else could Aditya think? Wasn't he right in feeling that Ketaki was running away from commitment and playing games with him?

But this was just the beginning of the relationship. It had not even been a year since they had met. Commitment already? The wish to bind oneself now. Wouldn't it be better for Aditya to assess her properly?

Why was Aditya in such a hurry?

She wanted to think a thousand times before living with him or making any kind of commitment. Once they did so, that relationship would become permanent. Then, it would be difficult to have regrets or end the relationship. Ketaki did not want to be caught in that trap again. She was just not capable of facing that pain again.

Aditya wanted to know Ketaki's intentions before a full physical union.

Even though they desired each other, both held back due to their nature, doubts, and fears. Still, in Navabhum, it is common for lovers to have a complete physical union. If they really want to, then it is easy to find. The couple must know what they want.

This is what Ketaki was saying to herself. Yesterday, again, I learnt that love fades away like old clothes. It is not worth giving to a beggar if it is in tatters. Still, everyone searches for love in life. We put it on enthusiastically, as if it were a new set of clothes, and flaunt it. We want people to know it is new. People may wear anything—satin, silk or cotton—but every cloth has the same fate. First, it is stroked and caressed by the body. Then it is beaten, it tears and gets crushed and dies a slow death. Still, what is new is new—unique, stylish, novel. The search for love, as also the story of love, is endless. What is worn out, tattered, and boring becomes new when a person connects it with himself. Ketaki is not going to accept someone else's leftovers. She is getting drenched in the fresh outpourings of her emotions.

Since Ketaki is experiencing whatever is happening for the first time, everything is new. This entire treasure trove of experiences is hers. Only hers. Her property alone. Then why should she not enjoy it to her heart's content, pick it up, and play with it?

Sanyog
Union

Romantic Love

Since we have considered classifying separation as a semi-union, it would be correct to consider sanyog or a union a complete union, a union of mind and body.

Navabhumis call the union of body and mind romantic love. In romantic love, there is more desire for the body, and that desire is for one who is unattainable. Which means the desire disappears after marriage. Therefore, to maintain this romanticism, the Navabhumis started subverting the institution of marriage long ago. Now, in this era of complete freedom, lovers have no restrictions. Do whatever you want. There are so many options. Stay together, live apart, stay in the sky, remain on earth. Even homosexual love is now legal. Same-sex marriage, too.

One thing to be noted here is that no matter how much openness there is regarding sexual relationships, there is a moral code that lovers have to follow very carefully. Here, too, personal morality and social morality are two different things. The interesting thing is that while sexual relationships become acceptable on an individual level, openly discussing them at the social level, especially in the case of extra-marital relations, is considered a violation of morality. You must have heard of the story of the President of Navabhum—as soon as someone exposed the story of his extra-marital sexual intercourse, the opposition party got the opportunity to go after him. Then, he lost face publicly on national TV. But still, the situation in Navabhum does not worsen to the extent that fatwas and death orders are issued. A commotion or ruckus is made, and that is the end of it. After that, it is up to the lover to live with his head bowed down or, if he dares to live with courage, his head held high, his gaze directed straight at the beating heart of society.

So it is only marriage that means complete union. The amazing thing is that, while it is acceptable for the people in Navabhum to live together, the romanticism does not seem to be destroyed when they do that. As soon as they get married, they feel that a yoke has been placed around their necks, and they start struggling to get out. In Purabhum, the union of body and mind is forbidden until the entire ritual of marriage is complete. The lovers there have to cross many mountains of caste and class, ancient and modern, religious and unreligious;

I don't know how many mountains they have to cross. The hearts of the lovers meet, but for the bodies to meet, they must be patient through all of their youth or take refuge in a secret union. That is why many lovers run off, away from the eyes of society, but if they are caught, all hell breaks loose. They can be hanged. Although religion is becoming the enemy of the union of lovers even in Navabhum, in the new era, the biggest enemy is a career, which destroys any chances the poor lovers might have.

On these grounds I would also like to expand the definition of sanyog or union in the present-day scenario, especially in the context of Navabhum. The most popular form of union is the open union, which is accepted after marriage or after the hero and the heroine declare themselves to be boyfriend and girlfriend. After that, one gets social recognition. Although only marital union gets full recognition, in Navabhum, if the hero and the heroine decide to live together even without being married, society accepts it as if it is marriage. There is no need to take recourse to the law when ending the relationship. By the way, now in Navabhum, these extra-marital or non-marital relationships have legal status. There was a famous case in which a film actor's partner initiated legal action against him. Matters became complicated because not only were they living together but they also had a son. Now that such relationships have become common, open unions can also be put in the same box as marital unions. The only problem is that those who enter into a union without marriage want to avoid the traditional name, for they consider marriage a bond only in name and want to give a new name to their relationship that suits their era and feeling, or they want to live beyond the legal bond that marriage is. They also find comfort in thinking that there is a door and they can leave whenever they wish; so they never suffer from the problem of suffocation. Otherwise, in today's times, the contagious disease of feeling suffocated by marriage has become so common it is spreading like wildfire across an entire generation. It is natural for everyone to want to protect themselves from this disease.

What can the poor things do? While inflation is increasing and the sources of income are decreasing, ambitions are growing. Earlier, it was only a question of men's ambitions. Now that the women's liberation movement has gained momentum, women must also have a career. The problem is that the age for establishing a career is the same as that for love. Prasad, the famous poet from Purabhum, has even said that a flower withers when a garland is strung. The hero and heroine of this story can find the time for love only after establishing a career. They do not feel that the flowers have withered. Their minds are full of excitement and enthusiasm, but still, their career is more important to them than love, there is no doubt about it. They also believe that *bhukai bhajan na hoi Gopal*—there can be no devotion on an empty stomach—and since love is worship, how can you do it on an empty stomach? So, a job first, then love. A job means not only earning money but also finding oneself. Especially if you get a job that aligns with the desires of your heart, you take part in society, discover yourself, and make a name of your own through it. The poet's statement that the flowers die would also mean that the flowers of mature love blossom but do not have the freshness of those of tender age. One love is foolish, and the other has the gravity of thought added to it. But there is some degree of blindness in both of them because, without blindness, love cannot flourish.

The thing is that, before the era of women's liberation, since there was no question of a woman working, she would go wherever her male lover went. Now, when both have careers and the heroine is as knowledgeable and skilled as the hero, who will leave what for whom? A new type of marriage has started in Navabhum for such lovers; it is called a commuter marriage. Commuters, i.e. people who travel back and forth. So in such marriages, the hero and the heroine remain in their own geographical areas, but their marriage is solemnised at a particular place. They visit each other during holidays or weekends and meet. Then they return to their own town.

Such marriages are becoming very common in Navabhum. There are benefits to it, too. Especially in terms of its containment of the infectious disease of suffocation, which has spread due to marriage;

an excellent cure has been discovered in commuter marriages. Whenever you feel that you are starting to suffocate, just run away to the city where you work and all the symptoms of the disease will disappear. But people in commuter marriages also suffer from many other diseases; for instance, they may wonder what the benefits of such marriages are when you do not stay together. They are deprived of complete union and thus become victims of the disease of loneliness. Not just loneliness, they become victims of many other afflictions as well. They end up looking for other relationships in the absence of each other's constant companionship, then looking for excuses to justify those relationships and then the complications of always trying to end or maintain the relationship.

People from Purabhum living in Navabhum have also started having commuter marriages. They are satisfied that they are officially married, yet their lives go on as usual. They don't even have to give up former or future lovers.

Many forms of union have also become common to suit the needs of the times. The aspect of union with which we are concerned is the cohabitation and consummation of the passion of the hero and the hero. Generally, cohabitation and sexual intercourse go together, but as we have discussed earlier, the lover and the beloved are often not able to live together and sometimes they still get the opportunity to have sex. In a commuter marriage, the lovers decide the amount of cohabitation and sexual intercourse depending on their mutual needs and the requirements of their jobs.

Sexual intercourse is a complete union, in a way. At least on the physical level, there is a complete union between the hero and the heroine. It is, of course, another matter that despite being united on the physical level, the lover and beloved cannot be united on any other level, such as the intellectual or emotional one.

As far as I know, all the heroes and heroines can and want to be united on every level. Especially on the emotional level. As far as physical intercourse is concerned, the matter is not so simple. According to the general definition of love, the desire for physical intercourse is the most powerful in love. Many scholars have called love a disguised form of sexual desire. That is, according to them, love does not exist but physical lust, when it surges, presents itself like the many forms of love, disguised in tenderness, emotion, and sweet words. The impersonator performs a lot of tricks, and tries to be as entertaining as possible. Then, in the end, he reveals his true colours. Many people are not able to tell whether their lust is playing tricks on them or they are getting caught in the trap of love. They understand this only much later, when the lust cools down and love evaporates. There are very few people in this world who know the true form of love and who truly love. A lot of poetry is created from the basic source of love and considers love the root of life. But love is not for everyone. It is even more difficult today because the demands of love are becoming very difficult. On the one hand, life is becoming more and more complicated and, on the other, love is also becoming more and more bewildering due to this complexity, because now lovers do not know whether they are really in love or whether it is their low IQ or some mental obstacle due to which they are not able to manage their life properly or are being hindered from running as fast as they want to run in the world of business. Their hearts also do strange things, forcing them to make very different decisions from the ones they used to make before, which did not happen so much earlier.

Yes, we were talking about the union of the body, which has its roots in lust or desire. Aditya and Ketaki did experience desire. But the experiences of this loving couple living in Gaurbhum had made them somewhat doubtful about sexual intercourse. The thing is that physical union is a very common thing in Navabhum and people do not hesitate to roam in the garden of physical union even without love. Both Ketaki and especially Aditya had been in situations in Navabhum that involved loveless sex. They were now at a point in life when they had no enthusiasm for such sexual intercourse, and they first wanted to experience love on the emotional level; then, if it was natural to have sex, they would allow it to happen. What I have called a loveless union initially gives the illusion of being love. Seeing the moon in the morning makes it seem like it is night, whereas day is about to dawn in a short time. Similarly, the morning of that illusion dawns very early as well. Ketaki also wanted to decide whether it was night or morning first. That was why neither of them wanted to make special efforts in this direction. That did not mean that they did not want sex. The flame had been lit within both of them. It could not be extinguished.

But there are also early stages of sexual intercourse, when the conversation does not go beyond kissing, hugging, and seeing each other. The union of Ketaki and Aditya had been restricted to these stages; they were afraid to move beyond it.

This fear is an ancient one. Most often in the past, the reason for this fear was that the heroine would get pregnant and face disgrace in society. Not that these fears do not exist nowadays, but after a profusion of contraceptives became available, they decreased to a great extent. In the past, especially in Gaurbhum, due to diseases like AIDS, lovers kept a tight rein on their sexual desires. When experts suggested that the use of contraceptives could prevent this disease, lovers started insisting on using prophylactics. The government and the industry here also became so cautious about this that they started producing contraceptives in factories that had earlier produced chocolate candy for teenagers. The government would distribute free contraceptives day and night to students of universities, colleges, and schools. Once, during Halloween celebrations in Navabhum, I went to the student centre of my university and found some baskets full of products wrapped in shiny wrappers. Sweets to celebrate Halloween are commonly available in offices and schools, so I picked some up thinking they were sweets and discovered that they were contraceptives. Then I picked up a few, thinking they would come in handy. I gave some to Ketaki, but Ketaki got angry with me and said, "What rubbish have you given me?"

Be that as it may, one effect of the government's prevention campaign was often visible to the human; used and discarded contraceptives full of semen could be found on the benches of parks meant for the public, on footpaths, in subways and parking lots behind shopping malls. The sanitation department's workload may have increased somewhat, but it must have curbed the spread of epidemics.

Aditya and Ketaki were not particularly concerned about this because they were very cautious in these matters. They had their blood tested every year. The results were always negative. As far as pregnancy was concerned, Ketaki started dreaming a bit later that she would be able to enjoy the happiness of motherhood with Aditya.

She often dreamt a mini-Aditya was taking the tips of her nipples in his mouth and biting them. Her body would become tense with the intensity of desire. She started imagining what a complete coming together of her body with Aditya's would be like. If they wrapped themselves around each other, if their bodies merged into each other. Two individuals become one. An intense desire would arise within her. Her whole body would start to tremble, she would want to hide and become invisible in Aditya's body, with not a single part of herself left. She wanted every single drop of her to dissolve in Aditya's existence. Her body was becoming a burden that she could not handle, like a branch laden with flowers. She wanted to hand over everything to Aditya. Her all. Her flower garden. Her sexual being.

Only by handing herself over completely to him would she become light and start flying again. Aditya would take her burden and give her wings. She would fly and start singing as melodiously as a koel. Her body was eager to fly, sing, and dance to the beat and rhythm.

Ketaki was suddenly overcome with fear. If intercourse can be a climax, it can also be the end of love. Just as after an explosion, what is left of a bomb is only a few burnt pieces of iron, similarly, all a man is after sexual intercourse is a slimy substance. That had been her experience of date rape. You must know what date rape is. It is very common in Navabhum. The media have widely covered one or two legal disputes around date rape. After all, rape is a crime. Ketaki had not taken legal action against this friend because the values of Purabhum ingrained in her told her that she would unnecessarily get humiliated. The date rape happened in Navabhum and the man who raped her was also from Navabhum.

Aditya's fear was of a different kind.

Aditya also wanted to merge. He wanted to enter Ketaki inch by inch like colour spreading across her. But he did not want Ketaki to surrender completely until she was fully immersed in his love. The more he was attracted to Ketaki and the more he craved intimacy, the more he thought that a physical relationship with her was not what allured him. At least, he would never give priority to an attachment like that. He wanted to make this relationship last from one birth to another. He would only want to have sex with Ketaki when she had melted and dissolved in his colour, when a desire for him became Ketaki's passion, when Ketaki was only his at heart. Otherwise, he did not want to move forward beyond semi-union or ayog.

Perhaps this has to do with growing older. People start over-thinking. One does not blindly run after one's desires without weighing and assessing what one is doing. On the contrary, thought drives desire. Then both of them come face to face. They come to blows. The one who wins gets the upper hand. Often, victory and defeat are not well defined. The match is a draw. Then, when it comes to everyday decisions, sometimes one comes out ahead and sometimes the other. The fighting continues. Sometimes the voice of one speaks and sometimes the voice of the other. Sometimes one dominates and sometimes the other.

Aditya and Ketaki also begin to realise that it was important for them to give their love the chance to have a perfect union because their desire for each other was as fierce as a burning rocket—they were at the centre of their desire, they were each other's moons. When an old girlfriend wanted to meet Aditya, he said he couldn't meet her and added with a smile, "I am deeply in love with someone at the moment."

He only wanted to meet Ketaki. Every moment, every second. Suddenly he had become aware of his surroundings. When he saw the sunrise in the morning, he wished she was with him. When he saw the moon at night, his loneliness troubled him. When he was at parties, with his friends, whenever he talked to someone, Ketaki would be on his mind and he would not feel at ease anywhere. He was always calculating when, where, and at which conference he could meet Ketaki. Whenever he got an invitation from a university to give a talk and it happened to be near Ketaki's city, he would say yes immediately. To the extent that he would happily agree to go to places where he never went if there was the slightest chance that he would meet Ketaki there. Many of his friends were surprised at the change in him; now the fellow was turning up in places he had always refused to go to.

There may or may not have been obstacles in their path. As far as a union for a limited time was concerned, that was certainly possible. One could meet anytime, anywhere for a day or two. But a permanent or long-term union was not possible. The reason for this was that many decisions had been postponed or, rather, thinking about them became too much of a burden, so they had been eliminated from the mind for the time being. I said earlier that solving these questions would be difficult thanks to women's liberation. One of the people in love must come out of their geographical circle, but these two were so firmly fixed on their axes that it was difficult for either of them to move.

A limited-time union can also be called "having an affair" in today's language. In fact, an affair is devoid of seriousness and there is a special emphasis on physical relations. That's why both of them found the word irritating; they considered their feelings much more sublime than that. They did not want to have an affair with each other. That was why they were very conscious of the relationship. Ketaki said that Aditya was her only love; she did not want to sully him with the dust of an affair. With Aditya, she had got to know of love's all-pervasive form, which could be physical but could also not be. This relationship was for life. If there were a life beyond life, she would want Aditya's company there too. Aditya wanted to marry his love and make her his life partner.

The union that the two could achieve looked like a short-term union or an affair when seen from outside. But, from within, its appearance was different. Even if that union was limited in time, its consciousness and impact kept every moment of their lives fragrant. Usually lovers do not have control over how or where their story goes, whether theirs will be a happy ending or a tragic one. Overwhelmed by circumstances, they sway to the blows they face. Fortune and misfortune keep coming their way and moving them. No matter how many plans Aditya and Ketaki make, is their destiny in their hands?

Rainbows and Streams

They say that where there is a will there is a way. That means it is in the power of the hero and heroine to give another dimension to their relationship or not. But, just as streams of water ultimately meet in the ocean, no matter how much our hero and heroine kept weighing and thinking, it was inevitable that the currents of the mind would meet the ocean of the body.

An opportunity to meet arose, and they decided to do so on a small island near Navabhum.

Curiosity, excitement, and anxiousness had turned Ketaki into a nervous wreck. Firstly, there was the newness of the person; on top of that, it was an unknown place; thirdly, she was travelling to another country alone. She was afraid that something could happen to Aditya on the way that would prevent him from reaching the destination—then what would she do alone in an unknown place? Sometimes she felt that Aditya was waiting for her in somewhere and she could not get there. Her flight was late and no one knew when it would take off, or whether it would take off. She was worried about getting a message across to Aditya. There was no phone anywhere. Nor did she know exactly at which number she could find Aditya. Sometimes she felt as if a ship had stopped at some unknown island and she had no clue where. Was this where she was to get off or was it somewhere else? She couldn't tell whether she had dreamt all of this or whether it had been just a thought in her mind.

Aditya said that he would make all the arrangements, Ketaki just had to catch a plane and get there. He also addressed her fears by saying that there seemed to be no possibility or good reason for him to die right now. But it would be a different matter if his flight got delayed by a few hours. He would try to book a flight that got in before hers did. He also comforted Ketaki by saying nothing would happen to her or him.

Both would return safe and sound. After all, she had roamed around the world. Why was she suddenly getting scared? It made him happy inside to know, while he tried to find the psychological reason for her fear, that Ketaki loved him, which was why the fear of not meeting him or losing him made her say such things.

Aditya's flight reached earlier. He had already booked a very comfortable room in a nice hotel on the shores of the Caribbean Sea. He had arrived a few hours earlier and checked all the arrangements. He had also booked a taxi for them to get around in. Then he started counting each moment till she came. Ketaki's plane got delayed. He kept thinking of going to the airport. Then he tried to convince himself that if Ketaki failed to spot him at the airport and took a taxi, she would worry when she reached the hotel to find that he wasn't there. He left a message at the reception saying he was sitting in the lobby and sat on a chair near the large, wide glass window overlooking the ocean. He ordered a gin and tonic and fixed his eyes on the boats sailing in the water.

The hotel was built upside down on a rock. That means the lobby was on top and one had to go down the elevator to get to the rooms. It was a special feature of that hotel and the tourist guide specifically recommended watching the sunset while sitting in the lobby restaurant. It was just noon and Aditya had already chosen his favourite table, where he would sit and watch the sunset with Ketaki.

The biggest event of that day was the arrival of Ketaki. Aditya was scared till the last moment that Ketaki would change her plans. When she stood there in front of him wearing a long, flared, black cotton skirt and a flimsy off-white coloured blouse with lace edges, just right for the summer weather, Aditya felt as if he was still dreaming. He was just about to get up when Ketaki leaned down towards him him. He raised his face, kissed her lips, and was about to pull her into his arms when he realised he was in the lobby. Regaining his composure, he stood up and said, as if testing Ketaki, "Would you like to go to the room and wash your hands and face or should we watch the sunset first?"

"I have left my luggage at the reception. There's no need to wash up."

"You sit here. I will ask the porter to take your luggage upstairs—I mean, downstairs."

Ketaki plopped herself on the chair in front of Aditya and started looking at all the birds in the sky.

As she became aware of her surroundings, she thought Aditya had chosen a very beautiful place to stay and involuntarily smiled shyly. By that time she had perhaps forgotten how to feel shy. It seemed very childish. She had a habit of talking boldly. Today, suddenly, shyness seemed sweet to her.

"What will you drink?" Aditya asked as soon as he returned. "Should I order some wine or something?"

"Already? No, no. We can have tea at sunset. Childhood habits do not go away. And the humid heat here is reminding me of Purabhum."

"The greenery, too."

"Absolutely! On the way here, I saw gulmohars, champacas, desi roses, bougainvilleas, and many familiar Purabhumi trees and plants. Many Purabhumis live here as well. It seems strange to come to an island miles away from Purabhum and find the same familiar faces in a strange country. They have the same features, dark complexion, and short stature, but their mannerisms and way of speaking are so different. It seems so familiar and yet so unknown. I am very curious about this place. The people here migrated some 100–150 years ago, so despite being like us, they have become something else. Just imagine what we, the foreign residents of Navabhum, will look like after a few centuries."

"Although many things get dissolved over the centuries, I can confidently say that the people from the old world will still retain their own identity. Even if it is in the form of a new variety of that identity. The Punjabis have also been in California for a long time but have not been able to give up their Punjabiness completely. I wouldn't be surprised if some mark or specialty remained. Even on this island, the Purabhumis have a distinct identity."

The sun was moving towards the heavens. As it disappeared from the sky, it seemed the entire sky was covered by coloured dust. Ketaki looked at the colours of the flowers in the lawn of the hotel and sometimes at the purple, orange, and pink clouds floating in the sky. She felt an unusual excitement at the thought of the evening. A sweet intoxication was permeating the atmosphere. The leaves were moving and swaying in the wind. Ketaki got to her feet. "Come on, get up, let's go for a walk."

When they got out of the lobby, one or two taxis were standing outside. Aditya talked to a taxi driver and signalled to Ketaki to sit in the taxi.

"Let's go to the beach. You like walking on the sand, don't you?"

Shivers ran all over her body when the surging waves touched Ketaki's calves. With a sigh she grabbed Aditya's hand with her own and found his hand trembling. It felt as if the entire ocean was eager to break through the walls of the body and pull them out.

As evening fell, the colour of the clouds became darker. The sky was now trying on new makeup.

"It is rare to be able to watch the continuity of day becoming evening and evening becoming night. Even though the same routine is in reality repeated daily."

"We don't have the time to notice continuity."

"Nor the patience."

"You know, I have tried many times to note the change. Especially when one travels towards the east and the dawn of a country is awakening. I keep my eyes fixed on the sky to see when the darkness turns into dawn and the dawn wears the guise of sunrise. I have seen the sun rise many times but not the night dawning. When the eyes open, either dusk has already arrived or it is dark and the eyes close automatically."

I feel that, when Ketaki was saying this, somewhere inside her, some other parallel conversation was going on, which perhaps was not clear to her, as if while talking about day and night, she was also talking about life and death. It might have had a very deep connection with her own life because one day she was telling me about the dream that she often sees at night even now, in which her father dies mysteriously. What she sees is him going from living to dying or the process of dying—she never sees him sick or in pain in bed. She never got to see the process of morning turning into night.

Is it possible to see the union of death and life?

This was a sad shadow on her union with a lover like Aditya.

Then she paused for a moment and said, "But today I feel that I can see everything and I want to capture every moment in my memory."

"Won't being captured hurt it?" Aditya smiled.

"I will keep exposing it to fresh air. I will not hold it too tight."

Aditya squeezed her.

"You know, I love you very much, so much so... so much..."

"You won't be able to bear it," Ketaki added smilingly. "Do you find me so light?"

Aditya teased her, "Of course! So light that I could lift you on my fingers."

"No, Baba, don't you dare! If you make a mistake, you will regret it for the rest of your life."

"You consider me so weak! Okay, I might not be Hatim Tai, and I can't lift Mount Govardhan on my fingers like Krishna, but I have enough strength to hold a bouquet."

"Wow! Are you complimenting me?"

"I was afraid that you would object to not being called a flower and ask why I was saying 'a bouquet of flowers'."

"Then why did you say it ?"

"Because no single flower can do justice to the diversity and richness of your personality. When you appear as a scholar, you spread a different colour and fragrance, when you appear like this, by becoming my beloved, you have such an intoxicating smell in you." A sudden strong urge descended upon Aditya. He kissed Ketaki's cheeks, hair, ears, eyes and forehead. "You are not just Ketaki!"

"*Ketaki, gulab, juhi, champa, banphule...*" Ketaki quoted the old film song as if she were intoxicated.

"Yes, Ketaki. Not just a bouquet, you are the whole garden—flower beds, bushes, pruned trees, pond, lake..." and Aditya got lost somewhere in that garden!

The sky was royal blue. The moon and stars were sparkling like silver beads newly embroidered on freshly woven chiffon!

The sky leaned very close, as if a tent studded with stars was standing tall!

The wet and salty breeze of the seashore fluttered and flapped at their bodies. Sometimes they would get wet because of the splashing of the waves.

While the waves of the ocean were churning and trying to touch the moon, the whistling winds were pulling and tugging at the waves and the moonlight covered everything in its shimmering light, on the soft expanse of sand two wet creatures, drenched in the sweetness, tight in each other's embrace, free from the sense of being, were enjoying moments of existence.

Their not being was being.

Their being was not being.

Time, the horizon, and consciousness had merged into one point.

The heavens were watching them from all sides.

The stars had fixed their eyes on them and witnessed this game of chance.

Dew drops kept showering pearls on them all through the night.

Ocean waves drenched them again and again.

Ketaki's body would tremble. Aditya's arms would bind her in their serpentine grip. Like lines of smoke both would merge into each other.

Aditya would pay obeisance at the temple and offer flowers.

Both of them would fill up and empty. Then fill up and empty. Then they remained full.

It was as if morning and evening, evening and night had become part of some continuity. Everything around them was still. If anything was alive and pulsating, it was that point that had washed away all perception of consciousness.

"Ketaki, why do words seem inadequate when it comes to expressing feelings? No matter how much I search, I can't find the words I am looking for. I want to tell you what I feel but can't find..."

"Be quiet! Just be quiet! I heard you."

"But I want to hear from you. Whatever you feel... I want to hear that too."

"You think words come easily to me? But if there are no words, they can be stolen. In all the centuries of human experience, there must have been many who felt like us. Yes, I remember, when I was in college, I read a novel—*Islands in the River*—which I can't forget even today. I remember that the writer expressed much of what I felt but even he was not satisfied with his words. He frequently quoted English poets. His heroine Rekha used to say everything on her mind through English poems or Tagore's songs. The novel was in Hindi but one-fourth of it was filled with these poems. All those poems were beautiful, very beautiful. That was when I learnt for the first time that love is not just happiness but also anguish. And there is a lot of pain in love."

"But there is a lot of sweetness in Tagore's songs. May I suffer such sweet pain again and again."

"As long as there is meeting, there is waiting, there is sweetness in pain, but..."

"But will you and I always be together? Always. I won't let you leave, even if you want to."

"Really?" Ketaki had a sad smile in her eyes. As if she were saying, "I wish what you are saying were true or could be true."

Aditya pretended to ignore that and said, "You and I will only be apart like Jayadeva's Radha, who starts suffering when she does not see Krishna around and her friend tells her:

> *lalitala vangala tāpari śīlana komala malaya samīre.*
> *madhukara nikaraka rambita kokila kūjita kuñjaku ṭīre.*[1]
>
> A soft southern mountain breeze caresses trembling vines of clove.
> Arbours hum with buzzing bees and the cries of cuckoos and doves.

"So your friend is telling you as well that the season is very intoxicating and it is difficult for Krishna to reject lovers in such an atmosphere, so if you want to have control over him, meet your lover as soon as possible, otherwise you will keep talking about pain and Krishna will give you the slip."

[1] From the Gita Govinda, a collection of religious songs written by the 12th century Bengali poet Jayadeva. The poems are still sung at Bengali Vaishnavite festivals.

"What nonsense! You rascal." Ketaki giggled.

"Is that so!" Aditya got sentimental. "This is unique for me. I have never experienced anything like this in my life. I did not even expect it. Perhaps it does not seem wise to expect something so hard to get. What you have given me is the most precious thing in my life. The key to my life, the source of life. The inspiration to live. The stream in which I will cross over to the other side. I do not believe in any God, yet I will call you a divine gift because I have no other words for this unique experience."

"If there were words, I would choose the most beautiful words, braid them like flowers, and garland you. I would worship you with the offering of meanings and bathe you in the water of emotions. You are mine, Aditya. Just mine. I just want to be yours. Only yours."

"Ketaki, this is the first time in my life that I have known and experienced such beauty. I never want to lose it."

"Neither do I."

The next morning they kept roaming in the forest. It was a very dense forest, with many types of trees, bushes, birds, langurs. They walked on narrow mountain trails drenched in sweat, then cooled down in the cascade of a waterfall flowing from a height of 300 feet. As soon as the shower touched Ketaki, she started giggling and Aditya felt he was complete as he looked at her with delight. Jokes, jokes, dreams, wishes, peals of laughter. Aditya felt like giving the whole world to Ketaki and

Ketaki seemed enchanted and wanted to absorb all of Aditya within herself.

The moments of union are very short. Like moments of happiness are always numbered. After that, only memories remain. And a person keeps remembering the same memories all through his life.

Both of them were full of happiness. Happiness of mind. Happiness of body. Happy to savour wisdom. To savour devotion. The sweetness of love.

Deep inside their minds was the satisfaction that this relationship was not with just anyone but with a dearly beloved person. So the feeling of happiness and satisfaction reached its zenith.

"Adi, what is the peak of love... its limit? Have you ever tried to find out?"

"I am finding out now, thanks to you. I had heard that love finds its pinnacle only in the pity of the devotee, when the lover reaches the door of the beloved in the guise of a beggar. The crazy love of Meerabai or in Sur-Tulsi's song '*Tohi mohi nate anek maniyai jo bhavai*', in which the relationship between lover and beloved is fundamental and indestructible in every way, like between water and fish, or water and drops, ocean and rivers, clouds and rain. Ketaki, you and I dissolve in each other or cannot exist without each other. This is the last step of love!" Aditya's body's grip around Ketaki tightened like the tentacles of an octopus. Ketaki was melting like a wax statue in an iron furnace. What kind of heat is this that burns and at the same time quenches the burning of years?

Both of them kept opening up to each other. Their relationship had acquired a new dimension. They had found a lot to discover in each other. The flow of communication between them had started. And they kept dipping into that for hours.

Ketaki felt that her desire to be close to Aditya was increasing. The more she met him the more she wanted to meet him. Like when a seed sprouts and a plant starts to grow and keeps on growing, the plant of their love was growing in leaps and bounds.

"Did you ever imagine we would start loving each other like this? If you hadn't let me stay in your room that day, would we ever have met?"

"Well, to be honest, after I read your first book I was keen to meet you. Your insights made a deep impression on me. I would have tried to meet you."

"But it wouldn't have been a meeting like this, such a dramatic one."

"Perhaps the drama is still affecting us."

"But now, so many new scenes have been added to it," Ketaki said jokingly.

"Actually, Ketaki, I never thought I would experience anything like this at this age. All that was left in my life's journey was work. That my body would ever feel so young again was beyond my imagination. Now it is as if a twenty-year-old boy's heart is beating inside me. All of this is very alien. The pace of my life has changed, it is heading in an unknown direction. It is as if I have started living anew. You must find what I am saying very weird."

"No! Not weird at all. It is very beautiful. I feel rejuvenated as well. All my sadness, loneliness, the monotony, everything has disappeared. As the excitement, enthusiasm, and desire to fly have awakened, I just feel like running in endless fields covered with green grass. I want to hop and skip, leap like a deer, swing like a peacock, chirp like a bird, quack like a duck, loud enough to make the whole pond echo. I want to hang on the branches of trees, to look at the clouds for a long time and get drenched in torrential rains, to turn myself into a stream of water. Never stop, just keep running, keep flying."

"When you fly like this, it gives me pleasure too, Ketaki, I also want to fly with you. Will you fly with me?"

"You are with me in my flight but you become the kindling that blows me away with its power. Just like a rocket. So much fire is generated to make it fly, and then the rocket flies with only the energy of that fire. This is what happens, Aditya, the energy of your love makes me sit in a Sputnik and fly away."

"If I honestly were capable of that, I would be very proud of myself."

"You have no idea what you have done to me, Aditya."

"Listen, take me along the next time you sit in a Sputnik."

"I am in a Sputnik right now. Come with me."

But Aditya was not where Ketaki was. The hearts and minds of both of them had been woven from different fibres. Aditya did not fly like Ketaki did.

Often, when Ketaki was flying, Aditya came to his senses.

When Ketaki was being sensible, Aditya started weaving a world of fantasies.

After a few moments, Aditya said, "Ketaki, what is it about you that gives me so much affection, so much peace? I feel as if I have reached the place I have been trying to get to all my life. Now I can't go anywhere else."

"Will you just come and stop at me?"

"Yes, my whole world revolves around you. There is no going anywhere from here."

"I don't want to go anywhere else either. You are my resting place, destination, the essence of my being."

Aditya caressed her and asked tenderly, "Will you live with me?"

"Yes, I can't stand the thought of being parted from you."

"But will you be able to live with me?"

"Why not? There is no other way now. It is getting harder and harder to stay away from you. When both of us are eager to be with each other, why should we live so far apart?"

"Would you like some more time to think about it?"

"Thinking will waste time."

"Are you certain, then?"

"Absolutely certain."

And Ketaki covered herself with her bedsheet and was ready to sleep. Aditya teased her, "Why do you need the bedsheet? It is so hot."

"No, I can't sleep without covering myself with a sheet."

"Leave it. Let's sleep naked."

"Shh. What are you saying?"

"Why? What do you have to hide? I have seen everything already."

"It is an old habit of mine to cover my body when I sleep."

"Habit?"

"Yes, since childhood. When you grow up, that's what you are taught at home."

"But now you have grown up."

"Habits don't leave you, do they? However much I try, I can't fall asleep without covering myself. Does that seem strange to you?"

"Well, don't put your clothes on then."

"How is that possible? Either both of us are sky-clad, or neither."

"Clothed in white. You have brought a kurta pyjama. Put it on and get under the sheet."

"I will not be able to sleep now."

Both of them were giggling.

A Fresh Start

On the way back from the island, Aditya could only think of one thing. They had to start living together. Being with Ketaki and feeling her touch was breathing new life into him. Any time spent apart from her was time wasted.

Ketaki was restless as well. She kept thinking of things she wanted to say to Aditya all the time. She kept bringing up the subject of living together.

Aditya felt he had to do something so Ketaki and he could spend the rest of their lives together. One day, he asked Ketaki on the phone, "Should I ask at my university whether there is a position you can apply for?"

"Is that possible?"

"Well, you only find out if you ask."

"But listen—"

"You have no objection to living with me, do you?"

Aditya felt it might be wise to check if their words were still valid in the clear light of day before taking any concrete steps.

"That is what I want. I have told you that already. But I don't know why I also feel a bit apprehensive."

"About what, Ketaki?"

"About leaving my city, my world, and making a fresh start all over again."

"Would you prefer that I come to your side of the country? You could find out if there are any opportunities there as well, but I could create something for you over here. There's nothing wrong with trying."

"No, don't do anything yet. I'm not ready. I will let you know when I am ready."

"But I don't get why you are hesitating. If you think my living with you is unreasonable, let me know so I can adjust accordingly."

"Not unreasonable. I want some time to think. Give me some time."

"Let me put it this way. If we start working on it now, it may take a year or two before it is practically possible, even longer. "

"I get what you are saying. But I need some time to think."

Aditya was a bit disturbed by what Ketaki was asking for. If they loved each other and wanted to live together, what was the need for such careful thought? Did Ketaki not love him enough to be ready to give up everything for him? Was it an unreasonable expectation on his part? Was he prepared to give up everything for Ketaki? The answer that rose within him was pretty straightforward. Yes.

Ketaki was a lot more hazy and unclear inside. She has never given me clear answers when I have questioned her. There seem to be some murky shadows lurking there—a tiny little girl... sitting on her father's shoulders... he tosses her up sometimes, then catches her and holds her tight... the sky above resounds with their laughter... but then that person disappears. The girl asks her mother, "Where is Papa?" The answer is standard—"He has gone on a trip." "When did he go?" "In the morning." "Where was I?" "You were sleeping." "Why didn't you wake me up?" "Don't be stupid. How could I wake you up that early and deal with you? You keep me from sleeping anyway." She would fall asleep at night longing for her father. He wouldn't be there the day after, either. She wouldn't ask anything. Mummy would scold her. Or give a negative answer.

This happened time after time. Papa was there. And then suddenly, he wasn't there anymore. For a long time. Then he came back. And left again. So she stopped hoping to see him. When he arrived, she went out to play with her friends.

Maybe she was also asking herself whether Aditya would always be there for her.

A Heavenly Bird

Ketaki sat surrounded by flowers. Heaps of blossoms gazed at her with caressing eyes. Today was the first anniversary of their meeting—the night of their union. She had just come back from university. Aditya had sent her a huge bouquet: lilies, roses, irises, anthuriums, and birds of paradise. Colours and fragrances filled her room. A note from Aditya was attached to the bouquet. The first sentence was, "There are only flowers in this bouquet, no thorns. May our lives be like this."

Yes, there were only soft petals on the flowers; any thorns that may have been there had been removed. Tender green leaves were wrapped around them. There were no thorns on them either.

Ketaki's eyes were focused on one flower. A bird of paradise. A bird ready to take flight rather than a flower. Its beak pointed towards the sky. Ketaki repeated the words to herself, "Bird of paradise." Why do they call this a heavenly bird? What a beautiful imagination the person who named this flower had! Maybe because of its splendid colours—yellow, purple, blood-red, green—and the elegant shape. Birds are beautiful as well. She had seen so many colourful, pretty birds on the island. But none like this. Which is why this unique bird must only exist in paradise. Flowers that turn into birds and fly.

Ketaki felt all the flowers had turned into birds and started to fly. They were hovering about in her room. And she had joined them and was flying too. So was Aditya. She could take off with the flying birds. Beautiful moments of life—that belonged to her, to Aditya, to these flowers. A life without contradictions. Aditya was right. Aditya's love was like a bird of paradise.

Paradise. She had never tried to find out what that could be. And now it had spread itself in front of her.

It brought back vivid and fragrant memories—they were in the sea, riding the waves. Sometimes they chased after them, and at other times they ran ahead of them. Sometimes the waves knocked them down and washed over them. Aditya clasped her in his arms, preventing her from falling while the waves slapped at them. Aditya's feet were firmly planted in the sand. He jumped above the waves and pulled Ketaki up with him, making her jump. But a wave washed over Ketaki. Her hair covered her face. Aditya moved her hair away from her face with one hand. She could feel gritty sand in her teeth. She pulled her hand away and cupped it to rinse her mouth with seawater. The brackishness of the salt scraped her tongue. Her eyes are stinging slightly. And then another wave knocked the two of them over together. The wave retreated. They stood up, waiting for a new wave to emerge and immerse them in the water. They were laughing themselves silly.

Then, they sat on the sand and built sand castles. Aditya made a big one with many rooms. A veranda and a long path from the gate to the veranda. Ketaki looked at it in surprise. Her sand castle was just an igloo-shaped room. Aditya asked, "Will you live in my home?"

Ketaki crushed her house with her foot. "Make a castle for me like that one."

"But this is yours as well."

Meanwhile, a big wave came, and Aditya's castle turned to sand in the flow of the water. Ketaki began to clap. "Look what happened to your house. Wow!" Aditya didn't laugh. He didn't say a word.

Then, they headed out to sea in a tiny boat. Ketaki suddenly felt they had gone too far. They'd left the shore far behind. She was scared. "What if a big wave comes and turns the boat over? Will we sink?"

Aditya notices her fear. "Why? We will swim back."

"Will we be able to swim that far?"

"Should we go back?"

And all of a sudden Ketaki's fear disappeared. Was it because Aditya was with her?

"No, we don't have to go back. And if we do drown, so what? We'll be together."

"Have you thought about what you are saying?"

"Of course. Let's try drowning together."

"Then we have to go back. In the deep waters here, we won't be able to find you. If you are to drown, at least do it where I can find you."

"How then?"

Aditya flashed her a naughty smile. "In the bathtub." And in the lovely sunshine, Ketaki felt a thrill rush through her. Aditya's touch was tender like warm water.

Aditya changed the direction of the boat. Ketaki was looking into the distance, where the sky met the seashore. A big semi-circular horizon encircled them on three sides.

And then they had spent such a long time at the seashore. They were looking at the aquatic birds, listening to the racket they made, and collecting heaps of seashells.

Suddenly, he stood up. "Come, let's go snorkelling."

They fetched snorkels and went out to sea again. In the water this time. Lots of colourful fish gleamed in the sunlight. Ketaki had never seen such pretty fish in her life. There were fields of coral in the middle of the water. All kinds of marine plants. Another world was revealing itself to her underwater. It was a first for her.

Aditya's snorkel kept filling up with water. They returned to the shore shortly.

Ketaki was not satisfied yet. She would have spent hours under the sea's surface looking at that mysterious world if she could. Colourful fish were dancing in front of her eyes. It was such a new experience. After a while, she said, "I am going to go back into the water."

She covered her nose and eyes with a mask, put the snorkel tube in her mouth, and went off to see the fish. Blue and yellow, red and blue, white and red, green and yellow, purple, orange... fish of so many colours!

Aditya waited by the shore.

When Ketaki emerged from the water, her face was glowing with the success of a victorious campaign. She removed hair from her eyes and looked at Aditya with a smile.

Ketaki's wet body was gleaming in the sunlight. Aditya's eyes rested on the parts of her body not covered by the swimsuit. He could not stand being apart from her for such a long time. When Ketaki came closer, he dropped her onto the sand and covered her with kisses.

"I thought you had become a fish and started to live with them."

"Leaving you behind?"

"Do you know what I feel like right now? I want to rip off your swimsuit and—"

"No, I know we are abroad right now, but in civilized society, one doesn't do such things in broad daylight."

And Ketaki dragged him into the churning water.

The sound of a phone ringing startled Ketaki. She ran. She thought it might be Aditya. And it was him. "I was celebrating my anniversary with you," was the first thing Ketaki said.

"How?" Aditya asked in a relaxed tone.

"How..." She was taken aback. "You were with me. Just with you."

"But how? I am two thousand miles away from you, longing for you and wondering why I can't spend the day with you." Aditya's voice was filled with the joy of getting hold of Ketaki on the phone and the anguish of being apart.

"We know magic. That is how you came here through your voice."

"I can't concentrate on my work. I left the meeting and came to talk to you."

"Should I tell you how I was with you? You were on a chariot heading towards me. A chariot with horses. The chariot descended from the sky, and I swayed in the wind. You saw me and stretched out your hand. I grabbed your hand. You pulled me into the chariot. The chariot was moving at quite a speed. The horses were galloping in the air. I saw that you did not have the reins in your hands, but the chariot didn't flounder, and we set off at great speed. We were heading for the sky, and suddenly, it began to rain flowers. There were so many flowers, so many flowers that the whole sky was covered with flowers. Suddenly, the flowers sprouted wings, became birds, and started flying."

"Okay, so what happened then?"

"Well, the phone rang, and the bird is still in my hands, but now I will tie its wings and put it in a vase-shaped cage. So when you come..."

"When I come?"

"You will set them free. When are you coming? I am with you anyway, in the air, sky, water, everywhere. But I need your physical presence—the sense of touch has its own needs."

"Do you know what I was thinking about, sitting at that meeting? That day, when I came out of the bathroom after a shower, you were being naughty and pulled away my towel. Just like that..."

Ketaki was overcome with shyness. She felt her cheeks blush.

"Okay, okay. Finish your meeting and call me."

"No, listen! I want to touch all those flowers with my hands, smell their fragrance, listen to them chirp with my ears, and learn where the bird of paradise perches. Its dense black silken woven nest—"

"Stop it! Are you trying to compete with the poet Jayadeva?" Ketaki couldn't stop laughing.

"I wouldn't dare to do such a thing."

Motion and Discovery

Some more time had passed.

Aditya was planning to spend a long time with Ketaki. But would she like it if he left everything to go and stay with her? Until she asked him to do so, he would not be able to go there on his own. Ketaki kept talking about living together, but the last time they met, she said she wanted to visit the old country and see her older sister. She didn't want to decide anything yet. She would do that when she returned. Maybe travelling far away would give her mind the clarity to determine what she was to do next. Aditya wanted to see Ketaki bloom, grow, and flourish. Not get forced into anything. Ketaki would do what she wanted when she wanted. That is what made Aditya happy. Happiness is accepting happiness. Does happiness have any other form of existence? If it does, let it. Aditya's happiness lay only with Ketaki and anything to do with her.

But as soon as Ketaki was far away, her mind was filled with doubts. Doubts about herself, doubts about love... she started to understand it again... love... Aditya... everything that came under the noun 'love'... everything that she felt... that she knew or didn't know but wanted to know... and all those questions... what would this love transform into? Is transformation when two people become one in the flesh? Or is love something else? Something beyond companionship and intimacy, vowing to spend the rest of one's life together. Above all of that. If there is love, it has to be above all of that. Living together does not mean that love will flourish. It can be something else. Should she take such a risk? Why should the salvation of every emotion lie only in its embodiment, and why should its embodiment only be in words or physical exercise? Isn't the feeling everything in itself? Isn't it enough that it exists? Isn't it enough to know and enjoy the happiness of having it? Does it need a physical form?

She told me, her narrator friend, about Aditya. "For the first time, I have loved and been loved. He is a gem. Pure 24-carat gold. A wonderful man. And a great scholar. I feel like leaving everything and worshipping my love, nurturing it. But then I can't do it all the same. I keep procrastinating. Aditya has asked me to make up my mind many times. What shall I do? Will our love get lost?"

I responded,"In matters like this, you should only listen to your heart. What does your heart say?"

"My heart? My heart says a lot and vacillates, it's fickle and uneasy."

"Does making up your mind and accepting Aditya end that uneasiness?"

"Well, yes, it does, but how do I know that another kind of uneasiness won't start?"

"I don't get you... You lot are from another generation. We had to stand by the person we marry for the rest of our lives."

"Love is not a question of standing by someone, the premise of love is to keep love alive, to keep the flame burning. If love dies, there is no meaning in staying together. If you are in love, there is no meaning in living together. That is not a condition for love. Yes, if society demands it, that is another matter. But society is not demanding it of me. It is a personal decision I must make. And on my own."

"You are getting more and more confused."

"I am suffering; how do I explain it to you... or myself?" And Ketaki burst into tears.

I, or the narrator, could see the little doll in Ketaki, the doll who was sadly waiting for her father and thinking that he would maybe never return. And she is teaching herself to live without Papa. With other uncertainties. To leave Papa and go far away.

In a letter to Aditya from Purabhum, she wrote, "I need to understand love. I used to think that love was an illusion, just air, a figment of imagination. I have to live on this earth and grasp what is true, but now it seems that the feeling in my heart for you is love. But the feeling doesn't regard you simply as a sweetheart. You are a complete person. Who knows in how many layers and in how many ways I am connected to you? I can challenge you, confront you, fight with you, rebuke you, even. If I fall, you pick me up; if you get hurt, I stroke and comfort you. If there is an argument, I can defeat you, but I do not hesitate to accept defeat. Is this all within the boundaries of love? Isn't love another name for constantly wanting to be close to someone? All of this exists in my heart, and yet there is more than this. To be contained in you and yet be able to stay apart from you. Both. To find you and to lose you. Sometimes, I scare myself, Adi. I mean, what is it I feel? It is love, right?"

Aditya stared at the letter before him, thinking for a long while. He sympathised with Ketaki. It pleased him that she was thinking about love. So she was drenched in his love, even if it bewildered her and kept her confused. Love had been planted in her like a truth. There was no time to answer the letter. Ketaki was going to return in a day or two.

Ketaki had returned from the old country, but did not contact Aditya for a long time. A strange lassitude lingered in her body. Aditya kept waiting to hear from her each day and was bothered; surely she had returned by now. What had happened? If anything had gone wrong with the flight, it would have been in the papers. Had she stayed on for a few days?

But the university term had begun. She had to go to work. In the end, he gave up and called her one day. Left a message on her answering machine and got no response. Called again, and Ketaki took the call. When he asked why she hadn't called, she said, "I still have jet lag."

"That usually ends after a week. Surely, you have been back for over ten days now? When did you get back?"

"I came back as scheduled."

"Then why haven't you called all these days?"

"I told you I wasn't feeling well."

Aditya sensed a strange feeling of alienation and exhaustion in her voice.

"Are you avoiding meeting me?"

"Why would I avoid you?" Irritation rose as she spoke.

"I am heading towards your town—"

Ketaki thwarted him immediately. "No, please don't come right now. I am not ready."

"There's nothing to be ready about. I am not going to stay with you. I was only talking about meeting you."

"I am feeling very lethargic. It happens. It takes me longer than usual to get back to normal. That world is something else. It absorbs you like raindrops on dry earth. Or like those reeds, you know, the ones that catch hold of a thin dupatta so that you can't disentangle it again; it might tear, but it will not come loose from the sharp thorns."

Doubt began to seize Aditya's mind. *Is there someone in the old country whom Ketaki has met, who has unsettled her like this? An old friend? An old lover? Or, she may have met someone on the trip back. Now Ketaki isn't interested in Aditya anymore. Is she so unstable? No, that can't be possible. This is just my mind going crazy. But something is up. Ketaki isn't saying something.* Ketaki was so confused that she had no idea what effect it was having on Aditya's mind.

Had the fear that her father might not turn up at all found a home in her heart? The tiny child had given up all hope of seeing him. When Papa came, she ran out to play with her friends.

Dreams and Desires

Aditya asked Ketaki the same questions again and again as if he did not believe that Ketaki was still wholly his. He felt there was some dilemma in Ketaki's mind that she did not talk to him openly about. Her inner turmoil was reflected in her poems. But she never said anything that could create a rift in the relationship.

After two or three months, when Ketaki came out of her shell, they met at a seminar where both had been invited as experts in their respective subjects. Aditya had gone prepared to meet her face-to-face. "Listen, Ketaki…"

"Hmm."

"Whatever happened between us…w as there anything you were disappointed about?"

"Why are you saying this?" Her mind and body blossomed like a sunflower when she saw Aditya.

"You do still love me, don't you?"

Ketaki felt as if a young child was asking his mother for approval. "Did I do everything right?"

Ketaki started to laugh. "When you were little, did your mother scold you a lot?"

"She still scolds me. Do this, don't do that, one doesn't do things like that. She keeps giving me some lesson or the other as if I still don't have the sense to understand."

"Have you not been able to prove to her that you are intelligent even though you are such a great scholar and professor?"

"I don't know. I have always thought she thinks my older brother is better. She loves him more. She would always tell me to be more like him. As a matter of fact, I have been a lot more successful than him in real life. But I was very rebellious and naughty; my brother was quite simple. He would listen to Ma. I would always oppose what she said. So, Ma did not consider me very responsible. She didn't trust me fully. Even when I did something right, she thought it was inconsistent with my nature. That may be why I left the country and came here. In my mind, I wanted to tell my mother that she should care about me and respect me. But now my mother complains that I don't care about her, that I never write letters, and that I don't go to meet her. Meanwhile, I go almost every year. I may not write letters, but I do call."

"For mothers, meeting once a year is never enough."

"Yes, and then one has to meet one's family in the same period one meets one's friends. My mother and brother constantly complain that when I go there, I only go to see my friends, not to see them. There are always loads of complaints."

"But you still want your mother's approval!" Ketaki burst out laughing.

Talking about his mother had made Aditya turn serious. But he was aware of Ketaki's teasing mood. He joined in her laughter and said with a smile, "I know what you are trying to say."

Turning serious, Ketaki said, "If you visit your mother every year, isn't it because you keep trying your best to make her happy even if she keeps complaining?"

Before she had framed what she wanted to say, Aditya understood that she wanted to make fun of him, to show he needed constant reassurance in love because he had such a complicated relationship with his mother. He said immediately, "Well, certainly, madam. I want to take every opportunity to keep you happy as well. Unless you have any objection to that."

"Well, I am very pleased with the fellow," said Ketaki, wrapping herself around Aditya. "Listen, I would like to meet your mother."

"Will you come to Calcutta? I will introduce you to my mother and brother and everybody else. My mother will be pleased to meet you."

"What kind of a relationship did your mother have with your first wife?"

"They didn't spend much time together. I had come here. The marriage took place with my mother's approval. She selected her—the spoiled daughter of a rich family. I hoped my wife would be very different from my mother, but she was just like my mother: a mix of expectations and complaints. Every person in the world looked better to her than I did. She saw flaws in everything I did. That's why it was not possible to live together."

"And your son?"

"She wanted to keep him away from my shadow. I pay for his education. Sometimes, he comes and sees me in his holidays."

"I wonder sometimes what life would be like if I were your wife."

"What does it look like?"

"I can't see anything clearly. But I am such a pessimist. I can only see conflict. At the same time, it is not certain that you and I will quarrel. Many issues bind us together. But I am also scared that what can break us once can break us more easily the second time. We've both been through this."

One could not deny the truth of Ketaki's last sentence, but the state of mind Aditya was in, he was hurt. Yet, without getting discouraged, he said, "We can understand each other's needs like no one else can. Working together, we can inspire and support each other.

If a person has reached the right place, then where does the question of breaking up arise?"

"Do you think so?"

"Yes, there is no doubt in my mind."

"You may be right. When I am with you, I am fired up and radiant. I get a lot of inspiration from you. Whenever I come home after visiting you, I get back to my work with a vengeance. If it stays like this, why shouldn't we live together?"

"That's what I say."

"Do you want to marry me, or are you talking about living together?"

"Whatever you prefer. I am free. I have nothing to tie me down. I can marry you any time."

"Oh my god! I will be a bride again."

"Will you feel weird about being a bride?"

"No. It's not about that. To be honest, I would love to be your bride. I will live a new life. Aditya, the joy you feel in every experience you have when you live with the one you love is greater. I can see you and me standing together... loads of people are congratulating us... your friends, my friends. Neither of my parents is alive now. I don't know what they would have said. But I am sure Papa would have been proud of you."

"I am picturing you in my social circle in my city and wondering what you will make of them. What will your reaction towards all of them be? Our lives will change drastically. What will my friends feel when they meet you?"

"I don't know any of your friends."

"Well, they know of you. Just a couple of close friends of mine. To whom I talk about you."

"I feel like talking about you as well. I have one friend. She is writing a novel. I speak to her now and then. Sometimes, she nags a bit too much. But after talking to her, my mind becomes lighter. Otherwise, the way I remain preoccupied with you might have driven me crazy. How do you feel after talking about me?"

"It's a joy. Sharing memories of you with someone gives me special joy. A chance to relive experiences. To repeat the joy of happy moments one has lived through. I have always talked about my innermost feelings with these two friends of mine. We were at college together. At school, too. Bosom buddies."

"I am thinking of old friends. How we would tease each other if any of us dared to speak to a man. We all wanted to share secrets but to hide them as well. If you started speaking about something, the others would guess what had happened before you finished the story. I could only find one friend like that after I came here. You can only have intellectual discussions with the others, not talk about matters of the heart. I must be so thirsty for such talk. That is why I talk to you so much about my feelings." Then suddenly, as a thought occurred to her, Ketaki asked, "What colour saris do brides wear where you come from? White or red?"

"A white sari with a red border."

"The next time you go home, will you get me one?"

A bit startled, Aditya looked at Ketaki. "Come along with me. Then we can buy the sari of your choice together."

"I will wear it when I go to visit your mother."

"And Ma will bless you." Aditya framed Ketaki's face in his hands.

"My God! Look where you have taken me. It sounds like the story of a Hindi film." She wrapped her arms around his neck and was swaying.

"Not at all. Getting lost in the world of imagination brings a pleasure of its own." Aditya had started swaying with her.

"One should not deprive oneself of any other pleasure either."

"Getting lost or flying away is when we get to know what we want. If you aren't capable of imagining something, you can't achieve it in reality, either. I enjoy entering the world of your imagination."

"I enjoy taking these flights of imagination with you, too. Talking with you makes me reach where I want to be."

"That's how it should be. We should be able to fly until we reach a point we are heading towards."

"But the higher we fly…"

"Yes?"

"The harder we fall…"

"Why should we fall? We are only examining our imagination, getting to know our dreams. There is no question of falling here. We haven't even started trying to come close to our dreams yet."

"Well, you have discussed a position for me at your university."

"I have. You will have to apply."

"By when?"

"When it is ready."

"Great. I will start thinking of it."

"Don't take too long. Send it in as early as possible."

"You are always in a hurry. I need time to think. I will have to tell them here as well. Oh, Aditya, it won't be easy, all of this. First, all the running around to get tenure. And now that it is done, to uproot myself again."

"People do change jobs, you know. If your position here corresponds with your position there, it shouldn't pose any problems."

"You are right. But I have my own life here. I have made a place for myself. I will have to start afresh again. My friends, my work, it is all here."

"Are there people here you can't stand to leave behind?"

"Yes, there are. But one can leave them as well. Why can't you move here?"

"I am looking into that as well. I asked you about it. Suppose there was anything for me over here. I have no problems about coming here to you. But there has to be an opportunity. How else will I put the bread on the table?"

"I am quite capable of putting the bread on the table."

"I know you are. But I will not give you that right. I want to look after you. I need to have a steady source of income."

"That's it! What a typical male thing to say."

"I like looking after others. That's all. I do not want to lose my ability to do so. That's not how I was brought up. I never could and never will be able to do that. I was raised to believe that looking after the woman and children is my responsibility." An innocent smile lit up his face. He hoped that Ketaki would not take his concept of being male as an expression of machismo.

"Well, good. I will stop working and only write books."

"Sure! You are free to do exactly as you please."

"I should marry you, right, as soon as possible?"

"That's what I am saying. Should we fix a date for next month?"

"Why not tomorrow?"

"Let me call the airline and see if any tickets are available..." Aditya tried to get up from the sofa, but Ketaki stopped him.

"But we haven't decided yet whether you are coming here or I am going over to you."

"Decide then, won't you? At least I have assured you of a position, so your coming seems more appropriate."

"You may be right, but I am not ready yet." She had shifted a bit further away. She put her hands in her lap.

"Tell me when you are ready. But be careful when you joke with me. I am ready to fulfil everything you say. So, as soon as you are ready, I will send you a ticket. You are the one who needs to think."

"I can see that. I must think carefully before I say anything to you. You get ready to do whatever we discuss the minute we bring it up. I was joking."

"I know that. But be aware that one can get caught in a joke of one's own making. Because I don't take what you are saying as a joke. Do you understand?"

"Yes, I do understand." Both of them burst into laughter.

The Play of Memory

After short meetings, they had to part. The whole business of sending messages started all over again.

When our hero and heroine wanted to send messages to each other, the phone wires acted as messengers. They don't have to disguise themselves to enter the inner sanctum. And they deliver the message in a completely pure form. Free from anyone else's interference. Just as they are.

They fixed times for morning, afternoon, and evening conversations but still needed to leave a message in between.

Sometimes, the fever of emotions burnt in our hero's head. Then Aditya would issue a series of rambling messages dripping with desire. Rounds, bumps, triangles, wetness. With many adjectives, similes, metaphors, and figures of speech. Ketaki listened. Her whole body would start to tingle. Streams would begin to flow.

Aditya left a message: "Do you know that you are very playful? The memory of fooling around with you makes every nerve in my body tingle. What is playful called in Hindi? In the dictionary, it says 'khilandari'. That word does not suit you. A Sanskrit word, 'ramani'—the one who delights—seems more appropriate to me. There is a sense of playfulness in it. So, I can use that word to describe you."

Then he would think of a dozen other names. Any beautiful name he had heard. He wanted to call Ketaki all of them. Ketaki teased him, "It looks like a Krishna is hiding in your mind with desires for all these gopis. How will we manage if you want to slake your passion for all of them and just be with me?"

"I want to see you and enjoy you in many different forms. All these are names for you—you are Madhuri, you are Radha, you are Kamini, and you are Kanupriya. I love you in every form. As much as I might see you, know you, love you, enjoy you, I will never get enough of you. Not in this lifetime.

"A poet has said:

umr-e-darāz māṅg ke lāī thī chār din
do ārzū mē kaṭ gae, do intizār mē

A long life I asked for, of days only four
Two of them I spent in hope, two in waiting.

"That is Zafar. He put into words exactly what I feel."

Aditya wanted her beside him every minute of the day. If he had to go to another town, he would insist Ketaki join him there.

Once, Aditya asked Ketaki to come to Wanshitown, the capital of Navabhum. He was to receive an award at an Asian studies conference to be held there. Busy with work, Ketaki could not go. At the reception after the award ceremony, instead of greeting fans and friends and joining in the conversation, Aditya went to the phone booth in the hotel lobby but he could not get hold of Ketaki, so he spoke to her answering machine. "You didn't come to the awards ceremony. I knew you wouldn't, but still, I kept looking for you in the audience. Many women were around me, but I was not interested in talking to anyone. Lots of people came up to congratulate me, and all I kept thinking was what you would have said to me had you been here. I want to celebrate this important occasion of my professional life with you."

After the night's programme, he locked himself again in the phone booth. He did not mind that Ketaki was not able to take the call. He could still express his views. "There was a classical dance performance in the evening. I kept imagining you in the body of a dancer. In her drooping eyelids, in the movements of her body, in the rise of her breasts, I was searching for whatever I wanted from you. But I have returned empty-handed. You know, right now, the fragrance of your body is driving me crazy. I want to listen to your breath very closely. Want to smell your hair. I want to feel the softness of your lips and breasts. You are teaching me what loneliness is. I genuinely don't feel like meeting anyone. I am constantly lost in thoughts of you; I have been thinking about you, and this is all I feel like doing. Had you been in the audience, I would have taken genuine pleasure in receiving the award. Now, this will just be an incident to narrate to you."

Ketaki was captivated by Aditya's messages. She waited for them every moment of the day. Wherever she was, even if she got a few minutes, she immediately started listening to the messages on her machine, using any nearby phone. When there was no new message, she would listen to old messages. She would spend her entire day on this. She listened to messages and left messages. When she was not listening to or leaving a message, she would repeat some lines of Aditya's, think about some lines of her own, or start planning what she would say in the next message she was going to send. Messages like sparklers from which sweet sparks kept falling every moment.

She was incredibly happy. Her heart, mind, and body were full of excitement and energy. It was as if life had become a fountain in a royal garden that ran twenty-four hours a day.

There was just as much attachment and restlessness in that life as consciousness and passion. It was as if she kept repeating one thing:. *When will the distance between us be reduced?* Then she would leave messages, restless, sad, full of desire. "I have no part in your life. Your days, your evenings, are only for you. Or they belong to those close friends with whom you chat, eat, or go out for a drink. Where do I figure in your life? Tell me. What kind of relationship is this between you and me? I don't even have as significant a share of you as your friends do. Then how is this a lifelong companionship?" And, then she leaves a message as if reciting a poem:

"*Your history is your own, your waterfalls, chants or babbles, satisfactions and dissatisfactions, screams, dormant memories, forgotten or awakened, of your history, all yours. Your present is your own. Your own is the bustle of your mornings, the rush of the day, the noise of work, the sweat, dust, ink, or your present that drops from the stars. I am not a part of your rushed or bored mornings. Your evenings full of meetings, parties or gatherings. In the conversations or raised glasses of those evenings. Not even in those lonely sobbing nights. Perhaps not in any scene, in any part of that life that is apparent. Still, those moments touched by you, by your memory, by your closeness, by your desires—the churning of the universe, all the tremors of the earth, the whole of history, the hopes and fears of what is yet to come, merge into those stunned, tangible moments. Past, present, and future halt; I live at that point. I squeeze the essence of so many lives into a moment which is only mine, yours or the collected existence of both.*"

Aditya responded, "Were you saying that, despite loving each other wholly, we cannot share many aspects of life? Why? I am ready to share everything with you."

"I know you will say, 'Why doesn't she make up her mind?' That you have left the door open. You have even sent an invitation. But I don't go anywhere easily, I don't move from my place until I am forced to.

"That's not to say that I never felt any compulsion. Many times, I have felt like breaking away and running off. But I get defeated by my own mind. I have all kinds of fears. There is a camp of ghosts inside me. Who knows when and how they come out in moments of decision? As long as I keep nurturing love from a distance, it keeps growing; it may suffocate when I come too close. How can I explain to you that it is not easy to free oneself? It took many years to build myself up, gain my identity, and find myself. How can I lose you like this? No, I do not underestimate your value. You are invaluable to me, all my happiness and the whole of my life is centred around you. I will miss you by moving away from the centre.

"What I am myself is what I can't understand. Perhaps nothing. That is why I recognise the centre: maybe I see my own existence only in the light of the centre, yet I am running away from that centre: what is happening to me? Aditya, take care of me; please take care of me.

"I couldn't sleep all of last night! I just kept missing you. I kept thinking of and reliving the moments we spent together. When will we meet again?"

Aditya got worried about how she left mixed messages, full of contradictions, again and again. Was it so difficult to know oneself? What was there inside Ketaki? Why was she so confused? Could Aditya solve this mystery? Would he not get messed up himself in the process? He tried to sympathise with Ketaki and her internal conflicts. But sometimes, it also seemed that Ketaki had chosen to retreat behind a protective shield.

Why would anyone do that? But she kept on declaring her love for him as well.

At times, when Aditya listened to his answering machine, he felt she was not leaving messages for him; she was talking to herself. She found it easier to say to his machine in his absence whatever she could not say to his face.

One day, she had put on Bhimsen Joshi's song Piyā milan ki ās' and left the receiver of her phone by her speaker.

Aditya listened to it and wondered whether Ketaki had reached the level of emotion he was at. Would Ketaki ever get there? Then, eager to get his love across to Ketaki, he left her a sad message. "When I am far from you, I feel so lonely, sad, and desolate, Ketaki. You'll never be able to comprehend that. Perhaps you can't grasp to what extent I love you and how I suffer without you. My nights are spent in sleepless, deserted, desolate wandering. Being away from you is turning into a curse, Ketaki. Did someone curse me? Am I Kalidas' Shakuntala? Why do only women get to suffer in literature? Such a lot of suffering. Nothing can describe what I am going through. I will have to say it to you in the language of women. It feels as if in this relationship of pain and suffering, I am the woman, and you are the man."

Aditya could not know what Ketaki felt. But her reply was: "It is true that there are many Radhas and Meeras but only one Yaksha. You have forgotten all the ghazal literature. There, it's only men who are bereft in their longing. The fundamental relationship of love with pain is in the roots of ghazal. Remember that couplet of Ghalib's:

ishq se tabīat ne zīst kā mazā pāyā
dard kī davā pāī dard-e-be-davā pāyā

From love did my mind the joy of life procure
A cure for my pain, and pain that had no cure

"And when he cries, blood flows, not tears. The truth is that a man exaggerates his pain. That's why he says, 'If there is no dripping from the eyes, then what is blood?' Nature has also given woman a much higher capacity to bear pain. She is the one who has to be a mother. I remember how whatever Ma was going through, she would never say a thing. But if Papa had a slight headache, the whole house would come running with tea and espresso.

"Let me say one thing. Pain is the mother of creation. That is why you are thinking of such creative things. Perhaps the sleeping poet in you has awakened again. If so, this love will not prove to be so futile."

Aditya felt that it had all turned into an exchange of taunts and jibes. Did Ketaki really know the intensity of his love?

He deliberately called Ketaki when he knew she would be in the university so that he could express his feelings bluntly and his real point would not get lost in Ketaki's arguments. "You are very good at making fun of others' emotions. I do not believe that men exaggerate their pain or feelings. The truth is that men have always ignored their pain and hidden their weaknesses in an attempt to prove themselves physically stronger. The literature of every language is full of men who displayed bravery on the battlefield. Man's inner self, his world of emotions, has been completely ignored. Men aren't even allowed to cry. Therefore, they swallow their pain until they feel the need to shed tears of blood. That's why the world needed Freud. Unless a man recognises his inner so-called weaknesses and accepts them, his mental world will continue to be complex, dragging him towards destruction. Both man and woman reside within every human being. If pain is woman and bravery is man, both live within us. It's a matter of waking them up. The women of today have achieved bravery, but men must compromise with tears."

How could Ketaki lose the argument without saying her bit? But she also sent it to him only when he was at university. "Wow, you are excellent at this. You haven't started writing poetry yet, but what you are saying is true poetry. The poetry of an intellectual has a unique flavour. This time, you've surprised me. Let me make a little joke. Don't feel bad. There is still some Bengali sentimentality left in you. But I like a man who is a human being from within, not someone with a lot of false bravado. That's why ami tumi ka bhalo bashi. You are lovely, truly a good human being. Absolutely genuine. Like 24-carat gold. Lots and lots of love."

This time, Ketaki's message was bubbling over with love. Aditya felt a sweet coolness inside, as if a refreshing breeze had come up from the river and caressed him. Why did he start thinking about Ketaki in such a negative way? She had her own unique style of loving. When Ketaki had a style of her own, why wouldn't her love be special? Why didn't he try to understand her? He made her doubt every little thing she did or said. It was Ketaki's good nature that let her tolerate so much.

Then, there were no messages from Ketaki for a few days. They had some hurried conversations. Partly because he was working on his book and Ketaki was busy with the department's work. But suddenly, Aditya became very restless. Something was happening in Ketaki's life that she did not want to share with Aditya; she wanted to keep it hidden. One day, again, in the same restlessness, he left a message: "You don't leave messages on my machine these days. Do you have nothing to say to me, or are you bored with me? Are you bored because you have heard my messages too often? In that case, I should not leave messages for you. Is that what you're trying to hint at by not leaving a message?"

Ketaki immediately called him and said, "How strange you are! I had nothing special to say, so I left no messages. How did you interpret this to mean that I was bored with you? Why do you have so little faith in yourself? What do you think? That you are not worthy of being loved? What is this complex in you? You are not conscious of your own value."

Ketaki's words did not console Aditya. He said, "I know my worth very well. That's why no one has the time to talk to me."

Ketaki could sense his anger. There was assurance in her voice when she spoke. Perhaps somewhere deep inside, she was also starting to understand Aditya's need. "At least you cannot say this about me, who keeps waiting to talk to you every moment. Our tragedy is that we do not live together."

"We haven't even tried to live together."

"Should we do so now? But how? When we are busy with our work like this?"

"Do you want to live with me?"

"Sure! What could be greater than that in life?" Ketaki's mind was open. Aditya felt they could only resolve all these dilemmas if they decided to live together. He said in a very decisive voice, "Okay, let me take care of the arrangements."

Aditya kept thinking of new excuses to meet. A few days later, he called. "This time, let us celebrate your birthday together."

"Where?"

"I'll come to you."

"You'll come all this way just to celebrate my birthday?"

"What do you mean by 'all this way'? Even if I have to go to the stars for your birthday... what about Sputnik? You were taking me with you, right?"

"You are being very romantic!"

"The unfortunate thing is that you throw me to the ground when I start getting romantic. You refuse to sit with me on the merry-go-round."

"Someone must be on the ground, right? Otherwise, we will fall off it together."

"So what? All that will happen is we will get hurt."

"One can get injured so badly that it is difficult to get up again.

"So you will never sit on a carousel because you are scared you might get hurt? I will have to go on my own."

"Then go and see. If you feel the place is worth going to for both of us, call me. I will join you."

Ketaki was laughing loudly. Aditya also laughed and said, “Look how selfish you are being. If someone has to fall, then this gentleman should fall alone. Why would you get into trouble?”

“If both of us fall, who will help us? One of us must be fit should this happen.”

“We were talking about your birthday.”

“And I don’t celebrate birthdays with anyone.”

“What kind of thing is that?”

“I mourn my birth.”

“So let me join you.”

“No, no one can participate in this.”

Aditya felt he was floundering when Ketaki refused to let him come. Once again, he thought that Ketaki was far away from him. She would never be able to reveal many of her inner feelings. She would never wholly be Aditya’s. When she talked like this, she scared Aditya away.

But still, in his mind, he had decided that he had to do something so they could live together.

That day, when Aditya suddenly told her that he was coming to spend the next week with her, Ketaki was utterly stunned. Aditya’s arrival should have brought her happiness, but suddenly she felt unprepared. She had become used to living alone. Everything she did was dependent on her needs and wishes. If she put something somewhere, it would remain there until she moved it herself. Nothing would move from its place. It didn’t matter to anyone what time she slept or how long the room's light was on or was switched off, whether she went to bed or fell asleep with the book she was reading on her chest.

The turmoil of sharing life again with a new person and anxiety was valid.

Aditya said, "You did not even apply. It would have shown that you were interested in settling in my city. The rest I would have looked after. Now, such a thing is not possible. So, I will have to make the move." Before Ketaki could respond, he added, "I will spend three months of the summer with you."

"What! My God! I don't believe it. How did you manage this?"

"The book is with the publisher. Meanwhile, I have prepared a new project on economic globalisation. I have to start research on it. A lot of material will be available in your library."

"You haven't mentioned this before."

"I didn't know whether it would be accepted or not. Now it's more fun to surprise you."

"And what if I had to go somewhere this summer?"

"I asked you, and you said you were not going anywhere."

"But I could go."

"If you have to go, go. I'll finish my work by then."

"And your son also comes to you during the holidays, right?"

"He has gone to India with his mother."

"How strange you are. Why did you not consult me about this in advance?"

Aditya was getting worried about Ketaki asking so many questions. Wasn't she happy to spend a long time with him? He felt a little let down but didn't want the matter to move in an unwanted direction. Perhaps to tease Ketaki more, he asked, "Will you find an apartment for me?"

"Won't you stay with me?"

"I don't want to violate your privacy."

"What is hidden from you? Are we not intimate friends?"

"I don't know."

"Why are you being like that?"

"I thought you would be happy if I came."

"I am happy. Do I have to perform a song and dance about it? I have barely had a chance to spend time with you, how can you think I wouldn't be happy?"

"So I get there on May 20."

"My work will not be finished before May 30. I have one or two dissertations; their defence is scheduled for the end of May."

"Work goes on, and you will be able to find some time in between."

"Okay, just come." Suddenly, Ketaki was bursting with excitement.

A Fellowship Ceremony

When Aditya appeared at her bedside in the morning with a cup of tea, Ketaki smiled even though she was half asleep. What a happy day. She couldn't imagine a more beautiful morning than this.

"Let's sit outside on the balcony. Today's newspaper will be at the door."

Taking the cup in her hand, she got out of bed and went to pick up the newspaper. Sipping her tea, she said, "Waking up with a cup of tea made by someone else has its own charm."

"As long as I am here, consider morning tea my responsibility."

"Really? Will you wake up so early every morning?"

"I am in the habit of getting up early, and making tea is the easiest task in the world."

"Won't you get tired of making it every day?"

"I won't, but you might get tired of drinking tea that I have made."

"No. If you keep serving me morning tea, you can live comfortably in this house."

"All my life," Aditya teased.

"Absolutely. I will not lose the habit of drinking tea for the rest of my life." Ketaki laughed.

"Remember these words of yours."

"You too."

Ketaki insisted that Aditya stay at her place.

Just knowing that Aditya was coming to Ketaki's lonely household suddenly filled that tiny apartment with excitement, and fragrance.

It was like Ketaki had noticed her home for the first time. She looked at it as if through someone else's eyes. The room's design, the windows, the colour of the curtains, the furniture, everything. Simple but elegant—she said to herself. Everything matches. As soon as one entered the apartment, Ketaki's hand-made paintings were displayed at the entrance. On the wall was a whole row of pictures of her mother that she had painted herself. Mother lost in thought, mother cutting vegetables, mother in an armchair, mother at the dining table, mother watering the plants, mother lying in the bed reading a book.

There were paintings by local artists in warm colours in the living room. A Kashmiri carpet and paintings by some Purabhumi artists. Some brass and bronze statues.

A vase and a few inlaid boxes on the coffee table. There was a still-life in the kitchen with some whole and some chopped vegetables and a knife for cutting vegetables.

Her apartment had three bedrooms. She had made one a guest room. The other one was a study. Many Madhubani paintings were hanging on the walls of the study. The shelves were filled with books by leading thinkers from around the world. Although she was not interested in decorating her apartment, keeping it in good order was still important. A comfortable, elegant, and clean home where one could move about, think, and work.

Now Ketaki was inspecting the entire house as if Aditya was roaming around in that house and not her. After seeing the living room and bedroom, she moved towards the bathroom. She felt thrilled preparing and cleaning the house for Aditya. When she put new soap in the soapbox and a new set of towels for Aditya, suddenly, the hotel room where she met Aditya for the first time flashed in her mind, along with all the thrills of that night. Even then, the feeling of being close to each other's bodies had thrilled her. She thought about the fact that all her things would touch Aditya's body. While putting new sheets on the bed, it was as if she was looking at Aditya lying in front of her. While she was dusting the sofa, Aditya would stretch out comfortably there, sometimes opening the newspaper and sometimes sitting and sipping his evening whiskey. While wiping the dining table, she would make Aditya sit there and feed him the best dishes she had made. Sometimes, sitting opposite him, she would nibble on the edge of her sandwich.

She had not even touched a duster for a long time. A Spanish-speaking Caribbean woman would clean her house every Thursday. The woman was good at cleaning. Ketaki neither said anything to her nor did she know how to speak her language. In fact, Ketaki would go out whenever the cleaning woman had to come to the house so that she could clean the house in peace. The woman was huge. She was very tall, her hair tied tightly at the back, and she always had a smile on her face. The way she enthusiastically beautified the entire apartment gave Ketaki a lot of pleasure when she sat down or roamed around the house after she left.

When there was order in the house, there was a feeling of order in life, too, but that day, suddenly, she started noticing small issues with the the cleanliness and order of the house, and she was trying to fix them.

Aditya had told her that he wanted to enjoy domestic happiness with her. When he spoke to Ketaki on the phone, he would often stand in his kitchen, sometimes in the garden, and express his desire for Ketaki to be with him at that moment. Ketaki shuddered at the mere mention of those moments. The happiness and thrill she felt in her body made her wonder whether one could find happiness even in keeping house. Maybe there was happiness in only imagining that happiness.

She still did not know which domestic life or family life Aditya was talking about. There was a new kind of happiness in whatever she was doing.

She went and bought a lot of food enthusiastically and thoughtfully—fresh vegetables, fruit, dry fruit, cheeses, bread, biscuits, cookies, and meat. After coming home, she put away everything neatly.

She scrubbed the kitchen counters, stove, floors, cupboards, and drawers till they gleamed.

She had cooked some food and kept it so she could spend as much time as possible with Aditya. Still, she had yet to fully prepare everything because she wanted to serve freshly cooked kebabs and things like that.

When Aditya came, Ketaki was in the same state: she found herself torn between looking at him and at her home.

After setting the table, she prepared fresh chapattis and fed him. Aditya ate the food with great relish, and when he started praising her, Ketaki said, "By the way, I have made the chapattis especially for you. I usually make do with Middle Eastern pita bread."

It was as if Aditya was a dream come true. She kept following him around. Even when he went to the bathroom, she would wait for him to come out. She did not feel like sleeping at night. If Aditya slept, she would wait for him to wake up.

When she was cooking, Aditya would come and stand near her and say, "Tell me what to do. I want to cook too."

Ketaki would hand him onions, garlic and ginger to chop and say, "I don't like chopping vegetables. I can't manage to cut vegetables properly so they are fine and nice. Will you do it?"

"I like working in the kitchen. Whatever you don't want to do, please give that task to me."

"Do you know how to cook fish? Hilsa in mustard?"

"Can you manage to eat a fish with so many bones?"

"I love it."

"That's settled, then. Tomorrow, I will be the chef. The menu will be fish curry and rice."

"Wonderful."

Morning Games

bītī vibhāvarī jāg rī.
ambar panghaṭ mẽ ḍūbo rahī
tārāghaṭ uṣā nāgarī

Night is over, wake up, my friend.
Dawn is breaking, and the stars
Have started to hide in the sky.

Aditya was standing at her bedside with a cup of tea the next morning.

Ketaki blinked and took the cup. "How do you get up so early?"

Aditya smiled. "*Jo jāgat hai to pāwat hai, jo sovat hai so khowat hai*. She that is awake receives, she that sleeps loses. I want to spend every waking moment with you." He moved forward to kiss Ketaki's forehead while she lay resting on her pillow.

"Do you love me more than sleep?"

"Yes, if you want, I could sacrifice the rest of my life's sleep for you."

"Will you keep me awake, too?"

"Without that, what joy will I have in staying awake?"

"Then we should talk of sleeping for the rest of our lives."

"That's also possible, but just to reiterate, sleeping could be tantamount to losing."

"But by sleeping, I don't mean becoming unconscious, only a long rest."

"That is, waking rest. I have no objection to that." Aditya snuggled in with her. "Sleeping or waking up like this suits me."

The teacup in Ketaki's hand wobbled. "Look, look, don't get up to any mischief, the tea will spill."

"Let the tea rest, too."

"You were talking about waking up and getting to work."

"Now this is also work—the biggest goal of life. One of the four main purposes of life."

"Early in the morning?"

"The morning hours are the most beautiful moments of life when hope, joy, and liveliness are all opening up and blooming. Tiredness has disappeared, and one is completely ready to welcome life. Love is the greatest happiness ever."

"So all that talk about waking up and gaining..."

"There is no contradiction in this." And placing his lips on Ketaki's ear, Aditya started whispering, "Look, even Radha is not saying anything out of shyness,

paśyati diśi diśi rahasi bhavantama,
tvadadhara madhuram adhuni pibantama

In her loneliness she sees you everywhere
Drinking honey from other lips.

"But she searches for Krishna all over, eager to let him taste the juice of her lips.

nāth hare jaya nāth hare
sīdhati rādhā vasugṛhe

Lord Hari, hail Lord Hari
How long must Radha suffers in her bower.

"There is no need to hide your longing."

Ketaki's breathing started becoming heavy. Aditya continued, "And let me tell you about Radha's longing. Radha has become so emaciated when she can't find Krishna that she can hardly take two steps. That's why I have to come to you. Look what Jayadev says.

vihita viśada visa kisalaya valayā
jīvati paramiha tava rati kalayā.

Wearing bracelets made from lotus shoots
Thinking of your skilful love, she stays alive.

"Wearing bracelets of lotus shoots, weak and in despair, lovelorn Radha stayed alive by remembering Krishna's dexterity in love. Ketaki... my Radha."

Ketaki felt some delightful, wavy, colourful music, produced by silken strings and fragrant with the scent of incense, was playing in her ears. "Keep talking, keep talking..." Ketaki was feeling intoxicated. Aditya's voice was becoming so slow that it was as if he was whispering:

> *candraka cāru mayūra śikhaṇḍakamaṇḍala valayita keśaṃ*
> *pracura purandara dhanur anurañjita medura mudira suveśaṃ*
>
> Peacock plumes kissed by moonlight crest his hair
> His clothes like a rainbow on a water-laden cloud.

"Radha is yearning for Krishna. If she waits too long, he will slip out of her hands. Enjoy the happiness of complete companionship right now. The air is intoxicating with the touch of vines laden with flowers. It is resonating with the music of cuckoos and bees this spring. My beloved is only with me. Am I not lucky?"

"There are no gopis here," teased Ketaki.

"You are the one, Ketaki; you are all those gopis, whatever their names are. Your personality is new; you are new every day. I will always hunger for you; my thirst will never be quenched. My desire for you will not go away. Your image moves like clouds in the sky. You bloom like a garden caressed by the wind. Out of control like the rolling ocean. What are you, what are you, who are you? Have I ever known you? Will I ever know? My puzzle. My sky. My perfection. My incompleteness. What should I tell you? Who are you? I could drown in you! All of me is lost in you. I cannot separate myself from you. I am nothing when I am apart from you! A waterless drop, a fish out of water, that's how I am!"

Suddenly, the sky, the earth, the room, the curtains, the light, everything disappears. No smell, colour, or shape, nothing can be sensed. The only sound is that of breathing. Two creatures and the trembling of bodies.

The Swamp of Darkness

There was a beautiful spot a couple of hours' drive from Ketaki's apartment. Ketaki sat on a rock on the banks of a quiet lake, surrounded by hills. She was talking to Aditya, sayng many things, listening to him say many things.

"Tell me, have you ever loved someone before?" She had asked this question earlier and it had already been answered. She wanted to see whether the answer was the same or had changed. Perhaps his love was not unquestioning and blind any more.

"Why are you asking all this?"

"I want to get to know you from a different side."

"I have handed myself over to you like an open book, read it as much as you want. You still think you don't know me?"

"I want to know more, more, more, a lot more."

"I have probably told you this before. This is the first time I have fallen in love as an adult. When I was nineteen years old, I was attracted to a girl, and that relationship did not last more than a few months. After that, I had other relationships and we thought of marriage but not love. It happened at the physical level as well. No one could bind me. My heart could not find anyone as crazy as me. What I have felt with you is indescribable; beyond words, it drives me crazy. You are my precious undertaking. I don't want to lose you."

Ketaki saw that Aditya's eyes had become wet.

Her gaze remained fixed on Aditya's eyes for a long time. She felt herself melt inside.

This time, Aditya asked, "Tell me about your past."

"What about it?"

"Whatever, from the time before you met me."

"Nothing worth telling. After getting divorced from my husband, perhaps I was waiting for the right person... so I found him. Now I have no more demands from life, no more waiting. My present is the most beautiful part of my life."

"Didn't you fall in love with someone else?" Aditya also knew he had already heard the answer to this question, but still...

"Probably not! When I was nineteen, I thought I was in love with a boy, but it was just infatuation. The intoxication wore off very quickly."

"I hope this is not infatuation now."

"No, this intoxication does not seem to go away." She smiled, understanding what Aditya was hinting at.

One day, when Ketaki was at the university, Aditya needed some books, which she had taken down from her shelf and kept on the table. He was flipping through one of the books when he saw an open letter in it. The fact it was addressed to "Darling" startled him. And he read everything in one breath without even thinking about the fact that it was someone else's letter.

Ketaki had told him that she had never loved anyone, and here was a love letter addressed to her. He looked at the date; it was from five years ago. He tried to guess the name from the signature and figured that it was the signature of some Ajay.

Aditya's head started to ring. When they had first met, she had mentioned having lunch with Ajay one day. That day Aditya was mad at her for not being near her phone to take his call. So this was how Ketaki was playing games with Aditya. Pretending to be in love with him and having relationships with many men simultaneously. What kind of love was this? It was all a lie. Obviously, she did not take Aditya seriously. Just for the sake of physical pleasure or for some psychological need, she had been flirting with so many men. Love was nothing. That was why she was afraid to commit. She talked about being together and then retreated. Was this what was called liberation?

Aditya felt as if she was making a fool of him. Oh, why couldn't he have seen all this earlier? It was as if some sharp instrument had pierced him. How could he bear this pain? What was he to say to Ketaki? He could not maintain a relationship like this. Why was Ketaki doing this?

He loved Ketaki. He would not allow this simple thing to let unnecessary doubts enter his mind. He would talk directly to Ketaki.

Ketaki returned a little later than she had said she would. Seeing Aditya silent, she thought he was perhaps angry with her for being late. She said, "Some students came. It took time to answer their questions."

"Well, that happens. No problem."

"Then why are you so silent? Are you angry?"

"Angry? No."

When Aditya stayed in the living room and studied till late at night, Ketaki felt that something was troubling him, and she would not be able to sleep if she did not know what it was.

Aditya quietly placed the letter before her and said, "It was in your book."

"Oh."

When Ketaki saw the letter, she shrugged and said, "Yes, it was written five years ago. Did you see the date?"

"I am sorry, but you had lunch with this person a few months ago."

"So?"

"That day, you did not come to talk to me on the phone. I was waiting for you."

She kept looking at him in silence as if he were deciding her fate.

"You said I am the only one in your life, whereas you had a relationship with this person."

"Don't be silly. Does having lunch with him mean I am in a relationship? What nonsense!"

"Your letter speaks of the relationship."

"That was in the past."

"Then why do you meet him?"

"There is still a bond of friendship between us."

"Well, now I don't want to say anything more than this. I feel very small if I do this to myself. I will never raise this issue again."

The matter went no further after that day, but it had stuck in Aditya's mind.

He would often start examining Ketaki's words and behaviour in light of this event and suddenly stop himself when he became aware of what he was doing.

It was not that Ketaki had not noticed the change in Aditya. She, too, was scared deep inside. Then suddenly, one day, she said, "Adi, often a strange fear enters my mind that you will not be able to bear the intensity of your love. As if suddenly, you will want to end our relationship one day."

Aditya burst into laughter. "No, I will stay with you until you drive me away. Let me tell you about this girl; she sent me away when I was nineteen years old."

"That is childish. I had infatuations too and they ended."

Ketaki was relieved. It felt as if Aditya would be with her forever, for life, from this birth to the next. She said, "I will never ask you to leave."

"Is that the truth?"

"You couldn't be the first man in my life. You may be the first in many respects because you showed me what love is, but you are the last and most important man, too."

"That's what I want to be, Ketaki. The last and most important."

Then Ketaki changed the subject. "When you are emotional like this, your eyes are lovely. Has anyone told you this?"

Aditya's mood was a little lighter, and he said, "There have been comments about my eyes before, but never because I have been emotional about anyone like this."

"Stay like this; I always want your eyes to look like this."

Rocky Terrain

Aditya had been at Ketaki's for over a month and a half. Much of Ketaki's work still needed to be completed. She felt they were spending a lot of time talking and going out. She would be disappointed that she hadn't finished her work when the holidays were over. When she mentioned this to Aditya, he said, "Okay, from now on, you do your work, and I will work as well."

But it was not so simple.

Suddenly, things seemed to change.

Ketaki started telling him about the smallest things to do with her university colleagues, the staff, etc. She felt that Aditya was her guest. She considered it her duty to entertain him. It became necessary to talk about something or the other all the time. Even the slightest silence made Ketaki worry that Aditya may feel she had nothing left to say or that their relationship was failing instead of growing. She consulted Aditya on every minor matter, perhaps to keep him engaged.

"Pranab Pal is asking me for an article for his journal. Should I write it or forget it? There are many deadlines now."

"Do it; it's the summer break."

"But you are here right now. I'd rather spend time with you than do all this."

Aditya was happy that Ketaki loved him more than her work. Still, he also suspected that Ketaki was doing this because he was a guest. Had they been living together, would she have done the same? He did not want her to drop her work for him. He had once said to her, "It is my deepest wish that both of us move forward together, doing our research work, supporting each other."

Ketaki liked this very much but often felt like leaving everything behind and focusing on loving Aditya. However, after some time, she also realised that quitting the university job would frustrate her.

"Frank Coppola called. We are working together on a project. He has a meeting all day tomorrow. I won't be home all day."

"Okay. I also have to work on my chapter."

Almost every day for the next week, Ketaki had to stay out until the late evening in connection with a new project. If she returned late, she would go straight to bed without stopping to chat with Aditya. After a break of two or three days, she had to leave again. She broached the subject carefully. "My chairperson has called a meeting. If I don't go, I will have to explain myself. I can't say that my lover is here."

Aditya said jokingly, "And why can't you say that? By the way, I am not saying you should skip the meeting for me. It isn't a big deal. Do whatever you think is right. I don't want to interfere with your work."

"I am on holiday. No one can force me to go. After all, how could I be present if I were somewhere outside the city? But it seems tricky not to attend when I am here."

Reluctantly, Aditya had said, "Then it's okay, go. I can go home if you have any problem with my staying here."

Ketaki was shocked by Aditya's attitude. Feeling upset, she said, "What did I say that made you think I had any objection to your staying with me? But I do have to work on other things."

"You have no objection. I was just saying it." Aditya did not want the issue to escalate. He had planned to go to the beach that day. He had also made a hotel booking. He hadn't mentioned it to Ketaki because he wanted to surprise her. But now, he did not say a word. He felt sad that Ketaki was busy all the time. For her, he was just one of her many activities, while he had left everything and set up camp here.

He, too, could have been happy at home in his city, but what had stopped him? Why was he trying to make Ketaki happy and killing himself in the process, while Ketaki had no idea of the intensity of his love? The compulsion of his love, which had brought him here, did not make Ketaki forget her less critical work and consider it necessary to spend as much time as possible with Aditya.

A few days later, when Ketaki said Dave Smith wanted to work on a project with her, Aditya couldn't keep it in any longer. "How many people are you associated with? How do you manage so many people at once?"

Ketaki could not figure out whether he was taunting her or speaking his mind. She said with the same ambiguity, "What are you trying to say? These are all my friends."

"Friends!" There was uncertainty in his tone.

"Yes, one can have a lot of friends."

"Is it just friendship?"

"What else? Do I have so many lovers?"

"Why can't you? Women can have more than one lover. Especially for the women I know, it's no big deal. Rather, it is normal for them."

"Do you take me to be a prostitute?"

"There is no question of prostitution in this. All this is the language of social morality. I do not consider it immoral to have relations with more than one man. I have probably told you this before."

"If you don't consider it immoral, then what do you think about it?"

"Being naturally monogamous or polyamorous can only be a question of attitude, a question of nature. I am not concerned with what society thinks about it. I am concerned about you because I love you, so I need to know everything about you."

"You know that I have broken off whatever relationships I had in the past. Apart from you, no one will come into my life, nor will I let them come. I love you and you only; I have never felt for anyone with such intensity. I only want to get lost in you, Adi."

Aditya kissed her face as she stretched towards him. "I want that too, Ketaki!" And both merged into each other's existence like water-filled clouds ready to pour rain.

A Serpent and A Demon

Moments of sanyog or coming together can be strange. When two people are together for some time, they start wanting to step outside of themselves, away from each other, as if the union is a permanent situation. It is necessary to escape from it for a while and have fun elsewhere. One of the primary reasons for cracks in the relationships of most lovers is that they consider sanyog a permanent life state and start looking for protection from it. Once they come close to each other, it seems to them that this union is the most significant reality of life. This goal achieved, they think of moving ahead. Unions are left behind and the perspective changes, whether it becomes focused on their jobs, the pursuit of other interesting people, or similar things. After a perfect union, i.e. marriage, the root cause of divorce is that the lover and the beloved often live under the illusion that the union is equal and permanent. And because some people also think that stability is death and changes must be brought into their circumstances to maintain the flow of life, they feel the need to change. Some sensible married couples keep moving or travel for a change of scene. Similar principles have roots in the 'madhu chandra' or honeymoon concept.

Ketaki was a scholar of political history, but she had a passion for telling stories. The sleeping artist in her was stirring slowly. You have already read some of her poems. She often thought of writing a story, even discussing the plot, but never wrote it. Still, the new plots that came to her mind kept her excited, and she often started discussing them with Aditya. "Adi, I think I should write a story. I am thinking of a fascinating story. A girl is staying alone in a hotel. She often sits alone in the hotel lobby as if waiting for someone. All the men passing by are very curious and try to talk to her. They ask her whether she is staying in the hotel or has come from outside and is waiting for someone. I am still deciding whether she has come to the city to meet her lover or alone on business. I have not yet been able to determine whether she is married or not."

Aditya interrupts her. "Let me tell you: make her a call girl. She has a relationship with all the men simultaneously, but no man knows about the others. Then that girl accidentally gives an appointment to two men together and—"

Ketaki cut him off "This is all you can think of. Why can't there be a focus on love?"

Aditya nudged her and said, "Did I upset you?" Then, teasingly, "That's not guilt speaking, is it?"

Ketaki was furious. "The snake is always sitting coiled inside you. I know you think the same thing about me, too, that I don't know how many men I have been with like this simultaneously. You are waiting for the day when you suddenly catch me with another man. Understand this today: that day will never come because this is all an illusion of yours. But how long will I keep on explaining myself? If you want to believe me, then do so; otherwise, you will continue to suffer. I don't know how often I have to tell you that you are the only person in my heart and mind. I cannot even imagine giving any space to any other man."

Aditya was contrite. "When you say things like this, I start believing you."

"Then why do you doubt me?"

"That could be my weakness, a whim of my mind; perhaps I don't believe someone can love me so much. Any woman who came close to me eventually became someone else's. Apart from me, some other man was also present in her life. That is to say, she kept saying that she loved me and yet was in relationships with other lovers... perhaps that is why it is so difficult to trust you. There is no one else in your life. And yet, you meet people all the time."

"I meet them for work."

"Okay. I accept what you are saying."

"So, you believe in me."

"I will not question your statement."

"Will you listen to me carefully?"

"What?"

Ketaki took his face in both her hands. "It's a figment of your imagination. I love only one man, and that is Aditya Ghosh."

"Ketaki, I do not doubt your love. I know you love me."

"Then?"

"It's just that you prioritise many other things or people besides me."

"Like?"

"Like... I don't know how many... What do you say? Every Tom, Dick and Harry. You give as much time to everyone as you give me. How should I interpret that?"

Aditya felt that he had said whatever he could in symbolic language. He neither knew nor could say that he genuinely suspected Ketaki had relationships with other men and that her love was not of the standard he expected, like the love he was giving her. Pure, from the bottom of his heart.

Ketaki did not have any misgivings about making any mistakes in her lovefor Aditya.. She believed that 'slow and steady wins the race' and tried to be as balanced as possible in her behaviour. So as to appear neither crazy nor indifferent. Was this balance of hers making Aditya feel unbalanced? Ketaki's behaviour led him to believe that he was not special to her, that she was sacrificing her life for him... perhaps this was what was troubling Aditya. Would it be better if he went back home?

Then, one day, he suddenly decided to return home. Even before the deadline, he felt that Ketaki wanted him to go, as if his stay had gone on longer than necessary.

Ketaki tried to convince him to stay and said that she would have more time for leisure the next day.

Aditya felt that Ketaki only talked about the future. The moment at hand would be lost in other preoccupations. What a strange kind of nature she had.

He told her, "If this relationship cannot survive at the level on which I want it, then let's break up."

"Which level are you talking about?"

"You know very well that when I am here, you start running away from me. Does everything have to be expressed in words? Can't you see this yourself?"

And he didn't even wait to hear her answer.

Viyog
Parting

Disappearing Lines

The dividing lines between separation and union are disappearing for me. My hero and heroine's minds are connected even without a union. And yet, in moments of union, when the hero threatens to leave the heroine, or the heroine starts thinking about things other than the hero and talks about other people, cracks or separations appear.

Now, let us talk about the suspicious attitude of the hero. In the old country, if doubt enters the hero's mind, all love and affection vanishes. And the heroine is despised as if she has no value, like a potsherd under his feet. You must have heard the story of Gautam Rishi. As soon as he developed suspicions about Ahilya, he cursed her and turned her into a stone. There, the hero does not even reach the point of doubt; he knows intuitively that Priya has had sexual intercourse with another man. Similarly, when Ram doubts Sita, she is first tested in a fire ritual. When she does not burn, and there remains no reason to doubt her, the poor woman is thrown out of the palace. Once doubt raises its head, the poor heroine does not stand a chance; she is not even allowed to explain herself.

But our hero himself has left the heroine's house and is now burning up inside. His suspicious attitude has added some complexity to our story. I am afraid of what will happen to their love now. Will it last, or will it die an untimely death? All because of doubt! But what is this? Our hurt Ketaki is sending him a poem in an envelope. Aditya receives the poem shortly after his return.

One More Sun

Another sun born from this pain
who will not hide from clouds
nor shy away
from seeing his face
in the mirror of murkiness
He will spread a web of rays
so that every corner
will light up in the sunlight

Then, in the dark of night
standing in the corner
silently
he will wait for the morning
firm in his faith

that the morning will come
it is his character
his nature
his destiny

He understood. He knew that Ketaki's reference to the sun probably referred to what his name meant. Did she want to woo him? Was she trying to convince him? She knew deep down inside that Aditya was angry with her.

Would he give up his anger? He always melted anyway! No matter how angry he was or how many complaints he had.

But somewhere deep inside, his mind was not wholly convinced. Or the assurance was only temporary and would get shattered by even the slightest shock.

He felt a strange restlessness constantly, no matter how much he tried to divert it into activities. A peculiar emptiness had arisen in him. Ketaki's arrival in his life had been like the coming of spring, and he knew that this would never happen again. If it came with Ketaki, it would leave with her. There would be no second chance. Life would be filled with a kind of emptiness. Did he have the right to deprive himself of that privilege? Was it not necessary to involve Ketaki in this decision? Was his self-esteem so valuable that two people's lives had to be sacrificed? Yes, self-esteem. Why wouldn't Ketaki be utterly devoted to her man? That was the fundamental problem. He wanted to punish Ketaki for her actions. But what had Ketaki actually done? Did he have any evidence against her or any way of putting the blame on her?

Aditya could not remain silent any longer. But he had to find the words with which to respond to the poem. What would their weight be? Which words, which expressions? What would convey Aditya's state of mind to Ketaki? Aditya did not write poetry. But he could write letters. Lately, he had also had many dreams, and in those dreams, many faces blended with each other. He couldn't understand whether it was Ketaki or someone else. Had some old faces started resembling Ketaki's face? Sometimes, it was Ketaki's face but with someone else's hairstyle: sometimes, Ketaki appeared in his dreams with a bun, but she never tied her hair up in a bun. Was it Kanak, a previous lover, who was giving a new shape to Ketaki? Or was she putting Ketaki's truth before Aditya?

But it was not easy for Aditya to change his decision. The same old story of pain began again. The constant wait and Ketaki's abiding unavailability. His pleas for love and Ketaki's arguments. His efforts to move forward were Ketaki's efforts to move back. How would they adjust?

Aditya wrote to Ketaki, "I don't think we will ever be able to live together. You are afraid of putting all your eggs in one basket. You can never give your all to anyone. I want to understand why and for whom you want to preserve yourself. I have waited a long time for you to reach me. But now I am losing courage. Perhaps I can't bear any more pain. You were right; this love is just pain. Lonely, one-sided suffering. You will not move ahead from where you are standing. Many things encircle you from which you cannot emerge. We are not meant for each other, Ketaki. Here's wishing you all the best for your life and me all the best for my life. It is better for both of us to part."

This letter may have sounded a death knell to Ketaki. She remained sitting there motionless for hours. She couldn't move her hands or think a single thought.

What had happened to Aditya? Her fear had come true. She had known that one day, he would destroy everything. That was what had happened. That was what she had tried to explain to him, why she was afraid of getting involved... of drowning. And Aditya also had to do the same... how would she bear it now? She had already drowned without saying it... it was just a matter of convincing herself that she would not drown... that she would remain free. What kind of freedom? There was only pain here.

Why did Aditya think like this? Why couldn't they live together? She would change herself. She would convince Aditya somehow. She knew Aditya loved her. What if she expressed her love for him and her need for him? Then it would not be possible for Aditya to end the relationship like this. He could never be so cruel to himself and Ketaki.

But how was she to she respond to this letter from him or tell him to think again about what he wanted? Did he really want to break up? Had the future they imagined they would have together not left a single trace behind in his heart?

What could she say?

Perhaps it would be best for her to also remain silent. Then it would become clear which side the camel was sitting on.

Maybe Aditya himself would write or call.

Maybe he would say that all of it was meaningless, that he had written it in a fit of excitement. He didn't want to do anything like that, he could never end the relationship with Ketaki, it was all an act of momentary anger.

A week passed. Aditya made no conciliatory moves at all. Ketaki's unease continued to build. This meant that Aditya had broken the thread. Then why would Ketaki take the initiative? If this was what Aditya wanted, then this was what had to happen. Ketaki was not going to die. If Aditya knew how to live without her, she could live without Aditya too. *Okay, let's see how long he remains silent.*

Then she remembered all those memories she associated with Aditya—Sputnik, flying together, their dreams of living together, moments of happiness, the dense shade of the redwoods, waterfalls touching the sky, being careful on mountain trails. Leaning on Aditya, sometimes holding his hand while walking. Aditya constantly walked ahead and warned her of dangers. They would look at each other to their heart's content as if they could see deep inside each other with just one glance. Efforts and difficulties to recognise each other's inner self. She sat for hours, thinking. *You talked about being together. I asked where the wings were. You said "I will give you wings." I started flying. Then I wondered, where are the wings? You said, "Look at that; I have put them on you." I started flying again. Suddenly, a stormy wind blew. I got scared. I asked again, where are the wings? You said they were there. "Keep flying." I started searching here and there for wings. I fell on rocky ground, into thorny bushes. You said you had no wings, but you thought that by flying, you would grow wings. Then I saw that you were also flying without wings. The wind was under your control; the sky was in your arms. Lying on the ground, I don't want to wait for you to fall. I don't even want to see you moving. Will you also grow wings? Or will you struggle, drop to the burning earth, give up your strength or desire to fly, and start agreeing with me? And you will forget flying or the flight which was yours and mine.*

Ketaki had gone crazy. She couldn't think of what to do. How could she fix what she had destroyed? Through her own carelessness. She spent all her time writing poems. There were no messages on the phone now. There were poems on fax—what is love? The manipulation of words, the poetic outburst, or the deaf Beethoven's Ninth Symphony invoking the ocean. What is suffering? Liquid drops of dew, the suppressed breath of a volcano, the dissolution of the night or the turning of a mountain into dust. What is a song? The scream of the intestines, the remarkable coordination of crawling ants, the trembling touch of shaking fingers or the sweetness of rhythm. Ketaki continued to write. One day, the paper got stuck in the fax machine. Aditya received an incomplete poem.

> Relationships break up, not people,
> Leaves fall, not trees.

Then she wondered whether to send the complete poem to Aditya or leave it lying like that. She did nothing for three days. She kept going to the computer and busying herself with other work instead of printing it out. One evening, while working on her research, she suddenly printed the file containing the poem. She put it in an envelope, put a stamp on it and dropped the rest of the poem in the post box.

> Because
> when a person breaks
> nothing is left
> neither tree, nor leaf.

It was as if she was doing all this work under the influence of some unknown inspiration, as if she was walking in her sleep. However, she was careful not to fax the poem, so it would take some time to reach Aditya. It was as if she hoped that, by the time it reached Aditya, she would think of something else. She also knew that if she sent it by post, Aditya would eventually get it. Craziness was taking its toll on her.

Aditya did not end his silence, and Ketaki felt she could no longer bear it. It was necessary to blame Aditya for his foolishness.

The next day, she sent him another couplet in the post, one of Ghalib's couplets.

ghālib vo na samjhe haĩ na samjheṅge meri bāt
de aur dil unko jo na de mujhko zabāṅ aur

Ghalib, she neither understands nor will understand what I say.
Change her heart if she won't give me her word.

Ketaki felt that her inner turmoil, the excitement and restlessness driving her crazy, had settled down a little. Sweet expectations and hope were forming in her mind again.

Aditya, however, had thought a lot and then steeled himself before sending his letter. Still, he kept pacing like a mad person throughout the day. He did not feel like going anywhere; he was not getting any work done. Somewhere in his mind, he hoped that Ketaki would consider that letter a joke, a light tease. She was not to take it seriously and end the relationship. In his heart of hearts, he kept hoping she was not angry with him. That she would take his words lightly.

He was afraid to write anything else because he could not predict Ketaki's reaction. What was he to do? Waiting was perhaps the safest option. Ketaki would surely send him an answer. He would have to respond accordingly. When nothing happened for a week, he feared Ketaki would never respond. Maybe she had been relieved and said good riddance. Or was she so angry that she would never contact him again, or did she want to hear from his mouth that it was all a joke? But it wasn't a joke. It was true, which was why Aditya had written what he had. But what was he to do now? How burdensome, how meaningless, how unbearable life would be without Ketaki.

And then, one poem after another from Ketaki washed away all the dirt from his mind. He could not stop thinking about the flight and the relationship. He felt that Ketaki belonged to him. He had blamed her unnecessarily. Why did he do this? No, never again. He would give only his love to her. No doubts. No complaints.

He dialled her number. After beating about the bush for some time, he started talking about his feelings.

Aditya asked, "What is missing in my love? Tell me."

Sobbing, Ketaki said, "Trust me. That is all. There is no one else in my life except you."

Aditya's voice had become heavy. "Okay. I will try my best from now on. It would help if you also told me only the truth. Don't give me any room for doubt."

"Okay. Sure."

Aditya said, "Forget whatever I said. Let us start this relationship afresh. I will assume that you are what you seem, and you can trust that I will never hurt you. Maintaining the love we have given and received from each other is essential for us both to live; everything else is secondary."

Now Ketaki started thinking afresh: had she been somewhat reserved in front of Aditya? Had she tried to deceive Aditya? Did she not love him? But it was not like that; if she did not love Aditya, why was the mere prospect of losing him so frightening?

Perhaps earlier, she had not known that Aditya had become integral to her existence. Maybe she had only recently come to recognise the solidity of her love. Now, she would never question where Aditya was in her life or why. Now, there was only one truth, and that was that Aditya was there. He was there, and he would remain so.

Ketaki felt a tremor of pain in her heart. How long had it taken her to realise this? How much trouble had Aditya endured in the meantime? Now he knew... he could see the inner truth of Ketaki very well.

Now, there would be a new beginning. They would live consciously, knowing and accepting love.

Until now, the separation was temporary because, after being apart for a while, the hero and heroine decided to be together again. But ultimately, no love relationship can escape the consequences of separation. Now, we have to see how the separation makes its presence felt in our story. First, it is essential to know something about separation.

There are many types of separation; sometimes separation happens for good reason; at others, it's difficult to pinpoint the reason.

First, let's talk about the reasons. The most common reason is the hero going abroad. As we have seen before and heard again and again in many love stories, every hero has to find some work before taking responsibility for his girlfriend. Yes, if someone is a prince, then a job, etc., has no meaning. But he may have to go on an adventurous journey. After all, no one can become a hero without some enterprise. A hero is the one who takes the story forward. This is not possible without action. So, if there is no job, the hero will go on an adventurous quest, and only then will the seed of separation, i.e. the separation of the hero and heroine, be sown. Often, the hero does not have to go abroad; it is the heroine who gets upset and walks away. Even though it is wholly possible that the heroine may not want to separate, those moments spent sulking are just as significant as those of being apart. The hero's breath gets stuck in his throat, and the heroine waits for a moment for the hero to say something to convince her so that she can forget her pride and run into his arms. These hours become very long or seem long, and sometimes, this pride even takes the form of an actual separation. The hero cannot convince his beloved, which always leads to separation. Especially in modern stories, this kind of ego clash is a game that becomes serious; they get hurt for life, and the wound gets embedded in the hearts of the lovers. They never emerge from it and spend the rest of their life hiding the hurt from the world. However, this rarely happens, and in most cases, such separation occurs in union and then disappears after bringing about a miracle. In fact, Hindi poets have been very fond of such separation and have composed many interesting poems about heroines.

In this era of women's liberation, if the heroine can get upset, so can the hero. Similarly, if the hero can go to work, so can the heroine. The characters may have changed in these respects, but the situation remains almost the same. What did I say? Women's liberation is just a circumstance. Characters only change when circumstances change. The basic feeling probably does not change, but both the characters and the circumstances keep changing, and by being surrounded by them, the feeling also takes on a new form.

One reason for separation could also be that the beloved's family becomes a hindrance because of issues of caste or class and places shackles on the heroine's feet.

It is said that the impulse of love is like the water of a river, which starts flowing faster when its path gets blocked. Despite being in chains, the heroine keeps flowing like the pounding river of love. One day, breaking all family ties, she runs away with her lover.

But sometimes, the strength of the heroine's father is greater than the speed of the heroine. He diverts the stream, or the heroine herself jumps into the well out of fear of him. The third primary reason is the death of one of the lovers. Acharyas have specified these three main reasons for separation—honour, migration and death.

There is no scope for these three situations to arise in our love story. As far as migration is concerned, it is the very basis of our story. The hero and heroine already live in different cities and meet each other regularly. Since both are busy, they must travel by air to meet each other. One living in another town creates a situation of temporary separation between them, for which they keep finding solutions. This should not be considered parting or separation because they can talk to their heart's content whenever they feel like picking up the phone. Admittedly, due to being away, a longing and a yearning always remain in them, which is not satisfied by repeated temporary meetings. But if there is satisfaction in love, then where is the love? Therefore, this constant yearning is not a sign of separation but a sign of love when apart. We will discuss this in more detail later.

Now, to come to the matter of family obstructions. In Gaurbhum, parents usually won't impose their will on our heroine. In any case, our heroine doesn't have any parents alive. If she were a teenager, the parents would have had some role. But even if there were parents who said something to a daughter Ketaki's age, who would listen?

As far as honour is concerned, both of them find it childish, and death is inevitable for everyone. Therefore, what is the point of including such elements in this story? The storyteller is concerned with the living, with those who live. A story comes to an end with death. Therefore, even if death is mentioned, it should be treated as a phase of life so that the story extends from one birth to the next.

Many storytellers have used death, which is why love tragedies like Laila–Majnu, Sohni–Mahiwal and Shireen–Farhad were written. But now is not the time to die in the name of love. These days, people do not have the same strength, nor do they consider love such a precious and unattainable blessing that they are willing to sacrifice themselves for it, and if they were to accept it as a blessing and be ready to die for it, everyone would consider them mad or stupid. Instead of getting sympathy, they would become objects of laughter. Our love story would be doomed, so I don't want to take that risk.

The pain of separation is so great that it turns even thieves and armed robbers into poets. You must have heard the story of Valmiki. He could not bear being parted from a bird, and that made the poetry flow out of him. Imagine if he had been separated from a human—

what condition would he have been in? Through the separation from the bird, he understood the separation of man. The whole Ramayana became the story of the separation of son from father, brother from brother and wife from husband. It is incredible that the pain of Valmiki, which has survived for many centuries, was actually the pain of separation. Therefore, in this story, too, I do not want to deprive the subject of separation from getting its due.

None of the other things discussed and used in other stories happens in the love journey of Ketaki and Aditya. But their story is not without the feeling of separation. In other words, though they talked on the phone or, if they couldn't speak, left each other messages, there was still something inside them that remained hungry and continued to ask for more. What was it? Ketaki could not understand, nor could Aditya find a solution.

Even when he was with Ketaki, he often felt that she was far away from him, and he was desperate to reach her but could not do so.

Ketaki often felt that Aditya was moving away from her, as if she could not reach him even if she tried hard.

In fact, separation is the basic feeling of love. As soon as one falls in love, the first desire is to be united with your lover. Let's go by the definition scientists use. Love is that process of the body which brings the bodies of a man and a woman closer, and two bodies cannot remain together for 24 hours a day. Hence, parting or separation starts from the very first hour.

Much research has been done on this subject in Gaurbhum. Scientists say that this pain in the form of separation from the mother is present in every human being in some form or another from birth. The people of a country friendly with Navabhum have given many names to this by calling it this complex or that disease. They still call it mother's or father's love in Purabhum—they don't understand complexes like Electra and Oedipus there. For people in the Old World, a son who grows up and sleeps in the same bed as his mother is not a big deal. Here, he would be considered mentally ill. If anyone else finds out, they will send the son to a psychiatrist. If any lawyer learns about it, they will file some case or the other.

Readers should remember that this definition considers the human being a body. Scientists rely on the authenticity of what can be seen and measured, but our Old World hero and heroine have moved far beyond the world of their bodies. The hero is only concerned with the mind, and the heroine is more concerned with the soul. Thus, in practice, the mind and soul become self, personal identity, spirituality, state of mind, person, personal desire or emotion or opinion, and so on. When circumstances go against all these, suffering is born. The brain contains certain filaments that feel pain. If that part of the brain is surgically removed, one will not feel pain. It is another matter that, since the brain's structure is very complex, while removing the filaments of pain, one might end up doing some other damage. Now, what scientists should do is make such an invention for the welfare of humanity. My fear is that the only pain they can remove will be physical. Mental pain originates from the mind and soul; how can we eliminate it? Scientists have yet to learn where the soul or mind resides. They used to say it was present in an organ called the heart, but now the heart has been completely cut open, and a monkey's or artificial mechanical heart has also been put in its place in some cases. If there were a soul, then it would be visible somewhere. Operating the soul has yet to be figured out.

This means that the lovers will have to endure pain. Let us go back to the hero and heroine.

At the beginning of the separation chapter, you see that the relationship is about to end but then holds together. Enduring the pain of breaking up and coming back from it intact is rarely seen. Especially if the bond of love is genuine. But in Gaurbhum, relationships sometimes neither end nor come together completely. Lovers are neither wholly separated nor completely bound to each other.

The hero and heroine decided to stay connected to avoid the pain of breaking up. But do you think the problem has been solved forever? See what happens next.

Magic and Awakening

I feel that a seed of this suffering was sown that day. What happened in Ketaki's town was very normal for Ketaki. Even in Aditya's eyes, it would have been expected. And yet, it created a feeling of panic deep in Aditya's heart.

To be honest, Ketaki gave him cause for doubt, sometimes deepening and sometimes breaking the spell of her love. The magic of love rises, gets damaged, becomes weak, and then becomes strong again. If doubt ends it, then the desire for companionship connects it again—now we will have to look at it in more detail and consider all its aspects.

The situation had occurred many times in the respective lives of our hero and heroine. It was also a matter of habit. Like a spider's web, habits create many problems and trap characters. Ketaki was never that punctual, whereas our hero had become a Navabhum creature of the type that arrived early and was a victim of habit. So, this is what happened:

Aditya and Ketaki had agreed to talk at a particular time, and when the time came, Ketaki was not available.

Ketaki had no sense of punctuality. That often caused delays but it they were never longer than five to ten minutes.

Aditya kept dialling her number. The answering machine was switched off as well. Unable to leave a message, he sat beside the phone for an hour, hoping that Ketaki would call. After all, she knew he had to catch a flight to Purabhum that evening. He didn't know when they would be able to talk again.

Meanwhile, Ketaki saw that the agreed-upon time for talking had passed and thought that Aditya had probably left for the airport already, so she figured they would have to talk later. Still, she came home and waited for him to call from the airport. In his anger, Aditya did not call again. Ketaki tried sending him messages repeatedly. Sometimes to his machine Navabhum and sometimes to Purabhum.

The next time when Aditya mentioned that she had not been accessible on the phone, Ketaki said somewhat reluctantly, "Yes, a friend of mine had come over that day. We went out for lunch."

Aditya felt as if Ketaki was being very inconsiderate towards him. He got angry. "Had you told me, I would not have kept waiting."

"I didn't know you were waiting."

"Why not? Don't you always call me at that time? Obviously, I would wait to hear from you."

"Really? I thought I would call whenever free, nothing was fixed."

"It's okay. If you can't do it, then it's okay. Please let me know from now on so I don't keep waiting unnecessarily."

"Okay, I'll do that."

Ketaki could not understand why Aditya was so upset about such a trivial matter. Aditya had often waited long periods of time for her and had never shown any sign of displeasure. Why such a strong reaction today? Aditya's aggressive attitude made Ketaki's voice turn harsh.

It was true that he now knew a lot about Ketaki that he had not known before, as he had seen Ajay's letter, and Ketaki had told him about almost all her past and present friends. But she had told Aditya that she had no special relationships with any of them at the moment. Friendship, information, intellectual conversation with colleagues, or working together on some project—that was all.

On a couple of occasions after that, when she could not talk again for some minor reason, Aditya's tone insinuated that she was doing it to meet some man. When a few such incidents had taken place, if Ketaki was late even by a few minutes in meeting or talking to Aditya, she would start getting nervous.

Unconsciously, Ketaki's behaviour began to change. She would repeatedly tell him the reason for her being late in detail. She would begin to explain even if she were ten minutes late. Whenever she had to fix a time to talk to or meet Aditya, she would start giving a lengthy description of her daily routine. "No, it is difficult on Wednesday, there is a seminar the whole day, which will end at six o'clock and I will be tired. There is also a cocktail dinner in the evening. Classes will start again at 9 am now. They will continue till 12.30, and the Dean has called me for lunch at 1 o'clock. There's another class at 2:30 in the afternoon. I have to attend Peter Daniels' lecture at 4." And the list would go on and on. Instead of just saying she could talk at a particular time, she would list all the time periods when she could not. Often, their long conversations would be spent deciding the time, so much so that both of them started feeling like, instead of talking about any subject of their choice, they were busy figuring out when they would be free. Finally, one day, Aditya said irritably, "I am not interested in your daily routine. You think you can hide what's happening by telling me about your daily routine. Do I look that stupid?"

Ketaki was stunned. She mustered up her courage and asked, "Hide what's happening?"

Ketaki had received a blow. She didn't know what kind of woman Aditya believed her to be. Trying to keep her anger and sadness in control, she asked, "You believe I am spinning a web of lies? Why would I do such a thing?"

Aditya replied curtly, "How would I know? You might have such a need."

"Need? What sort of need? Do you mean I have some inner need to spin a web of lies?"

"What do I know?" Aditya said as if he had nothing to do with Ketaki.

"You are saying that either I have some mental illness or I lie deliberately."

"I am not a psychoanalyst. But you do not desist from hiding things even though we are as intimate as we are. You have repeatedly said that you do not do this intentionally. Then there has to be some psychological problem."

"So now you want me to go to a psychoanalyst and get treatment?"

Aditya was silent. Suppressing her irritation, Ketaki said, "You want me to tell him that my boyfriend believes that I lie, so I have come to get your help to figure out why I lie. Wow! Why don't you go and get yourself treated?"

"I—I—what do you mean?"

"Go and ask him why you don't trust your girlfriend. What is it in your mind that keeps you from believing that her love is true?"

Ketaki had turned the tables on Aditya. This sudden attack had him at a loss for words. His mind started to protest—Ketaki had slyly attacked him. He would not be fooled so easily.

One day, when Ketaki woke up in the morning, the dreams she had seen at dawn started troubling her. She felt that these dreams came to her often. When she talked to Aditya on the phone, she asked him why those dreams were recurring.

Aditya asked, "What do you see in your dreams?"

"Tigers and leopards. Five, six of them. They are around me. I am scared, and at the same time, I also have the confidence that they are not going to eat me. Like friends who mess with each other."

Aditya said, "Then they must be your lovers."

"What do you mean?"

"Why else would a tiger be a friend? It's simple."

"But there are so many tigers."

"Then you must know how many lovers you have."

"Aditya."

"I am helping you interpret your dream. Maybe it all means something else. Perhaps you should ask a psychoanalyst."

"I just told you about it by chance. I don't usually give much importance to my dreams. I don't even remember them."

"You are upset about what I said."

"Is that so strange? Things only mean one thing to you."

But Aditya's reaction was not a sudden one. It had been brewing for a long time. And the reason was not just the letter Ajay had written to Ketaki.

Many earlier memories were at the root of Aditya's anger. Some of Ketaki's messages had expressed her doubts about them getting closer or merging into each other, or perhaps it was Ketaki's letter, which she had written a few months after the meeting. He didn't know how many times he had read that letter. Her words are still engraved in his mind. "I don't want to be tied down... Relationships are not meant to bind one to someone... they are meant to open you up... Marriage is just a ritual designed to strangle a woman... I will not jump into that well again."

Aditya still needed to understand why Ketaki had written those things. Had she been trying to give him some signal? If not, then why would she write all that? And even if she had written it consciously, there must have been something in her subconscious that she wanted to convey to him. If it were accepted that Ketaki had been trying to tell him what he assumed after reading the letter, then the relationship had no future. But Aditya felt a great deal of hesitation and pain in saying something like that directly to Ketaki. If Ketaki didn't think so, and it was all just talk since Aditya hadn't felt any change or anything lacking in her love, would it be correct to say anything to her?

The turmoil in Aditya's mind did not go away. Ketaki did try to tell him that what she had said was not what Aditya was interpreting it to be. Would she express the dilemmas of her mind to anyone other than Aditya? He was the person closest to her.

But how could Aditya deny what he saw or understood? Why was Ketaki not there even after having made a promise to him? How could he not assume that there was something else in her life, someone else? Why else would she make Aditya wait like this? On the contrary, she would be waiting for him.

The thing is that every person can be judged by their behaviour. If you keep loving someone in your heart and never utter a word of love nor make any arrangements to meet your lover, how can a lover know that you love him? And this is what had happened to Ketaki. She believed that Aditya was her everything, and then she remained busy with worldly affairs; why would Aditya believe that he was her everything?

But this was also Ketaki's need. She wanted unrestricted, unconditional love. There were to be no time restrictions or promises. Her lover had to be mature enough to understand her every move automatically. If she didn't have the time to talk to him on the phone, she didn't. Why look for hidden meanings? Aditya should have known that she loved him. He should have trusted Ketaki. Such doubts were not supposed to arise among mature people.

Sometimes, Ketaki also felt that she could be the one in the wrong. Had Aditya started behaving like her, would she feel comfortable with it? Wouldn't she also start doubting him?

Ketaki thought that she would not doubt him even if she felt hurt.

This could be one of the expectations of freedom-loving girlfriends of Navabhum, to be loved unconditionally.

But I want to ask Ketaki whether she loved her non-commitment so much that she was even ready to lose Aditya for its sake.

I have understood from Ketaki's attitude that she was not ready to lose Aditya. She was not doing anything intentionally. Sometimes, things happened due to force of habit and sometimes due to carelessness, and matters got aggravated. She lost her balance just trying to justify herself.

Perhaps she spent a lot of time justifying things to herself. Like, even if she met Ajay, why was that a calamity? Why didn't Aditya understand that she saw nothing wrong in maintaining her old friendships? That did not diminish her love for Aditya in any way.

And Ketaki did not want to think or understand more than this. Because if she did, she felt that only the conservative customs and traditions of society or the formulae designed to keep a woman tied down came to the fore.

This was why she was ready to go to great lengths to maintain her independence.

Aditya's problem can be encountered in any land. But it is especially true of Gaurbhum that lovers insist that if someone loves them, it should be evident. Because in Gaurbhum, relationships between men and women are often casual and friendly. One meaning of love is the union of both body and mind. Or you can say that love is love, and only people who are in love can tell if they are in love or not. Often, the lovers themselves are not aware of it. But those unaware of their feelings can also be blamed for pretending not to know so they do not have to express their feelings. If it is true love, it is revealed in the same way that we know a new day has dawned when the sun rises or get a whiff of the fragrance of a flower. Others cannot see the fragrance of this inner being.

Aditya also says that other friendships dilute and weaken the intensity and concentration of the feeling of love; for example, if you keep adding water to milk, the quantity of milk will increase. Then you distribute it among many people instead of just one person. It will still be milk but it will have neither the same taste nor consistency.

Ketaki did not believe that there was anything amiss in the intensity of her love, in the strength of her passion.

The whole issue is that no one knows how to read the script that is running within the mind. Trying to decipher that somehow would necessitate a significant research investigation. Young psychologists say that they have invented many ways of understanding the mind. But their focus is on diseases only; all the research is focused on which diseases exist and what their treatment should be. Whereas we need art connoisseurs. Those who study the art of writing. Just as people have read the writings of the Egyptian civilisation, someone will know how to decipher the writings of the mind. But until then, what do we do? Ketaki would continue to speak her mind, and Aditya would speak his mind.

What is the real meaning of it all? In whose hands was this decision? If the decision was Ketaki's or Aditya's, then the matter would remain stuck where it was.

But how could anyone else understand the relationship between these two, who could understand the meaning of the matter and intervene? How would a third person understand when they did not understand each other even after getting to know each other so well? That was why Aditya gathered courage and directly asked Ketaki, "Is there something that you are hiding from me?"

"What do you mean?"

"I want the authentic Ketaki. One hundred per cent you... you, the authentic you."

Ketaki was shocked. What did Aditya want from her? Had she understood what he was saying?

"Do you want to say that this is not me, that you want another Ketaki?"

"You know what I am saying, Ketaki. You also know why I am saying this."

"You are irritated by my talk about being tied down."

"Why would I get irritated by anything you say? Remain who you are. Don't try to pretend to me to be something else."

"I am what you see. Nothing else."

"Don't fool yourself. First, consider what I have said. You can answer later. But I will repeat this, Ketaki, that I love you. I love you very much. Please don't lie to me. I cannot tolerate dishonesty."

Aditya's words hurt Ketaki. She didn't believe that she was living a lie. She also loved Aditya from the heart. Then why was there doubt in Aditya's mind? Ketaki thought she had never felt that she was not living a truthful life.

On the contrary, insistence on truth has always been a strong part of her life. Then what was Aditya saying? What kind of truth, what kind of lie?

When someone questioned her trustworthiness this way, Ketaki started to doubt herself. Did she not insist on the truth? Or was it because Aditya's vision was limited that he could not see Ketaki's truth? Couldn't recognise her love? Where was the truth? Aditya had, in a way, slandered Ketaki. Was Ketaki not an authentic person? Was she a lie?

What Aditya considered a lie, wasn't that Ketaki's mental state, something her fears had caused? Yes, Ketaki was afraid of drowning. Because after drowning, when the support of love disappears, the pain is unbearable. She wanted to love him but did not want to lose him. The pain of loss becomes more significant than every pleasure of love. And it settles in the heart and the mind. One can't think of anything else. Even the memories of happiness start causing pain.

Ketaki felt as if she had suffered this pain again and again and did not want to make the same mistake once more. So many incomplete memories were hidden in the dark recesses of her mind. The end of each relationship she had been in was a wound that remained a constant ache somewhere inside her. How many people she had lost! Life was a long string of losses. Many beads had been strung on that string for as long as she could remember. One such painful experience was the marriage of her elder sister. The person whom Ketaki loved the most was her sister. Her sister Rachna is ten to twelve years older than her. That part of the day when she had to be at school and away from Rachna Didi had been unbearable. Ketaki would be excited when she reached home in the afternoon because she could talk to her sister. After throwing down her schoolbag, she would immediately start to rattle off the stories of her day. Like a train, compartment after compartment, she would talk about what had happened in school that day, whom she had fought with, and who had said what. Whenever Didi came home late, Ketaki would wander around restlessly. She had to tell her sister everything. Otherwise, there would be turmoil within her.

Ketaki thought of the past. Perhaps the most significant event of her life was the marriage of her elder sister. She was her mother and father, her brother and sister. On the day Didi left for her new home, the whole house seemed deserted to Ketaki. Didi would write letters occasionally. She was utterly immersed in life at her in-laws'. She did not seem to have any intense feelings for Ketaki. At least, that was what Ketaki thought. Ketaki missed her sister for months. She yearned to meet her, but her mother and father said that her sister lived with her mother-in-law and father-in-law now, and it was not suitable for Ketaki to go and visit them. Didi came for a visit, but Ketaki's brother-in-law also came along. He was with Didi all the time. Everyone said, "Now, Didi is his." Didi never told Ketaki that she was still her older sister, that she loved her just as much as she did before. At first, Ketaki was heartbroken. But then she distanced herself. When her father got transferred abroad, she became even more isolated. Her sister's home then became another house for her, too.

Now, when she got emotionally involved with anyone, a primitive fear came alive within her—*maybe the support will not last; it will vanish at some point.* Mistrust and fear come with the charm of love as darkness follows the light. It was then that she found the insightful solution that having only one object of love was not the right idea. One should always have relationships with more than one person. Even if one goes away, the support of another will still be available.

Even after marriage, this same fear haunted her. Whenever she saw her husband in the company of a woman, she became furious. Then she said, "Do you think I can't find other men?" Perhaps it was to prove that that she befriended Ronald. Once, when she brought him home, her husband told her after he left that he did not like her meeting other men. "If you want to have male friends, leave my house."

Kartik came into her life after she left her husband, and Ketaki did not have any particular love for him. But there was an attraction between them. He was also capable of supporting her. At that time, Ketaki was looking for support. She had also promised to establish a lifelong relationship. However, she did not want to get involved in a new relationship after leaving one. And then, suddenly, Kartik stopped meeting Ketaki.

When Kartik went to India on vacation, he brought a bride home. A gorgeous girl, a little younger than Ketaki. It was only after seeing them together at a party that Ketaki found out about the marriage. The girl looked fresh off the boat and had been imported from the Old World. It turned out she was a model. Every part of her body was made up with great care.

She could not even directly confront Kartik. He had also moved far away. Their paths did not cross every day.

She saw Kartik again after a few years. His bride was not with him then. Kartik's three-year-old son was running around his father at the party. She heard it was Kartik's weekend to care for the child because the husband and wife were divorced. The reason for the divorce could have been anything. Perhaps it was the woman who had abandoned Kartik. But this had strengthened the fear that had settled in Ketaki's mind about man's dissolute nature. Her husband's similar behaviour had broken her heart. It was as if there was no escape anywhere.

Every man seemed to her to be here today, gone tomorrow. He might be her lifelong partner one day, and she would find him in someone else's arms the next day. Many of her friends also had similar experiences. Her close friend Priya's problem was that her husband tried to woo a new woman every day. Her husband's attitude was—what man doesn't fall in love with other women? He had also asked Priya why she would want to live with him if he couldn't prove his manhood? Poor Priya continued to live with him. Now, who knows where she was and how she was doing? They had not been in touch for a long time.

When Ketaki broke up with Kartik, she felt very unsettled. She wanted to go home to Purabhum to feel her father's arms close around her. The evening she reached home, everyone was sitting around her father's body, waiting for her arrival. How did all this happen so suddenly? Papa had no illness they knew of. No doctor could understand the real reason for his death. It was then that she learnt for the first time that those who loved her could leave her forever. They don't even allow you to complain, moan, or get angry. Even if you keep banging your head against the wall until you colour it red, the message will never reach them. How much she needed her father then. How helpless she felt. The very shelter which she had gone in search of had vanished.

Sometimes, she would search for her father in his library books and carefully read every note and comment he had written. Sometimes, to listen to her mother and uncles and aunts converse about her father, she would encourage them to speak about him. Sometimes, she would stare at her father's photos in the album for hours. Her mind wandered restlessly; tears would pour down and then stop, and sometimes she would stop crying for a while, but her eyes would fill up again.

Ketaki's misfortunes did not end there. Everything happened simultaneously, as if suddenly the whole sky was filled with monstrous stars. She had brought her mother back with her. She thought her father's passing was the reason for her mother's ill health, but taking her to the doctor unveiled another disaster. Her mom had cancer, and her days were numbered. Ketaki ran around to get treatment for her mother, but the cancer was at a very advanced stage. Her mother, who loved so freely, also had to leave for the world where her father had gone. It was a strange irony of fate. Had her father been alive, perhaps she would have blamed him for not caring for her mother. But now, whom could she blame? Herself?

How far can a person go to follow her dreams? Beyond a point, there is no turning back. One can just keep going onwards and upwards. There is no limit to the sky. But when did Ma or Papa ask her to return? They kept adding fuel to that fire.

And now the flames had started touching the sky.

This is what it is like when the sky is falling.

The comet of misfortune plummets to earth like this.

One blow after another. Wherever she placed her hand, it seemed flames broke out. Didi, settled in Purabhum, could no longer extinguish those flames.

Ketaki had become so lonely.

Then Ajay came into her life—an older widower. Ajay's friendship helped her a lot. She had become very dependent on him. She had once again gathered the courage to win the battle and was firmly engaged in her writing and reading. Ajay was attracted to her, and she even gave herself to him in her weak moments. But it could not be a long-lasting relationship. Ajay was sixteen years older than her. He was her friend and protector but not her love interest. He had also proposed marriage or living together, but Ketaki did not want that. She had told him clearly, "Ajay, I will always be grateful for the support you have given me in the weakest moments of my life, but I do not love you. It would be good if we could continue our relationship as close friends. But don't give it any other form."

But Aditya had descended on her sky like a moon or a sun. As soon as he arrived, he bound Ketaki with his magic. Only Aditya could be Aditya or the sun. When the sun rises, the moon and stars fade away. Everything becomes dim in its beam of light.

Ketaki had complete faith in Aditya. She wanted to have faith in him, and until now, Aditya had not given her any reason to be suspicious. There was no doubt in Ketaki's mind that Aditya was the most important person in her life. She could live in peace by handing her life over to him.

This was the first time she had felt this strongly about a man and trusted him this way. It was like she had been possessed by some intuition. She could not even analyse the feeling and ask why it was the way it was. It just was! That was why it was love. If it was not love, then she did not even want to know what love was. She considered the feeling love and wanted to live on that plane. Aditya had become a source of eternal joy. She remained enchanted, in a state of bliss.

She also wondered whether Aditya was experiencing the same inner joy that she was. Spontaneous joy? Enchanted, invigorating joy?

For one living this inner happiness to the fullest, time constraints become very illogical and meaningless.

Then, inadvertently, thanks to her nature, something happened, or she did something that caused Aditya to doubt her.

Meanwhile, despite this blissful state of mind, she could not free herself from that complex aspect of her psyche which repeatedly bound her to Aditya or made her tear away.

Therefore, it was also true that no matter how hard she tried, her mind worried about letting her give herself to him completely. As if she started reliving those past experiences unknowingly. Ketaki probably revealed her wavering state of mind to Aditya. Still, she did not knowingly say or do anything to do so. She would say something, and then Aditya would get bothered. Ketaki does not understand why, when, and how this happened. She could have prevented it if she had known about it in advance. But it was only after it happened that Aditya starts looking a little bad-tempered and angry, and she realised what had happened. Then, suddenly, she became alert. And then, there was only one thing to do: take the edge off Aditya's anger.

Something similar had happened that time as well. Ketaki was not aware that anything had happened. She sensed Aditya was pulling away. It wasn't usual for her to leave a message and for Aditya not to respond. But Aditya only called after she had left three or four messages, and he did so with indifference.

Ketaki said, "Why are you not in the mood to talk?"

The answer was, "Who cares about my mood? Whether I live or die?"

"What's the matter? Why have you started talking about dying?"

"Can we avoid dying? Everyone has to die."

"This does not sound like you, Aditya."

"Can't Aditya think of dying? Has he got some deliverance?"

"Something happened to you today. Otherwise, you wouldn't be talking like this."

Ketaki understood. Aditya was hurting. That was why he was out to hurt her as well. She told Aditya, "You need to tell me clearly what the matter is."

"If there was anything to say, I would say it. I know your answer, anyway."

"I don't understand. You have to spell it out for me."

"Should I tell you? Do you want to listen? Can you take it?"

"As bothered as I am now, I will probably be less worried if you tell me what's wrong."

"It's up to you. Once you know, you might decide to live with someone else."

"What do you mean?"

"Who knows what you..."

"Why do you try to hurt me like this? Is something lacking in my love?"

Now, he had calmed down. He was speaking very carefully. "I wouldn't say it was lacking. You love me; I know this, too. But you can't belong to just one man."

"Why?"

"If you find any man interesting, you will not hesitate to go to bed with him."

By this point, the mental state of our hero was becoming like that of the ordinary heroes of Navabhum. When the hero of Navabhum wanted to hurt the liberated heroine, he called her a prostitute. Since Aditya did not wish to say uncouth things like other heroes, and claimed to be modern, he limited himself to accusations of sleeping around. Despite being hurt, Ketaki disregarded what he was insinuating and insisted on a clarification, saying, "What do you mean?"

"I mean what I am saying."

"Just because I went to lunch with Ajay the other day and didn't wait for you to call?"

"Not just then; it has happened often."

"When?"

"At last October's conference, you tried to ensure I would not come. Once I was certain I wasn't attending the conference, you decided to participate and went there. You had been planning to prevent me from coming so that—"

"So what?"

"How do I know who you wanted to meet? It must be someone. Otherwise, why would you play tricks on me?"

"So now, along with being a liar, I am also cunning?"

"I am sorry. I have no right to say such things to you. You are an independent woman. Who am I to tell you anything? I don't have any rights. But when I get hurt, I see red, and it becomes necessary to convey what I feel. I'm not too fond of concealing differences in a relationship."

"You have already talked to me about this. Your mind seems to be stuck in this rut."

"How will it go away until we find a solution?"

"I have no hesitation in telling you I decided to go at the last moment. It is also true that I have to meet many people there. We only get to meet at conferences. After all, I am a professional woman. But who I meet and don't is my business, and I will not tolerate your interference. You are even more suspicious and narrow-minded than my ex-husband."

"You can analyse it however you want. I am suspicious. But if you can prove my suspicion wrong, then please do so. I am not narrow-minded. Of course, you can have a relationship with whoever you want, but the terms of our relationship should be clear."

"What terms are you talking about? I never imposed any terms on you. Nor do I find it right to be bound by terms."

"Look, Ketaki, every human relationship has some conditions. Whether they are visible or hidden, they exist.

There are conditions in the relationship between a child and a mother. A child smiles at his mother only when the mother gives him milk. There is a give and take in every relationship. If you want to have a relationship with other men, let us assume our relationship is not exclusive. Like you have other friends, I will be one of your friends."

"But that is not how it is, Aditya. No one else can be what you are."

"Then we will have to change the conditions. If you expect me to be completely yours, you must also reciprocate."

"And as far as I know, my heart is entirely yours, and I want to have you ultimately. But we do live in this society, after all. One has to socialise with other people."

"When have I ever stopped you from meeting others? You can meet whoever you want for work. You could also meet people for emotional and physical relationships, but this should be clear between us. I do not wish to get hurt suddenly. "

"You will never understand me. You fulfil all my emotional and physical needs. But I cannot give up on meeting my old friends."

"We are going round and round in circles; I have told you what kind of relationships I am talking about."

"And I am saying that I care for no one but you. Don't you feel that I am completely with you when we are together?"

"Well, yes, you are."

"Why would I be wholly with you if I cared about someone else?"

"You make me feel like one in a million. But my mind is still apprehensive."

"Stop all this nonsense. There is only one truth for me. That is, I love only you. No one else can take your place."

"That is what I want to believe, Ketaki. I also want this to be true."

Garlands of Jasmine

But once lovers become victims of misunderstanding, it becomes difficult to do anything about it. Sometimes, it is impossible. The thing is that we are all bound by our limitations. Human beings cannot look inside the minds of others and see reality as it is. They base their knowledge on conjecture, and this conjecture sometimes turns out to be wrong. But even where there is no need to guess, a person is often unable to acknowledge the whole truth.

Aditya said he knew what his mind wanted well and why it wanted it. He studied his mind consciously. For example, based on the needs of his mind, he read the thoughts of others, and only then did he decide whether that other mind would agree with his mind or not. When dilemma and doubts about Ketaki arose, a whole history came alive within him. All those experiences of his past life, which till now were buried under cold ashes, suddenly burst into flames. It was as if a sleeping snake had suddenly uncoiled, hissing.

It was in the last year of his teens—just one year before he became an adult. When the filament of love lit up within him for the first time, every hair on his body had been struck by lightning. The blood in his veins was surging as if it was about to burst out of his body. Her name was Kanak. Pleasant, delicate, radiant like a morning bud washed with dew, charming, untouched, intact. Aditya had fallen in love for the first time. As soon as he touched Kanak, an electric current buzzed through him.

Every evening when he went to see her, he took a garland of jasmine buds for her.

He would plait it in her braid or wrap it around her bun. Then, he would sit and stare at her face for hours. She would get embarrassed. "Don't look at me like that!" He would take her chin in his palm and place a small flower on her lips. Dreams of a lifetime came alive in those moments. His imagination was very young; his dreams were very innocent.

A garland of jasmine buds. Love was intoxicating. Love that caressed them like a light breeze.

Then, he did not know what happened. Maybe nothing. Nothing in Aditya's eyes. But something had happened. She decided never to meet him again. A few days later, Aditya saw her with another boy from his class. For days, he wondered why this had happened. Nothing was lacking in Aditya's love. Perhaps she was bored, or was it just her fickle nature? Maybe searching for someone new was her nature. Perhaps other men who came into her life also met the same fate.

It had taken Aditya a long time to pull himself together. Why had Kanak done this? Why had she stopped talking to him? Why had she deceived him? What had been the harm in telling him if she didn't love him? After all, he wouldn't force her to do anything against her will. She had been with him of her own free will. Had she been uncertain? Had she not been able to decide whether she loved Aditya or that classmate?

But if she had loved that classmate too, it was good that she had left Aditya's life. If she had truly loved Aditya, there would have been no question of loving someone else. What kind of love could it have been if she couldn't immerse herself in Aditya? Aditya did not like the idea of someone loving two people at the same time. Either you loved or you didn't. If you did, then gave yourself up completely.

It is not that Aditya did not recognise that, apart from black and white, there are shades of grey. One mixes portions of both colours for this. It is natural to be uncertain. Aditya had been plagued by uncertainty many times in his life. Even in the matter of Ketaki, Aditya had wondered for a long time, for months actually, about whether to move forward or not, whether to get involved or not. That was why he put off having a physical relationship with her. Because he wanted to make up his mind first. But once one had made a commitment, that was it. What was the dilemma then? Kanak had also committed herself, but despite that, she remained uncertain. If only Kanak had told him her intentions openly. Then he would have held her in high regard. He would have respected her wishes.

In comparison, Aditya had wholly opened himself to her. There had been no objection of any kind. But right till the end, Kanak had not given him any indication that she was in a relationship with any other man. When she had him she could not meet him anymore, Aditya had naturally accepted that she had other obligations. He had never imagined that there was someone else in her life.

Perhaps that was why he was no longer able to trust anyone. He examined Ketaki's every move to see if she is playing tricks on him and hatching some secret plan to throw dust in his eyes. Was he hurting Ketaki with his behaviour?

But how would Aditya know whether she was telling the truth? She had hinted at so many things time and again. She feared being tied down. When he brought her small drop earrings on her birthday, she smiled and said, "Look at the design you have chosen. A net of spokes has been woven in the circle at the bottom as if it were a cage, a golden cage. Why, do you intend to imprison me in your golden cage?"

Aditya had not liked Ketaki's comment. He found those drops beautiful. Once, when both of them had entered the jeweller's shop while wandering around together, he had found Ketaki looking at those drops with longing. Ketaki had later told him that she liked that pair of earrings very much. When she had brought up the matter of getting tied down, Aditya had taken it to mean that Ketaki was afraid that Aditya might tie her down.

Did Ketaki not love him, or was she scared of commitment, or did she have someone else in her life?

Aditya also did not think it was right for Ketaki to feel he was tying her down. He had no such intention. Aditya had to commit to the same extent if they decided to marry or live together. But he did not see his relationship as a shackle. He felt they were meant to support and help each other and share each other's happy and sad moments. He wanted to help Ketaki. To see her go further and climb higher. Where did the talk of tying her down come from? He wanted to give love intensely and receive love intensely.

Why did Ketaki think of it as being bound?

Ketaki had never made Aditya feel she did not love him. Ketaki desired to be with him all the time, her eyes tied to Aditya in moments of passion, and to keep him connected with her rapt gaze as she talked to him every day, a conversation that kept flowing like the current of a river. If there was an interruption, Ketaki became sad. She wanted it to continue for the rest of her life. Such hope and longing were pulsating in her, and Aditya heard and felt it again and again. If this was not love, then what was it?

But it felt good to be bound to someone in love. Wasn't Ketaki supposed to feel the same? If she genuinely loved him?

On his last birthday, Ketaki gave him a book by Rilke. Rilke's *Letters to a Young Poet.* She had underlined parts of the book in which Rilke had said something similar. Aditya still remembered those lines: "Love is at first not anything that means merging, giving over, and uniting with another, it is a high inducement to the individual to ripen, to become something in himself, to become world, to become world for himself for another's sake." Rilke advises the young poet that it is not suitable for young people, especially, to surrender or to merge into someone else because they need to preserve themselves for the future that lies ahead of them. Perhaps it would have been better if he had read Rilke when he, too, had been nineteen years old. But now, for whom would he preserve himself? Now Aditya wanted to drown, to dissolve. His faith was now in surrender. He wanted to surrender and demanded surrender as well. But Ketaki still wanted to save herself.

Was there someone else for whom she wanted to save herself, or was this stinginess just a natural tendency? Did she plan to never give all of herself in life? There are people like this, too, 'constipated' personalities. Is this the truth of Ketaki, or does the matter boil down to the doubts in his mind? Or is it all simply the effect of some garbled philosophy?

House and Garden

But why didn't Ketaki try to understand what Aditya's mind is seeking? This was the meaning of love. Getting out of yourself. Trying to reach the person towards whom your mind is oriented. Why was Ketaki so obsessed with the fear of losing herself? Is it permissible to remain buried under one's own demands despite asserting that one loves someone? I, the narrator, am a woman. Therefore, it is possible that I have particular sympathy for Ketaki and that I am not aware of it. That's why I also want to ask Ketaki some questions so that my male readers do not accuse me of telling a one-sided story. However, I am also mindful that I must not be harsh towards Ketaki.

It is also true that, as I am a woman, I must be a feminist. But I wanted to see how much truth there is in what Ketaki was saying, how much selfishness and deceit. Take this poem written by the storyteller, for instance—

'House and Garden', which Ketaki sent to Aditya. She also said, "I don't know why I am sending you a poem. But I feel like it. This may represent my state of mind. The desire for freedom or, should I say, the longing for an open sky. Sometimes, I feel like becoming an aerial element and merging into nature. Like air, sunlight, or fire, which have shape and yet do not. I want to spread like a liquid, a visible or invisible, latent substance; it can spread everywhere and get absorbed. I don't know what kind of strange state of mind this is… it is also unclear to me… I don't know what I want. Whether this melting is to dissolve in you, or in something other than you. I am unable to say. I am getting carried away. This poem will not be able to express everything that is in my mind. Still, something about it seemed to speak to my heart. That's why I am sending it (one more thing… I will be out next weekend, so we will not be able to talk)."

House and Garden

I don't want a house
I want to live in the garden
Don't give me pots and pans
Pictures for the wall
Tablecloths
Pillows and pillowcases
Brooms or dusters
Sofas and cushions
I want a garden and fresh air

Sunshine and rain
Feathers and branches.
Can you give this to me?

My love desires
The open sky
Rainbow colours
I do not want
colourful scarfs
Or saris of silk
I will clothe myself in history
Tangle with politics
Tear down the walls of tradition
I have to find words
That are only mine
That touch me
Turn me upside down
Give me a voice,
Give me a definition

I want to lie down
On the grass.
I do not want
A soft, cushioned bed
Or quilts of velvet
I want
The forest, birds,
Storm clouds

And a roaring sea
I do not want a house
Security or compromises
This readymade world.
Let me carve out
a new self.

Aditya was even more confused after getting the poem. What did Her Highness Ketaki want? She was forever sending him different signals. Did she want to say now that she did not dream of a home with Aditya? All those things said in Union and Purvarag were in the past. Aditya was very disappointed. How could he solve the riddle of Ketaki? Would she let him live, or would she continue to torment him like this?

Now, you may accuse me of feminism, but I must say that I felt Ketaki's demand was not just her demand; it is a woman's demand, echoing down history, through society, across civilisations—a demand that she should be given a break from household chores and also a chance to do something else and explore other paths. Aditya, enhanced with the values of the New World, could undoubtedly have understood Ketaki's demand. Nowadays, even some men from Purabhum have started paying attention to such demands.

Yes, Aditya understood the historical injustice done to women very well. Still, the pain he felt due to the lack of complete giving in his relationship made him unable to see that Ketaki's womanhood needed to maintain that feeling of liberation. This meant not suppressing one's desire for liberation despite loving someone. At the same time, she did not want love and freedom to be enemies of each other. After all, why is it necessary for us to believe that love binds us and does not free us? She would have liked to prove, through her relationship with Aditya, that love and freedom could coexist. But Aditya often did not support her in this mission and got upset that she gave freedom more importance.

He wrote to Ketaki, "I don't think that we can ever live together. You are afraid to put all your eggs in one basket. You will never be able to invest the whole of yourself in one place. You keep saving yourself so you can invest elsewhere should you get the opportunity. You don't want to take any risks."

"There are no risks in our relationship. I can still guarantee my love for you."

"Tell me, will you come with me right now? Totally? Until you are sure, there is no meaning to a guarantee. The decision lies in your hands."

Was Ketaki truly afraid of putting all her eggs in one basket? If they cracked, she will lose everything.

The point is that if there is a historical truth for a woman, then there is a historical truth for a man, too, and history has given priority to the man and has established only his viewpoint. Now, the history that had created Aditya could also demand that everything be offered to him on a platter. All the eggs together. Even if he forgot his history, did not seek any offerings, and continues to sympathise with women's history, he still had no control over the pain in his heart caused by that history for centuries! And that pain was deep as the length of that history, and it became too much for our hero to bear.

Both were buried under the burden of their respective histories.

Both of them had to free themselves from this. Only then would the train of love move forward.

Only then would the pace of our story increase.

Before that, I want to ask my readers a question. Can history interfere in human personal relationships? What is more significant—history or human beings? Can human beings ignore history? Can they forget or deny it? History is a part of the present, and how can anyone deny the present, that too an enlightened woman like Ketaki?

But do the feelings of the mind fluctuate with history? This issue is more complicated. Ketaki should have adorned herself with the awakening of women's liberation within her and then fought history. But would this harm Aditya's wishes and desires?

The fundamental question here has become political: love versus politics or, rather, the political philosophy of Aditya versus that of Ketaki. In Navabhum, lovers separate because they have conflicting political opinions. Yes, this is called political correctness or political propriety. If you are a supporter of minorities like the black community, women, homosexuals, etc., then you are politically correct. Otherwise, you are not a right-thinking citizen. This is Gaurbhum's leftist principle, or should we call it a liberal way of thinking?

Such conflicts have arisen in every land and will continue to occur. The conflicts of love and war, love and duty, have been at the core of the stories of Shakespeare and many such artists. Our hero and heroine are some of the more intelligent people of today's times. I don't think they should put their relationship through the wringer on these grounds. It would be better if things didn't go any further than this.

If we are talking about history, we should talk about personal history as well as collective history. First, how far should lovers be allowed to delve into each other's personal history? Aditya and Ketaki did not have the same opinion on this matter. Aditya wanted to integrate the past with the present. Ketaki felt that her past was only her own—why gave anyone any right to it, even if that person was close to her?

Once, during a conversation, Aditya had said to Ketaki, "You disown your history."

Ketaki pounced on him. "It is better not to talk about this. Women have a habit, or should we say compulsion, of erasing their history. I can't carry my history around. You can boast that you had a relationship with this one or that one, but even if someone hurts a woman in the name of a relationship, she will suppress it."

Should Ketaki get even slightly hurt, Aditya resolved that he would salve her wounds or take revenge on the person who had hurt her. He lovingly said, "Ketaki, there is no need for you to disown anything before me. We both have had relationships before. You can be open. That won't make you smaller."

"But maybe I will start feeling small. A woman is brought up from childhood to believe that even though she may be in love with someone else, she can only marry the person her parents choose. Everything is hush-hush and suppressed. She will have to deal with and suffer her marriage. At least her parent's lives and reputations have been spared. Now tell me, how does one get the courage to open up? After living in this country, I have gained enough courage to say that I have had relationships with more than one man. That, too, just to you. I wouldn't even want to talk about this with anyone else. Anyway, isn't it a personal matter? You, too, should not attack me like this."

"Sorry, I had started considering myself a part of you the way I consider you a part of me."

"My own private sphere can only be mine. You're here. But there are many things which are only mine. No one else can go there. I might open up more with time. I can't say. After all, I don't know a lot about many things."

Aditya understood this Ketaki, and he didn't. It was also true that he neither wanted to know anything about

Ketaki's personal relationships nor wanted to ask her about them. Still, he wanted Ketaki to be as transparent as clean glass. Her opaque personality depressed Aditya. Like a small child, he wanted to reach out his hand and touch a toy he liked, and the toy kept moving further and further away. He asked himself this question again and again: did he completely understand Ketaki's mind? And the answer he came up with was that he always tried his best. Could anything else be done? In the end, we are all bound by the limits of our understanding. Even if you try hard to escape those limits, it is not possible to do so every time.

The Hand and The Palm

When a man is set free, he starts creating his own boundaries and drawing his own limits. It's like the relationship of the hand with the palm—the hand writes, while the palm is that on which your destiny is written. Sometimes, we accept the consequences of our actions and surrender ourselves to fate. This is especially so when a person does not want to take responsibility.

A moment came in Aditya's life when his mother insisted he get married, and he handed her the responsibility of arranging the marriage as she wished. Somewhere in his mind, he had also decided that love was not his destiny. He had to do something else. Any woman he loved would always have another lover hidden somewhere. It was as if this old belief was rising to the surface once again. Was the same story being repeated here? Had Kanak returned to Ketaki's body? Who knew? The snakes of doubt rose from many corners and started attacking him. Was the same story being repeated again? Or was he mistaken?

Ketaki was the last chance he had in his life. He wanted to devote himself to her. He wanted to spare nothing so that he wouldn't regret later that his love had been lacking in any way. Each time he met Ketaki, it was like a festival for him. A celebration of the sort that came only once in a lifetime. He would celebrate it, exuding enthusiasm from every pore in his body. He would shower her with gifts and bring her clothes and jewellery.

Those moments would become moments of worship for him. Ketaki seemed to be a divine presence descending from another world. Aditya's mind was that of a humble devotee. Eager to sacrifice himself. Anxious to be robbed. But like an apsara descended from an unknown world, she was both very close and quite far away. In some other world, far away... far, far away. It was as if he couldn't recognise her. Touching her, shaking her. She was not be made of human clay but some other substance. What substance was it? He would try to check by touching, sniffing, turning her around... and he would be bewildered.

This happened often.

He felt that Ketaki could not give him the kind of free love that he desired. She was a closed flower that always covered its insides with its petals. Its pollen and nectar remain safe within itself. It did not open to welcome anyone from outside. The flower was there but closed like a bud.

Or a cloud that was forbidden from causing rain.

A verse that could not be put to a tune.

A song that could not become an anthem.

A waterfall that did not become a stream.

Joy that did not become laughter.

Moisture in the eyes that did not turn into tears.

Why was it so? He searched endlessly for an answer. Was he not worthy of Ketaki's love, or was it Ketaki's problem that she was afraid of risking everything for one person? She invested small bits in many people so that she didn't suffer the same pain if something broke down or things didn't work out. When there were multiple relationships, if one ended, the support of another remains. Meanwhile, Aditya, having poured out everything on Ketaki, constantly feared that she would reject him.

I am afraid there is a danger of the entire investment sinking on both sides.

Whatever Aditya thought of Ketaki, Ketaki felt that if she had dedicated herself completely to anyone in her life, it was to Aditya. There was no doubt in her mind. She was entirely at peace after surrendering herself to him. Having given everything to him, she thought there was no need to worry anymore. Only that would allow her to remain unperturbed. She would be able to sleep in peace.

The sweetness of love pervaded her every moment, and it had become the essence, the basis of her life. She also considered Aditya's doubts normal and felt that when he was convinced there was no place for anyone else in her heart, he would automatically become comfortable. This was Ketaki's truth, and she felt that the truth would make itself felt sooner or later. She was carefree and had no idea that the sting of doubt was still poisoning Aditya. She could see it only when Aditya said something hurtful unknowingly.

Ketaki also had a problem: whenever something started feeling routine or took the form of a ritual, she felt like breaking its mould. She wanted to keep love free from routine or ritualism so that it would always remain an element that enlivened, fulfilled, and uplifted her, which liberated and yet stayed free. If someone repeatedly said "I love you," it began to seem like a ritual to her, and she felt there was no need to repeat it all the time. Similarly, when Aditya was with her, she was always afraid that Aditya would also start seeming like a routine to her. That was why she wanted to love Aditya but keep him at a distance. Aditya could not understand this about Ketaki. How could she explain it? Aditya told her, "I don't doubt you love me. I believe that you do. The problem is that many other things in your life are more important to you than me, whereas you are the most important to me."

Ketaki knew that Aditya was most important thing in her life to her, but Aditya would probably never realise this.

A thought took root somewhere in Ketaki's mind and began to grow, to spread. She realised that Aditya, in fact, wanted her to sacrifice herself. He wanted to have her completely, which was why he talked about other important things in her life. Aditya wanted her to leave everything else and be near him all the time. He wanted to be able to see her at all times, to be present whenever he called. Only then would he be happy. Wasn't this an all-consuming love? The strange thing was that Ketaki did not need anything like that. She felt comfortable when Aditya was busy with his work, and she was occupied with hers. That way, they could be together whenever they wanted and remain engaged in different tasks when necessary. There seemed to be a harmony, a balance in her life. Life like that was ideal for her. But she felt that, whatever Aditya might have said, no matter how generous he may have been, his deepest desire was that Ketaki surrender wholly and remain imprisoned within the boundaries of his gaze.

A sharp thorn had lodged itself inside Ketaki. Perhaps the love and relationship she wanted with Aditya was just an idea. In reality, this never happened. Still, the situation was that they had to either stay together and strangle each other or stay far away and yearn for each other. Which condition was better? To merge into each other or to destroy each other?

Aditya found her attitude strange. He said, "Love does not strangle anyone. However, selfishness can strangle you. Love always wants you to be happy, to flourish. This attitude of yours is not healthy."

"A woman's feelings are different from a man's feelings."

"And you are only concerned with your feelings. You don't want to take responsibility for what happens inside another person."

"How can I be responsible for the feelings of others?"

"Even if that feeling is inspired by you or directed towards you, even if you are its only source and confluence?"

"I might be a source and a confluence, but the ocean does not know which streams have come and mingled with its waters, it remains where it is as it is. How can a human being know what was gathered to create him or what she became? How can I know someone else's feelings? I am not God, who knows people's inner thoughts and feelings."

"So you don't know what's happening inside me?"

"That's not true, but—"

"Look, Ketaki, in love, a man gives the other person a chance to see and know him closely. You see and recognise yourself in the eyes of others and find an identity. We define ourselves only in the context of others.

Since the person who loves us gets to know us closely by observing us, what he says and thinks, his approval or disapproval, become very important for our identity."

Suddenly, at that moment, it dawned on Ketaki that Aditya's love was as deep, dense, and scary as an ocean. She would literally drown in it. It wasn't a question of crossing it by swimming on the surface. Drown and get lost. That was the only way. Whether a good way or the wrong way, God only knew.

Ketaki also felt it was possible she would dive in, making her fear even more intense.

Aditya was sinking even further. "There are no external entanglements in this relationship. No in-laws. No disputes among relatives. No children, no money, and no property. There are only two people. You can make this as whole and complete as you want. It is in your hands and mine, it is up to both of us. Tell me."

Aditya was right. It was just the two of them. What kinds of obstacles did they have to face? Why couldn't this love find fulfilment? Like sugar dissolving in milk. If that is the fullness of love, why couldn't he find it? Why didn't he immediately seize that totality? Why couldn't she open everything inside layer by layer and fill it with emotion, dedication, cleanliness, and softness, as clean as a mirror?

That night, Ketaki had a dream. *She and Aditya are on an island, going out to sea in a small boat. She sees the vast expanse of the ocean and is thrilled. The boat is sailing slowly in the calm sea. The clear blue sky bathing the ocean with its blueness, glowing a lukewarm cyan that has been touched by the rainbow rays of the sun. Suddenly, the sky turns grey. Thick clouds turn the ocean water muddy. Ketaki is scared because they have sailed into the mighty ocean in a small boat. A calm sea is alright, but if the weather turns stormy, how will they save the boat?* Trapped in this feeling of dread, she opened her eyes.

The dream stayed with her for a long time after she woke up. What a scare! What a storm!

What was it about? The eagerness to give away everything and the stupidity of remaining frozen in fear!

Do humans have to live conflicted lives?

Humans or just her?

Is this just stupidity, or is it some flaw that disguises selfishness?

Not to let yourself dissolve completely, not to erase yourself, is that being selfish?

Or is it a vow to save one's soul?

Are self-preservation, self-indulgence, or being self-absorbed the same thing?

The tendency to care for oneself is just stinginess, smallness, and miserliness.

Wouldn't a strong soul also strengthen the foundation of love?

The building of lasting love can only stand in a solid and determined self.

What if these arguments have a negative impact?

But there is something else beyond these arguments. A blurriness that unknowingly takes over. Due to this, she remained unaware and could never give Aditya the correct answer about why she was afraid of being tied to him, of giving in completely.

Cut it open and see what's inside.

What is Ketaki?

Which knife should we use to cut—the blade of psychology, history, sociology, or biology? Or something else?

Will a knife only cut one layer, or will it cut several? Maybe several layers. But still not all.

Cutting will lead to destruction, and one will have to lay waste to everything before drawing any new conclusions. Can't one try without cutting?

Let us first collect the facts and then move the knife gradually.

We have gathered some facts so far; a lot has been revealed about Ketaki in many pages. If we still need to do something, let us divide it serially into the categories of classical science.

Basically, Panch Bhoot or the five elements are what make up a human being: kshiti, jal, pavaka, gagan, samira. Or earth, water, fire, sky, and air. The form of water that Ketaki matched could only be a river because you can't predict the course of a river. Neither Aditya nor she knew in which direction Ketaki was headed. Aditya could not determine what course of action he should take so that she neither flooded nor dried up. Like the sky, she is mysterious, subtle, aerial, and untouchable. Fire's nature, visible in Ketaki, was her passion towards Aditya, her work, the brightness of her talent, and her excitement. She was free, independent, and always ready to fly like the wind. If we look at the earth also, much has already been said but the earth is made up of the soil which is what holds all the rituals or cultures within it. So, what are the rituals of a Purabhumi person?

What are those values?

Ketaki reached into the past. She saw the faces of her father and sister. Whenever she connected emotionally with anybody, that primitive fear came alive inside her, warning her that perhaps it would not last; it would disappear. Disbelief and fear were linked to the hypnotism of love, like darkness followed light. She also felt that having one base of love was not right. She needed to always have relationships with more than one person. If one were to go away, the support of another would remain.

Even after marriage, this same fear kept troubling her. Ketaki's mind and her psyche had been nourished in both countries.

Her mother's domestic values and her father's free thinking. She didn't want to be like her mother and had spent her entire career trying to be like her father.

Her father's world was limitless like the sky, her mother's limited like the earth. Still, her mother's sensitivity kept her involved. Ketaki felt drawn by the attraction of her sister's limited world. As a result of all this, a world of expectations was created within Ketaki, which her husband broke down blow by blow. The combination of so many influences forms a personality.

This is just beating about the bush. Many women are born in such an environment. What is unique about Ketaki? Is Ketaki like other women? One could ask whether Ketaki represents a class or a group as a character or if she is an individual in her own right.

Whenever I see Ketaki, I feel that she is just Ketaki. Perhaps more women like her have been created or will be born in the future. I only know Ketaki, and that too, partially. I have only met her in Navabhum. What I know of her past is as much as she tells me or what I can guess. After all, I have come from the old country as well.

In trying to understand Ketaki's inner nature or attitudes, the fundamental question is: why was Ketaki afraid to jump? Was it because her father, despite giving her freedom, taught her to walk very carefully, or was it that, after breaking up with the person she was married to, she started acting more cautiously than necessary? She lived alone in a foreign country, so perhaps this was her expat mentality. On the one hand, being an expat brings with it a feeling of freedom or independence; on the other, there is a compulsion to walk with caution. After all, freedom also teaches you responsibility. Wilfulness is a process of losing freedom. Our wise intellectual Ketaki would not subject herself to that, or she was afraid that her father would not be around and she would be left alone.

I had heard Ketaki say some clichéd things occasionally, such as that men are generally not interested in permanent relationships. Once a man has got a woman's body, the woman gives up on herself and starts wanting a permanent relationship, whereas for the man, the opposite happens—he starts yearning for freedom.

When Ketaki put Aditya in the category of an ordinary man, her mind was not inclined to believe him. Then, when Aditya was just Aditya, she felt that he had given her the love of a lifetime and that their relationship is unbreakable and would last forever and for many more lifetimes. She also started believing in all kinds of love stories. Even the films on this subject, like *Madhumati*, *Mahal*, etc., seemed romantic and exciting to her.

Ketaki could not see any signs in her relationship with Aditya that suggested Aditya only wanted a temporary relationship with her. Her whole life was at stake. But it was hard for her when Aditya started looking at her with suspicion. Then she started to think that Aditya would leave her on this pretext and end the relationship, so why would she risk everything? If Aditya wanted to prove she was a liar and not keep up the relationship, Ketaki could save herself from much pain by not getting hurt. There was no hope for the future. Perhaps Aditya's feelings were not that strong after all.

It was all about the fear of getting hurt. Aditya feared that Ketaki would hurt him by becoming attracted to someone else and turning away from him. This fear of Aditya's was killing Ketaki.

The question is, why is one afraid?

And what is the cure for fear?

Psychoanalysts say that one can only get rid of fear by expressing it; otherwise, there is no cure for this disease. The identification of the disease is its treatment. Yes, if someone is crazy, they are given chemicals, but there is no other cure for these somewhat harmless fears that are embedded inside. With knowledge, a person can control such worries. That is the only way to deal with them.

So, are our characters aware of their inner worlds?

Could the fact that the little girl's loving father tended to get lost in the hustle and bustle of work be responsible for Ketaki's attitude?

Frankly, great scholars may unravel the most complex knots in the world, but they need help understanding the suppressed nature and tendencies of their own minds. Our hero and heroine are highly developed creatures. They keep trying to look within themselves.

Even if one has some knowledge, one does not always have control over the way one thinks. Aditya did realise what was happening, but only the doubtful mind seems truthful when there is doubt. He forgot that the suspicious nature of his mind was making him do this. Maybe Ketaki was innocent. That was why he wrote a letter to Ketaki again: "The more I think about it, the more I feel that one can't change one's nature. Nor should it be changed. For example, if you lock a lion in a cage in the jungle, how long will it survive? If he is going to end his life by hitting his head on the bars, then what is the point of keeping him tied? That's how you are, Ketaki. If you are tied down, you will not bloom and grow. You will suffocate slowly in your sadness. Now I understand why you didn't like those earrings and said I wanted to tie you down. I could not understand your nature then. When I understood it, I rejected it. I may need more strength to find a compromise. I will accept you as you are, with your true nature and attitude."

Finally, he added, "Try to understand me. Please don't lie to me. Whatever you want, do it freely. I will accept it."

Ketaki was furious when she read the last line. She was in a temper for days. According to Ketaki, Aditya's distrustful nature prevented her from trusting and getting attached to him. Now, he had accepted this as the real nature of Ketaki. *Well, then, go to hell.* Ketaki stopped talking to Aditya. She didn't call or pick up the phone when it rang. Instead she fumed. She stood next to the phone until it stopped ringing, and then she picked it up. She even switched off the answering machine for a couple of days to avoid having any contact with Aditya. Then, one day, she thought there could be important messages from work she was missing. Constant anxiety and restlessness within. She had forcibly imposed a silence on herself. A painful silence.

Meanwhile, Aditya was worried about what had happened to her. Was she very upset? He left several messages full of concern. They all reiterated one thing: "My love for you is immortal no matter what happens. It is impossible to end this relationship."

Now Ketaki could not keep from replying. One should be honest and not afraid to call a spade a spade. But still, she found it difficult to speak. She sent a letter, "What do you think of me? I have told you what I feel many times. You still think I am lying and dare not speak the truth. What rubbish! You are as truthful as King Harishchandra, right? If you don't trust me, what kind of relationship is this? If you don't trust me, we should end our relationship. Love can never flourish without trust. I am surprised how you have managed till now. When there is no base, how can anything rest on it?"

Ketaki's anger was apparent in her letter. Aditya turned weak when faced with her fury. He kept quiet. He did not talk of trust at all. He called her. They started having a casual conversation like they used to. Ketaki sensed a strange change in the tone of his speech. He sounded aloof. When she asked about it, Aditya said, “It’s nothing. There is no problem. You must be imagining things. I am eager to talk to you, as always. I am always waiting for you.”

Ketaki thought that maybe she had misunderstood the situation. Her anger disappeared. She started chatting, her words flowing in their usual way. She told him many things about the university, colleagues, and herself. On the phone, one only hears a voice; you can’t see the face and catch any expressions. Still, she felt that Aditya was not as open as he used to be. Something was not right. But there was no point in asking him. If she did, he would say, “Everything is alright,” and retreat into himself.

She started wondering why she was feeling guilty. Ajay had called her, but she had refused to meet him so she wouldn’t have to explain anything to Aditya. She met Ronald, and he invited her for lunch, but Ketaki said she was too busy. So why the guilt?

A bolt went through her. Why had she put herself in a situation that required her to give an account of all her meetings with everyone to Aditya? Meanwhile, Aditya told her she was free to meet whomever she wanted to. So what was going wrong?

And things got worse whenever she started giving him an account of her actions. Aditya thought she was guilty and she then tried to clarify matters to get rid of that guilt.

What was Ketaki to do?

Perhaps she would try to understand her thoughts and then speak to Aditya. You end up saying something when you want to say something else while talking on the phone. The matter gets entangled in useless arguments. It's as if the real issue is never discussed. Now, she would sit comfortably, write down everything, and narrate her feelings. Precisely what she felt, and without getting emotional. "No matter how hard I try, I cannot explain what I am to you. What is this relationship of ours? Despite giving my all, I wanted to hold 'something' in me. To tell you the truth, I have started getting to know myself only after falling in love with you. I am still searching. What I did not know about myself, I am learning now. I may be developing unknowingly in the meantime. All those conversations about getting tied down were wrong. Getting tied to you is a bond of happiness; it is getting bound willingly. A bond, by which I mean being attached to you, that only gives me a feeling of joy. I don't feel afraid. But you are holding on to this in such a way that it is becoming impossible for me to reach you. Tell me, which words should I use to convey what I want to say to you? You tell me what to do. When the one to whom I have given everything says that I cannot be his or do not want to be his, then whom else should I appeal to? I want to reach you; you are the one I want to tell everything to, yet you do not accept me as authentic. All these things of mine become meaningless in front of you:

The one I worship seeks shelter
my prayer is silent
I am in anguish
where do I go to worship?"

Even if Aditya wasn't entirely convinced about her after reading this, he sensed Ketaki's distress. He felt guilty at the thought that Ketaki had suffered such a lot because of him. He tried to understand and explain the whole situation differently. Ketaki got a reply to her letter: "Ketaki, I kept looking at my pain. I did not try to understand how much suffering I was causing you. I want to apologize for this. As I have said before, I never doubted that you loved me. I might have suspected that there were other people besides me in your life, but you told me it is not so, and I am putting my complete trust in what you say. From now on, I will try never to doubt you unnecessarily. It is also fair to ask why, if you were not mine, you would try to make me believe this again and again. After all, what are you getting from me except our one precious thing: our love for each other?"

Ketaki felt as if somebody had lifted a heavy burden from her chest. It was as if she had conquered the whole of Lanka and brought Sita home. It was only after the burden was removed that the seriousness of that burden became clear to her. Before that, she had started accepting and living with it. But no, she would not have to make such a compromise anymore. All those fears or misconceptions had evaporated like cheap perfume. Now she was free. Her Aditya was with her. Now, she would fly again. She would embrace the sky with her wings. She started reciting a poem:

The wind, the wind,
a spring breeze am I.
Listen to what I say,
I am unique,
quite crazy,
happy go lucky,
with no worries.
I am fearless,
I roam
wherever I want,
An intrepid traveller.
The wind, the wind,
a spring breeze am I.

And the thought of flying made her mind blow like a silk scarf in the spring breeze.

She felt a strong urge within her to be with Aditya. She became so desperate that she was ready to leave mid-semester to visit him. It was Aditya who explained to her that by acting so rashly, she could cause serious damage to her career. She understood but could not stop the churning within her.

As soon as the semester ended, she bought a plane ticket to see Aditya.

"Let's go on holiday together."

"How much time do you have?"

"As much as you want."

"Should we go to Canada or Europe?"

"Wherever. But it must be snowing there. How about Purabhum?"

"Let's go. I also have a conference there next month."

"I have one as well at J.N.U. Shall we go together? Let's find out about bookings."

"Where do you usually stay in Indrabhum?"

"Didi is there now. The rest of my friends are scattered here and there. Where will you stay?"

"First, I will go to Kalika City. I will meet Ma and then go to Indrabhum. I usually stay at the International Centre there. "

"Stay for a couple of days in Indrabhum before going to Kalika City. We'll do some sightseeing in Indrabhum together."

A Flight Home

Once she was in Indrabhum, Ketaki became so busy with her friends and relatives that she was never home when Aditya called from Kalika Nagari. One day, Didi said that a certain Aditya Ghosh had called many times. "Don't go out before ten o'clock today. He said that he would definitely call you before ten."

"But I have an appointment with a J.N.U. professor at 9:30."

"That poor guy has made twenty-five long-distance calls. Can't you postpone the appointment?"

Ketaki was pleased that Didi was taking Aditya's side. Her sister must have been quite fed up with his calls. When Ketaki had come to Purabhum, her sister had answered the phone for her all day. She had told everyone, "Yes, I am her secretary. Tell me whatever you want to say; I will give her the message."

"The thing is that it takes work to get someone on the phone here. I have to meet that professor. If Aditya calls, tell him I will come home early this evening, after 7 pm."

But Aditya did not call her that evening. When the call came the following morning, Ketaki picked up the phone. "Where are you roaming around all day long? It is impossible to talk to you on the phone here."

"Sorry, I seem to have missed your calls. Tell me, how are you?"

"I am coming to Indrabhum the day after tomorrow. Do you have the time to meet me?"

Aditya also had many meetings of his own in Indrabhum, but all his meetings took place between 9 am and 12 noon. Afterwards, he freed himself and was ready to meet Ketaki. Ketaki woke up late in the morning and then spent time chatting with her sister over tea; then, there were calls and meetings with relatives and friends throughout the day. Either she was not as well organised as Aditya or more people knew her in the city than Aditya. All her maternal aunts and uncles were here. After all, this was her city, she had spent much of her life here. She had gone to Gaurbhum from here. When she returned from Purabhum, it was to this city. One of her friends, Geetika, wrote, "As soon as winter arrives, I start waiting for just two things. One is you coming here, and the other is eating eggs."

Returning to Purabhum meant Ketaki would absorb the colours, smells, sounds, tastes, and everything she could from the place. She had to listen to the latest news from across the country, take part in political discussions, listen to the newest music, watch plays and concerts, watch desi films, go to familiar eateries and enjoy eating chaat, sweets, and kebabs (which included everywhere from five-star hotels to food stalls outside the Hanuman temple), buy saris with new designs, visit tailors to get blouses made. Apart from friends, she had to chat with her professors, old aunts, and uncles. No matter how long her trip was, there was always too little time. She was so captivated by the atmosphere of Purabhum that, suddenly, it became difficult for her to find free time for Aditya.

Aditya was from Kalika City. Hence, his school and college friends were not in Indrabhum. Instead, there were people associated with his work. He met them only professionally; there were very few people among them who were close friends. He was very excited that day. A friend told him he could get some land in the hills near Rishikesh.

"Ketaki, I often think of retiring, coming here, staying in a quiet place, and completing my unfinished projects. I have heard this place is lovely. Will you come with me and see it? We can drive there tomorrow or the day after."

"I have never seen Rishikesh. I would love to go."

Aditya's eyes lit up.

When they met for lunch the next afternoon, Ketaki said, "I have to go to Raghupur for some work."

Aditya suddenly got angry. "You should have gone to Raghupur when I was in Kalika City. I have made an extended trip to Indrabhum because of you. If you leave, what am I to do here?"

"You didn't come to Indrabhum just for my sake. You have meetings with others, too."

"No, but—"

"I don't want to go to Raghupur, but I rarely meet the people here. I do get to meet you over there, in the other country. But if you tell me not to, I won't go."

"No, I'm not stopping you. When will you return?"

"I am going for three days. It's a short visit."

Aditya was displeased. "Will you have time to go to Rishikesh or not?"

"Let's do it after that."

"The thing is that I wanted to take Amitabh along because I don't know anything about that place. He is the one who knows about land prices and all that."

"So, talk to him."

"He was ready to go tomorrow. After that, he also has to go to Chitrapuri."

"I will not be able to change my plans for Raghupur. Why don't you go with Amitabh?"

When Ketaki returned from Raghupur, she got a message informing her that Aditya had returned to Kalika City. From there, he would fly back directly to Navabhum.

In Purabhum, Ketaki could remain engrossed in what she was doing for days on end. She felt empty and terrible about Aditya's departure. But there were so many other people around her that she did not pay much attention to his absence. Then, she started preparing to return.

After returning to Navabhum, Ketaki did not call Aditya for many days. She knew he was angry and would not make the first move. But she felt tired and lethargic and kept postponing calling him. One day, when she picked up the phone, she heard Aditya's voice. "Are you back?"

He sounded tense.

"Yes! You came back before me."

"I had nothing to do over there. I was getting bored."

"If you had waited for me, we could have gone to Rishikesh together."

He sighed dramatically and said:

tire vāde par jiye ham to ye jān jhūṭ jānā
ki ḳhushī se mar na jāte agar e'tibār hotā

You promised to meet me, yet me you deceived,
from happiness I would have died, had I believed.

Ketaki sounded slightly more enthusiastic. "That is the problem. You do not believe in me."

Aditya planted his foot on the ground and said, "Had you said after you got back from Raghupur that you were going off to Timbuctoo, would I have been able to stop you?"

Ignoring the suppressed anger in Aditya's voice, Ketaki said, "I told you I would go with you. You should have waited for me."

"Just let it be. You only say things to keep me happy."

"Why are taunting me like this?"

"One person's pain sounds like a taunt to another."

"You are the one who hurts yourself. When you didn't wait until I returned, how can you blame me for not going with you?"

"I thought I would pursue a dream, but you didn't want it."

"You are being very poetic today. What has happened to you?"

"Nothing. I have just realised the truth of our relationship."

"Which truth?"

"I had started to think I was causing you pain; I was being unjust to you. But how much place do you actually have for me in your busy life?"

"But—"

"I thought we went there on a holiday together. But it seemed like you wanted a holiday from me."

"We also went to Purabhum for the sake of those who live there. You had work there and people to meet. It is not like that here."

"It looks like what you do here is also to please me. It doesn't make you happy. It's as if a sacrifice is being made for me. I want you wholly. Not if you suppress yourself and give up everything and come to me. I can't accept that."

"Don't you feel I am happy with you?"

"I do, and I feel extremely happy with you. That is why we have not been able to end this relationship so far. But the more I think about it, the more I feel something is wrong. Either you do not understand me, or I cannot understand you."

"Even if I am making sacrifices to make you happy, so what? At least you understand that I have put aside everything else and consider you the most important. I am becoming whatever you want."

"No, I would not want you to do anything to make me happy. Anything you do that does not make you happy inside will never feel good to me. You must understand that anything done in a spirit of sacrifice has a very short life. If not today, the sacrifice you made will start hurting you tomorrow. You will get jittery. You will try to free yourself from this self-made tangle of sacrifices. Your real personality will want to come forward, and then that sacrifice will make both our lives a joke."

After a moment, Aditya repeated, "Please don't burden me with this sacrifice. I would not like to see you living the life of a martyr."

Aditya's flowing speech had stunned Ketaki, and she could not find any words. She could not think of any correct answer; she was silent and surprised and kept staring at the empty wall before her.

But she had not dreamt that the same nonsense whose resolution they had gone to Purabhum to celebrate would again arise in Aditya's mind.

The Sky and A Shelter

Then, one day, Ketaki got a devastating message. "I am ending this relationship. You cannot be what I want. I cannot be what you want. Nor is there any scope for us to change at this age. You cannot open up, and I believe in being completely naked and exposed. I want to dissolve, and you want to protect yourself by wrapping yourself in layers. You want the sky, and I want shelter. You want to fly, and I need rest. You cannot understand the depth of my love, so we should end it here. This is too much suffering for me. The pain has become unbearable now. We are just hurting each other."

He continued, "I want to protect my love for you. I don't want it sullied. It is too precious for me. These doubts—or what I consider your truths—will kill it. I have to save myself, my love. So I must end this relationship."

Until now, Ketaki had felt it to be a challenge of sorts to win Aditya's trust. Because of this, whenever he expressed any doubt, Ketaki also became conscious of not wanting to do anything that would hurt Aditya. But all these efforts were tiring her. When Aditya kept repeating the same thing, Ketaki wondered why she was putting up with all of it. Wouldn't it be better to take a break from Aditya or let him say whatever he felt like saying and ignore it? But if you have to live day and night with someone, even from a distance, it is hard to leave him to his fate; it increases your distress.

After all, when you are at this level, one person's sorrow or happiness is also another's, right? How can Ketaki not feel whatever Aditya is feeling? No matter how careless Ketaki might have been, the concerns in Aditya's mind did not allow her to be thoughtless. She usually stopped and took the position that a solution to the problem had to be found. But this time, something strange happened. Yes, it was bizarre. Even Ketaki did not know that it could happen, that she could be or react like this. Aditya's message left her completely numb. She remained sitting. She could not move. She heard a silent sigh coming from within. Like someone said, "It's all over now. This time, you won't be able to revive it. Let the flame that was dying get extinguished."

She was tired of fighting.

What kind of love was this, in which the lover was being sacrificed to save it?

Something kept flaring up within her: *I have done whatever I could from my side. Now, the world is coming to an end... annihilation. Everything will be obliterated. Holi will burn in front of me. Fragrances, colours, memories, wishes, and flights will be sacrificed in the fire, one by one.* She would see her world being burnt to ashes.

There was no society that had created obstacles. So, the mind had taken over that role. It would have been better if someone else had stopped her; she could have blamed that person. The trouble with blaming oneself is twofold. One is troubled because things are out of one's control. The habit of achieving everything, of success, means that when we face defeat, we cannot bear it.

She missed Purabhum. Had someone intervened, they may have tried to convince them and bring them together again. But the stubbornness of the mind... when you fight with your own, who will take care of whom? This is elemental destruction.

Ketaki accepted that everything was over. There was honestly no treatment for Aditya. Nor would she go anywhere to find a cure. Now, there was no option left. She had cut herself off from everyone in every way. She had dedicated every moment to Aditya. Now, what else did she have that she could give to Aditya? If, even after she had given him all of herself, Aditya did not feel he had her completely, what could she do to make him feel that way?

She could not free Aditya from the feelings that went all the way down to his roots. In a way, those fears and feelings had won. Ketaki's feelings and her love had to give up. What else could she do? Ketaki hardened her heart and told herself she would survive no matter what happened. She would not contact Aditya even by mistake.

From that day onwards, she would never open the pages of that chapter again.

If she saw him, she would turn her face away.

She didn't know why she felt so betrayed. She had thought that their mutual problems had been resolved. Ketaki had accepted Aditya's way of thinking, and Aditya had come to terms with Ketaki's nature, or whatever he called it.

Then why? Why did he do it? What she had assumed was a life-long relationship ended without any notice. It was as if someone had dropped a nuclear bomb on a beautiful city, and the explosion was such that there would be no hope of raising one's head for centuries to come.

She kept wandering around like a crazy person the whole day.

She didn't feel like working. Did not talk to anyone. She just kept herself busy. Talked to herself. Sometimes it was in Aditya's voice, and sometimes in her own.

She kept explaining to herself that many other people in the world lived without love. That love was a thing of the mind. If you felt like it, it was there; if not, then not. She would never change her current attitude towards life. So, what difference did it make whether

Aditya was a part of her life or not? If he were, he would continue to live where he was; if he weren't, the situation would remain the same.

Just as Aditya came into her life without notice or warning, he was also now leaving. She wasn't prepared for this. Even if they had not married, the relationship could have continued. Aditya had probably got scared of the pain of relationships. He had ignored the weighing scales of relationships, on which happiness weighed as much as pain. It was as heavy, at least for Ketaki.

Perhaps the building had been demolished long ago. Only the ruined walls were left. She was holding the bricks protruding out in her hands when everything crumbled and fell down. Now, all that was left was a muffled sound of breaking, or a lot of debris. She was deceived into thinking that it was a building. Then she started thinking, *what if the relationship ends?* Relationships may end. But love does not necessarily end because of the end of a relationship. The sociality of relationships does not reach where love resides.

Relationships end, not love.
Leaves fall, not trees.
For when love ends
Nothing is left
Neither tree nor leaf.

Love goes beyond the boundaries of relationships. It does not die. It sleeps, it rests. Sometimes, it yawns and stretches and goes back to sleep.

It is stable and permanent. Put it on when you want, and put it to sleep whenever you want. Sometimes, it will listen to you; sometimes, it will not. It might sulk, get angry or upset, but ultimately, it will agree. And what if it doesn't agree? There will be pain, right? Now I understand why poets like Ghalib talk about befriending pain. When pain itself becomes a friend, then what harm can anyone do? Pain may even liberate love. Love will survive only on its own. There is no need to rely on anyone else for everything:

After you left,
Anything you
Touched or enjoyed
Became you.
That glass tumbler
From which you took a sip of whiskey
And placed on the three-legged table,
That blue-striped plate
On which you tasted dishes,
Or that corner of the sofa
Where you spread the *New York Times*,
Turning the pages
And spreading it out,
The books on the shelf

Whose every title you knew.
Gasps of your breath in the bedroom!
Dishevelled sheets
A dent in the pillow,
Your slippers on the threshold of the temple,
The questioning expression in your eyes.
Your soap stuck to the bathroom tile,
The toothbrush and that special toothpaste.
Those saris hanging in the cupboard,
The ones you saw me wearing.
Those ear drops,
Which at some auspicious moment,
You chose and put on me,
Where the touch of your fingers,
The caress of your eyes,
Still lingers on.
I wonder, where are you not?
Because where you aren't,
Is where I can be.

Maybe Aditya was right when he said in his last letter—that deathly letter—that it was necessary to end the relationship to save love. He didn't want his love to be tainted. He wanted to maintain the purity of his love. He wanted to protect it from any lie, deceit, or fraud. And so this relationship had to end.

Ketaki had also accepted that ending their relationship was the only way to save their love. That means permanent separation is essential to maintain love.

Not death, nor the inevitability of time. None of the three reasons for separation mentioned by the sages—honour, migration, or death.

It's still a permanent separation.

And the love of our hero and heroine will last forever.

After all, they took a step more painful than death to protect love. Is this what is called living death? But love did not get the death penalty. It is as alive as the morning sun, the evening star, the darkness of the night, the wetness of the rain or the heat of the fire. The lovers are killing themselves through the death of separation to keep it alive. That is the new ending of our New World romance.

Epilogue

If you want, you can also call it the madness of the lovers. If the lovers had tried to understand each other even a little or sat together and talked to each other comfortably, this story would not have had such a senseless and absurd ending. After all, they are highly educated and intelligent, and no one stops them from meeting or talking. However, internal barriers may be stronger than external barriers.

By the way, readers, if they want, can also reject this ending. There are infinite possibilities in the encounter between Purabhum and Navabhum. We can explore other options as well if you wish.

This story can have many different endings.

Ketaki may never contact Aditya, and this relationship may come to a halt right here.

But still, many questions remain unanswered. Suppose both of them do not contact each other.

The main reason for this, as you know, is the tension between the two, but there is no proof that this will break the links of the mind. The links of the mind can remain connected throughout one's life, which should be the meaning of rescuing love by sacrificing the lover.

The point is that readers demand a definite ending, and writers also have a habit of providing them with such an ending. But as we know, the only actual end of life is death. Life continues even after that, so I do not favour any definite endings. Anyway, there are many possibilities in this story.

For example, it is also possible that Ketaki may not break her vow of not contacting him, but will Aditya not try to contact her again? He hasn't decided anything.

It is also possible that both of them will connect again. After getting back together, the story of doubting starts again. So much has been said about this that nothing else can be achieved by repeating it. There can be three possible endings to this tale: one, based on my imagination; the second, based on my understanding of the way Ketaki thinks; and the third, from Aditya's angle. (Yes, I have to tell you a secret, which I did not tell Ketaki. When Ketaki started narrating her love story to me, and I started writing it, I thought I would never meet Aditya. He visited Ketaki often, but I only saw him from a distance. Never spoke with him. When their relationship ended so suddenly, I couldn't restrain myself, and one day, I decided to meet Aditya to know his mind.

After that, the story had to have a definite ending. I added the epilogue after talking to Aditya.)

[1]

As far as I remember, after several months Aditya sent a letter to Ketaki. It was probably not a letter but a card wishing her a happy new year. This may not be my memory but merely my imagination! There is little difference between imagination and memory. One is related to the person it happened to, and the other to that which has occurred. It's just a matter of points standing on a scale of time. When you read this story, everything may already be a memory.

Ketaki sent a card in response just as a formality (that's what she said to me).

What had she written on the card?

This question is a pertinent one. As I remember it, she had written, *With best wishes for a doubt-free life.*

That was not nice of Ketaki!

But do you know that Aditya said in reply to this? "A tasteless life, free of doubt as well as love. What if I say that I want to forget all those conditions of mine and start a new life with you? I will love you as you are, however you are. I will not make any demands on the relationship. Are you ready for a new beginning?"

Then, he had written, "The grounds of this relationship will be different. I will not expect anything from you that I have been expecting until now. I will be happy with whatever you can give. I want to start anew because I love you very much, and even a little contact with you is essential to keep that love alive and to keep it from drowning in pain. I am drying up inside, it is vital to nourish my inner being. Otherwise, it will dry up and drain me too. Having known love, I cannot deprive myself of it like this. It looks like we will have to spend the rest of our lives without it. I don't want to die of deprivation. I want to live with the fulfilment within myself that I have got from you. Tell me, will you let this happen? Everything is in your hands, Ketaki. You can give me life or declare me dead. Will you tell me what decision you take? Or will you maintain the same silence you have held onto for so long?"

Now, you all will be curious to know what Ketaki's answer was. When you started reading this story, Ketaki told me all this. She asked me for advice, saying that if she listened to Aditya, the same tensions would begin again, and if she didn't do it, she wouldn't get relief from her inner restlessness.

The lamp of love shines inside her just like it does inside Aditya. But she is afraid of getting entangled in the complexities of love again. Now please tell me what advice I should give her. Should she water and nourish it or let it dry? If not watered, it will either wither and dry up or keep taking sustenance from somewhere, making the romance smell fragrant.

[2]

I don't know whether this thought arose in the minds of the readers or not, but after listening to Ketaki's words, some questions appeared in my mind. Please pay attention to them and tell me whether my worries are valid.

Sometimes, Aditya's doubts are not misplaced because, based on Ketaki's words, I often think that Ketaki has neither completely freed herself from her old relationships nor given up the desire for new ones.

Doesn't Ketaki know that she, too, is denying something? It is difficult for her to accept that other men also have a place in her life. Perhaps she often imagines what life would be like if she were with someone else. If Aditya is suspicious of her, can't that be why Ketaki neither understands nor can explain? Aditya also feels something, but he can't put a finger on it; sometimes it's about the bond, and sometimes it is about not answering the phone.

Meanwhile, the real reason is something else; he doesn't know it, and she denies it. I can't say for sure, but maybe Ajay was with her at that conference when she was away from Aditya for a week. But she doesn't even dare to tell Aditya in case it makes him want to end the relationship. The relationship which has become her lifeline. She really doesn't want to lose Aditya, and Aditya is moving away from her because he feels rejected. What a deadly contradiction this is.

If Ajay was with her at the conference, then Ketaki has to accept that it is because of her temporary relationships with other men that Aditya cannot trust her. If you cannot change yourself, you can at least accept being the way you are. Aditya did not ask her to change, but he wanted her to accept her truth; then, the foundation of the relationship would be based on truth.

As a matter of fact, Ajay's mere attendance at the conference did not make Ketaki guilty. There is a need to understand the nature and form of their relationship, which Aditya can't do and Ketaki can't explain.

Ketaki feels that she loses her individuality by getting tied to the truth that Aditya demands. She loses her privacy. Aditya captures her innermost layers. Where can she go to escape?

Aditya had told Ketaki that "any relationship can only be happy and complete if we accept each other as we are. Neither ask for change nor to be anything else." He had often told Ketaki that he was ready to accept her as she was. Why shouldn't Ketaki also take him, with the doubts he has?

If one can understand and comprehend the heart using the brain, then many sources of pain will automatically disappear.

If one manages to awaken a feeling of acceptance of each other in a relationship, the relationship will never end. Here, Aditya and Ketaki wish to have a sound relationship. Then maybe this story, too, will end like this.

Wouldn't this ending please our readers, too?

[3]

But another ending is also possible.

I think Ketaki has been in touch with Aditya because, though she has looked sad for the past few days, her face suddenly glowed today. She glowed with the determination of one who has come out of a conflict and decided something. Then I saw something else... I heard something else... about something that happens years later! A new morning is glimmering with crimson hues and rays of light. Ketaki's tomorrow, Aditya's tomorrow!

I see those moments with my eyes, those golden moments in the distant future. The hero is 80 years old, and the heroine is 75. They have gone for a holiday to the hills of Purabhum. Both have retired from the university. The hero tenderly kisses the wrinkles on the heroine's face, and the heroine suddenly remembers a novel by a Latin American author she read long ago and liked. It seemed particularly special that their love reached its ultimate culmination at that age, not the boiling point of extreme youth. It is about those mature moments when love leaves the body and starts living in the air, smell, soul, and spirit. Ketaki was standing right before me, absorbing those moments.

But I don't know if she is dreaming of those moments, or if she is thinking of making them come true, or if she has made them come true.

The Storyteller's Postscript

While discussing love stories, I told you that in most happy love stories, the heroine reaches the harem of the castle, where the love story ends. Fearing that, I did not want to take Ketaki to the place where our story would end. Nor do I want to turn this story into some tragic story. I gave you a promise at the beginning of the book. Therefore, these are the three possible endings that I have visualised. Readers can choose whichever ending they want.